GW00760570

The First-Born of Egypt

The First-Born of Egypt

by

DEMOUZON

The Midnight Library

PEEBLES PRESS INTERNATIONAL

NEW YORK   LONDON

This Edition first published 1979 by

PEEBLES PRESS INTERNATIONAL, INC.

10 Columbus Circle, New York, New York 10019

First published in French 1976 by Flammarion et Cie, Paris

English Translation © 1979 Peebles Press International, Inc.
ISBN 0-85690-077-X
Library of Congress Catalog Card Number 78-54648

Graphic Production by Filmar Graphics, San Diego, California 92110

All rights reserved. No part
of this book may be reproduced in any
form or by any means, except for the inclusion
of brief quotations in a review, without permission
in writing from the publisher.

Distributed in the United States by
Farrar, Straus & Giroux
19 Union Square West, New York, New York 10003

Distributed in Canada by
McGraw-Hill Ryerson, Ltd.
330 Progress Avenue
Scarborough, Ontario

Distributed in the United Kingdom and British Commonwealth by
David & Charles, Ltd.
Brunel House
Newton Abbot
Devon, England

Printed and Bound in the United States of America

The First-Born of Egypt

1

Ernesto Biaggi had hardly changed. As massive and broad-shouldered as ever, he had kept his shape like a cannonball, a little deformed and hunchbacked; his appearance had, in the old days, earned him the nickname "Quasimodo." Certainly he was thirty years older now, not far from eighty, but he gave more an impression of a person who wanted to disguise himself as decrepit than of a truly old and wasted man. His eyebrows, perhaps a little less bushy than they may once have been, and his thick, short hair were of a shade of silvery-white that seemed artificial.

Was he afraid? . . . Had he understood, upon receiving the curious harbinger of Death? Could a man of his temper ever be afraid? And then, at that age, doesn't Death follow us daily — subtle, yes, but ever-present, looming dead ahead and yet incapable of surprising us?

Biaggi took several steps towards the middle of the courtyard; a shabby and worthless square, depressing, dark, stinking; a well surrounded by four anonymous buildings. It was a paved, gray hole, with nothing but the sky above, a sky forever the same shade of gray.

High above, Marcel watched through the rooftop gable, his two hands squeezing the stock of an old hunting carbine, as sturdy and well-kept as a regulation weapon.

Biaggi stopped to catch his breath, then continued on his laborious and obviously exhausting march. The sound of his cheap shoes, slipping and dragging, just barely scratching the cement surface of the yard, rasped like the sickly breathing that is as hard to take in as it is to let out. Biaggi's legs told his age better than his appearance did. Marcel felt a kind of pity for him. But it had always been his own way to find such sentimental thoughts cheap and useless. He grasped the rifle and raised it scornfully to his shoulder without haste, coolly, with no unnecessary gestures,

7

but with a courage wrenched only briefly by anguish — the courage of a man before the battle begins.

Biaggi stopped in the middle of the yard to put down the plate that he had been carrying. With the same painful difficulty, he squatted as much as he could on his legs, and finally, to save his back from an almost impossible movement, he stretched his arms toward the ground. The plate, released before it touched down, fell on the cement with a metallic ringing. Then the old man retraced his steps to the corner of the yard where he had taken over a crudely-built shed of used planks and sheet metal.

This was the moment.

The muzzle of the rifle, bulging with the heavy casing of its silencer, followed the old man to the door of the shed. Yapping and growling came from inside the ugly shack, and Biaggi swung open a low bar. A little white and rust-colored dog trotted out on a leash, its tail wagging and its tongue hanging down. Since Biaggi wasn't able to bend over to pet his dog, it put its paws up on its master's thigh and whined. Biaggi dropped his heavy hand onto the dog's neck and mumbled a few words.

"Poor Giocchi . . . we must make allowances . . . bad legs . . . It takes too long, I know, I know . . . but if you wouldn't pull so much on the leash . . ."

The dog seemed to accept this excuse and, the flatteries of his allegiance done, went over by the dish and sniffed out the ground.

Marcel remembered Blitz, a huge wolf . . . part German Shepherd, part Doberman . . . who had been Ernesto Biaggi's formidable and pampered companion in other times. Now the old man had nothing for his only relation, for his only friend, for his only company — perhaps for his only reason to continue — but this pitiful, mangy clown. A poetic fall. A lovely ending for anyone's life.

The second joint of his index finger glued to the trigger, Marcel took careful aim, instinctively adjusting his sight through the bulky presence of the silencer, and then, holding his breath, slowly released the safety.

The dog had attacked his mash with a ferocious appetite, lapping and chomping noisily. Biaggi, motionless and unoccupied, watched his dog.

The burning shot from the rifle punctured the miserable dog insensibly. Half an ounce of lead and copper hurled at a force of thirty miles a minute towards a living body performs impeccably, before and after, and kills efficiently. A terrible shudder passes in a thousandth of a second through the entire body, crossing through the vessels, the nerves, and all the vital fluids; a very clean wound. And certainly irrevocable.

The dog flipped over, his whole body trembling, and fell without a sound onto the plate. Biaggi, still motionless, his arms hanging uselessly alongside his body, his hands half open, seemed to have no reaction. Stunned, he saw the accomplished act without understanding; he also saw the almost invisible hole in the dog from which blood was beginning to ooze.

Above, in the gable, Marcel steadily drew the bolt of his gun, ejecting the empty cartridge which fell soundlessly onto the thick blanket spread in front of the window, and reloaded. Another bullet waited in the chamber, just to be sure, to take no chances, because this was all part of the plan. The second shot was fired.

The prey turned over again; a kind of sideways leap which seemed to mean that the dog was still able to jump, to play and run . . . that it was still alive.

But the first bullet had perfectly fulfilled its mission. The dog was dead. The second shot buried itself in a dead body as insurance.

Marcel lowered his rifle and put on the safety catch without ejecting. He rolled the gun and the first cartridge casing in the blanket and laid it diagonally in an old cardboard suitcase. He closed it up simply, without hurrying. Before leaving, he threw a last glance through the dormer window.

Below, at the bottom of the well, Ernesto Biaggi hadn't budged an inch. His body, petrified and stupefied, remained rigorously the same as it had been just a few moments before. A single, pale ray of sunlight piercing all the gray waste, threw an insolently joyful light on his despair. Marcel saw two thickly gleaming tears on the old man's cheeks.

* * *

On arriving at Kennedy Airport, Marcel Ribot reflected that all the airports in the world were alike.

This banal observation was tinged with the excitement of a first trip abroad. He had taken airplanes before, but only as part of the military. This time it had been different. There had been carpeting, comfortable seats, aluminum paneling, blonde stewardesses, dinner trays, and even a movie: a heavy thriller in which Lino Ventura played a fugitive Soviet spy. Marcel was about the only person who followed the story through to the end. All around him everyone else slept or read. Some businessmen in the neighboring seats told him that they had already seen the same film twice, the week before, while making the same trip back and forth. Marcel regarded them with envy and admiration — and also a little uneasily; what did he have to say to men who had been to New York twice in so short a time? He was experiencing an unknown world and he couldn't contain his pleasure. He had cleaned his dinner plate greedily, and he had followed the movie with riveted attention. As often as had been possible, and generally, he had called the stewardess over, just to admire her blonde hair, her soft figure, and her stereotyped smile. He wanted to savor every single detail of "the trip of his life."

His first contact with America disappointed him. He even thought for a minute that his trip had been a dream and he was still back in Roissy, outside of Paris. It was all the same setting, functionally modern and sophisticated, with the same cosmopolitan and jabbering crowd. He followed the two businessmen and their briefcases like a ghost. In their wake, he retrieved his luggage and went on to customs. They checked his passport, and then he had to put his suitcase and his bag on a kind of cashier's counter. A nonchalant and apparently senseless creep signaled him to open the bags. Marcel Ribot took out his keys and, unperturbed, proceeded to work the locks. The official searched briefly and clumsily through the small trunk and then swung open the lid of the suitcase.

"Hey!" he shouted in English, "What's that? A rifle?"

Marcel shrugged his shoulders. He knew perhaps thirty words in English (love . . . bed . . . fuck . . . wine . . . bloody son of a bitch), but he was completely incapable of producing a sentence.

Even less could he understand what had been said to him in such a nasal and intimidating voice. The guy pointed his index finger at the contents of the suitcase and raised his eyebrows with the exaggerated air of an interrogator.

"What's that for?"

Marcel shrugged his shoulders again. As if it wasn't obvious. He pretended to aim a rifle at game, and fired several imaginary shots.

"*Carabine!*" he said. "*Pour la chasse. Chasse! Caza! Verstehen Sie?*"

The cop (a lackey in a blue shirt with insignia and a cap couldn't be anything but a cop) yelled in the direction of a young man with a clerical manner who stood by in the background.

"Hey! C'mon over here."

The young man hurried over. The two officials fired several fast questions and answers at each other.

"How do you intend to use this weapon?" The young man asked in French with an accent that was more Mediterranean than American.

Marcel smiled broadly. At last — civilization.

"For hunting, of course. It's a sporting gun," he replied.

"What caliber?"

"Seven fifty-four."

The new lackey translated first Ribot's answer and then the cop's response.

"My colleague says that he's not familiar with that caliber."

"That's possible. It's not used much."

Another translation. Discussion. Re-translation.

"Can you put the rifle together for us?"

Ribot grimaced in annoyance.

"It's not a rifle, it's a carbine."

In a few simple moves, Ribot put his gun together. Other passengers were getting off the plane all around them; they hurried by rubbernecking, proud of themselves because they had no reason to be reproached.

Ribot laid his gun on the counter. Once assembled, it wasn't such a formidable weapon, especially to the eyes of the Americans who were used to larger guns with greater calibers. Had Ribot claimed that it was a showpiece more for women's use, no doubt they would have believed him.

The interpreter took a notebook from under the counter.

"And your passport, please?"

Marcel, perfectly calm, held out his passport.

The guy noted his name, address, age and passport number and asked for his address in the United States. Ribot hesitated for a moment and acted like he was trying to remember.

"Hell, I don't know the names of your damn streets. It's my buddy's place — he's probably waiting for me outside. I only know that it's in Brooklyn . . . Williamsburg."

"You have nothing more precise?"

He thought about giving a fake street number, but he knew that he had a poor shot at coming up with a street which really existed in the Williamsburg district. He felt pretty sure that his questioners would be familiar enough with it.

"I only know my pal's name, Joe Torronto, and his restaurant, El Cactucito."

"El Cactucito? Sure, I know it. And are you originally Spanish?"

"Yes," lied Ribot.

"Me, too!" said the other, with a foolish grin. "Hah! Actually, my grandparents were Spanish."

"Ah, really?" Marcel forced himself to pay a little more attention.

"Do you want to fill in the card yourself? Here — first the make of the gun, the caliber, the usage, the weight, the length."

Marcel took the card. Resigned, he began to fill in the boxes, concentrating on making as few mistakes as possible.

"I didn't expect there would be any problem about bringing in personal sporting arms. However, I ought to have asked about it beforehand."

"Oh, well, you don't have anything to worry about now. It's authorized. It's just a little red tape. You know, with all this hijacking and hostage business . . ."

Ribot smiled. After he had registered his bags at Roissy, the C.R.S. had come to the departure lounge to find him and ask him a few questions on the subject of the gun — which the electronic detector hadn't taken long to discover. The alleged reasons had been the same: hijacking, hostages . . .

Definitely all the airports in the world were the same.

* * *

Joe Torronto hadn't missed the rendezvous. After the hugging and back-slapping, he led Marcel to a parking garage where a young man with a deep bronze complexion waited — a young man whose body was long and thin like a girl's, and stuffed into cream-colored jeans and an orange T-shirt on which Marcel could read "Super Flavor, Life Savers, Five Flavors." This message intrigued him.

"What's that?" he asked. "A poem?"

Joe burst out laughing.

"No, it's an ad for chewing gum!"

Ribot tried to smile. From now on, it would be better if he didn't ask too many questions.

Torronto introduced them.

"Santiana . . . my shadow! . . . *Marcel, un amigo francés, un antiguo amigo siempre, cuando fuí en Francia y otros lugares. Digo: un amigo francés, no es yanqui ¿ientiendes?*"

"What — Yankee?" asked Marcel.

"I assured him that you are French. You'll see, it makes all the difference . . . *¿Donde está el coche?*"

"*¡Ahí!*" grunted the character named Santiana.

He made his way through the rows of cars, his hips gently swaying. From time to time he glanced back to make sure the two others were following okay. His little precaution added to the heavy air about him which Torronto began to explain.

"Santiana drives well, he punches fast, and he doesn't talk . . . but take the time and the trouble to understand what he does say to you. If you make him your friend, he'll cut himself into eight pieces to save your hide in a bad situation. I know what I'm talking about."

"Hold on — is there still a lot of fighting?"

"It happens from time to time. It's almost always over some crap like dope deals or faggots. The big times are over."

"In any case, you still do okay with French. Hell — a guy who left Europe twenty years ago."

"You know, at my restaurant I have a pretty regular French crowd. Besides, I have some contacts in the Midi who keep me in touch with things. And what are you up to?"

"Me? I've hung it up. I'm through with trouble — completely. A little peace and quiet is nothing to laugh at. I do enough to get by, but not much to talk about."

The two men faced each other.

Twenty years earlier they had set out in the same rough life, side by side, in a kind of camaraderie, taking a place in society that they themselves had chosen, according to their destiny. Since then, time had slipped away, and they had moved further and further apart. Joe Torronto had become rich, well-known, and happy. Marcel Ribot had gone into a miserable semi-retirement, obscure and embittered. The two men, from then on, had not been able to ignore their friendship forged under the hardest of circumstances, by nature too deep-rooted to ever be forgotten, or even to diminish. That time had broken them in.

"You haven't really changed, you know," Torronto remarked.

"And you not much . . . in spite of your fat life," Marcel answered, smiling.

He knew very well that he had changed and that Joe had changed, too. They were both the same age: sixty-seven. Like Ernesto Biaggi, they knew how to keep up appearances: squared shoulders, aloof attitude, a cool eye, rigid posture. But there were weaknesses: the pasty complexion etched with too many lines, some rheumatism here and there; lungs which were still good, but with no more stamina; sagging, red-rimmed eyes that remembered the fires and the drinking of other times, the sand and the dust . . . the signs of advancing age. One day, like Biaggi, they would present the world with the desolate spectacle of a superb carcass incapable of stirring and obliged to struggle grossly in order to conquer each bit of ground it crossed . . . like a huge worm.

Yes; they had changed. They made an exaggerated pretense to the contrary for each other's benefit but of course it wasn't enough to convince them, or to dupe them.

"Ah, here's the car," said Torronto.

Marcel whistled, admiring. Here at last was the America of his dreams.

The limousine couldn't have been less than thirty feet long, and magnificent, black and shiny like onyx. A beautiful American car like he had never seen before.

"What is it?"

"It's a Buick Electra . . . $9,000 to lease."

Ribot didn't ask anything else about the car. He simply remembered that it was a Buick. He was ignorant beyond that, and he didn't even know how to drive. So —

The three climbed into the car which rolled with silent ease onto a ramp. They drove for a long time, in the middle of a long line of automobiles moving at a slow speed which, here, seemed to be normal. Marcel took in the spectacle with the eyes of a child. But he could only see cars, Mack trucks, route signs, cement, asphalt, guard rails, and an occasional glimpse of the East River, surrounded by a wall of buildings. He saw nothing of the marvels he had expected.

In Brooklyn, things changed. They drove under the elevated, where all the pillars were covered with filthy graffiti and seemed to exist only for that purpose. The buildings and the cars repeated each other endlessly. Brick replaced the concrete and Volkswagens replaced the Pontiacs and Mercurys. They went up Broadway, turning onto Ditmars Street, and found themselves in Williamsburg, the most heavily Latin district in New York — therefore the noisiest and most animated, teeming. Without a doubt it was also the dirtiest, but in any case it was the most interesting and colorful part of the city.

Marcel felt instinctively that he would be comfortable here. The chaos and the crass exuberance of the streets reminded him of the crowded bazaars and alleys of other times. He liked things this way.

The Buick stopped in front of Torronto's restaurant, apparently a rather classy place. A red canvas awning hung over the walkway to the entrance, and caged trees bordered either side of the door. Ribot studied the sign: "El Cactucito Rest., Bar B.Q., Clams,

Shrimp, Lobster, Steak House; At 9P.M.: Algo Nevritón y Su Conjunto."

"Your place is pretty swanky."

"You think so? I live upstairs. It's a little noisy, but still it's the most convenient for taking care of business. By the way, what is it that you've come here for? You mentioned in your letter that you had some business."

"Yes, but I'd rather talk it over some place a little more quiet."

Torronto assumed a knowing air, and a gleam of interest showed in his eyes. The fact that Marcel wanted to discuss business in private certainly caught his attention. Soon he would see whether Ribot had really changed or not.

Santiana switched off the engine and opened the door. A lively Torronto signaled to his friend to follow.

They took a table in a corner of the restaurant, whose decor suggested a frontier cantina at the time of the Mexican wars. Santiana, a few tables away, busied himself with keeping a discreet guard while sipping a mango-lemon soda.

"So?" asked Torronto.

"It's necessary that I see Siragusi — "

"Siragusi? That's heavy! You must be serious. Which Siragusi?"

"Attilio."

"Ah. The one on the waterfront. What do you want with him? You know it won't be easy."

"I want to talk to him. He's the only one who will know where I can find what I'm looking for."

"You've got a debt to settle?"

"Sort of."

"Can you tell me about it?"

"No."

"Okay, however you want it. I'll see what I can do."

* * *

Attilio Siragusi had been out of the picture for a long time. It was his age as much as a distaste for all the crimes of his youth that made him decide to retire early, around sixty. One of his nephews, who went by the name Bo Dafman, succeeded him, after his two sons, Roberto and Dino, were dropped from the biggest of the New York Syndicates, "The Four Riders of the Apocalypse." Machine gunning hit men in four cars, "origin unknown," later got them (their riddled bodies were found sometime afterward). Attilio Siragusi had taken this as a sign from Heaven that it was definitely time to pass the gauntlet. People said that his retirement was as removed and ascetic as Charles Quint's to the convent of Yuste. Already the new generation had forgotten that he had been kingpin, a big-time bootlegger and racketeer, one of the founders of Murder Incorporated, friend and protector to Johnny Torrio, Joe Adonis, and even to the great Anastasia.

He agreed immediately to see Marcel Ribot in order to please Joe Torronto, whom he had known when Torronto had been no more than just another hit man, a punk affiliated with the Dockers syndicate. There had been a long list of jobs done for the organization (had it been the last song for Tim O'Shannegan? Buck Clarow? Toni Benzo? he no longer knew). When Siragusi took his first trip back to Sicily, Joe Torronto had also gone back to fight in his homeland, and was just in time to join the *Bandera*. He had risked his hide twenty times more there than he had done in New York. It was an ungodly way to hide out.

Joe Torronto came back to New York much later. Siragusi retired a few years after. They had run into each other at receptions and had talked about the old times. More than their former association, their longevity — in a profession where it isn't easy to live past fifty — had soldered a kind of almost friendly relationship between the two men, who had no connections of either grief or vengeance, which was even more unusual. So Joe Torronto had obviously been indulging in dramatics by pretending that it would be difficult to make contact with Siragusi.

Santiana and the Buick Electra took Marcel Ribot to Siragusi's sumptuous country estate in Poughkeepsie, about sixty miles north of New York City, through the vast suburbs.

Joe Torronto would serve as interpreter and mediator. He was hot to know what business brought an old Mafia chief and the small, powerless Frenchman together, in the dawn of their old age. He was not going to be cheated.

* * *

Siragusi waited in the "little salon," a room which he reserved for short interviews. It was a room about a hundred square feet, rich in paneling, carpeting, and Cuban leather. The furniture was kept to essentials — a few armchairs and a low table — and the place was equipped with small barricades, in case of a shooting spree. But this possibility didn't seem to worry him much any more. An old black servant had opened the door to the visitors, and while he announced them they waited, but at no time were they able to catch the furtive shadows of hoodlums sliding in and out of the corners of the halls, as might have been expected. Siragusi lived in isolation, a tired old lone wolf, waiting for the peaceful death that he didn't deserve. He didn't drink, he never smoked, and he lived almost exclusively on *spaghetti marinara*. Joe Torronto had taken the time to explain most of this to his friend Marcel, yet as it was also his first visit to Siragusi's retreat, he himself was amazed at the total lack of precaution which seemed to surround the old Mafioso.

Attilio Siragusi didn't rise from his chair. Ribot was surprised to find his bearing rather like that of an old country doctor who was running for Congress. Siragusi had neither the thick mouth of Capone, nor the vicious eyes of Dillinger, nor the arrogant eyebrows of Luciano. With his patriarch's beard and his arms relaxed along the easy chair, he reminded Marcel of the statue of Abraham Lincoln which he had seen in a photograph in a travel brochure.

Torronto made the introductions.

"What can I do for you?" Siragusi asked in a voice that was low and quiet and somewhat listless.

Torrronto translated. Ribot explained that he wanted to find Charlie Adams, who was also called Bonanza.

"What for?" asked Siragusi. "To shoot him?"

"No, I don't intend to kill him. It's simply to remind him of something that happened a long time ago. He once told me that you were old friends. I lost track of him; then I thought of you, and knew that I could find you through Joe. This way, maybe I can get back on the right path. . .but I assure you, I really don't want to kill him." Marcel's voice was almost sneering, and it made Joe wonder, and probably old Siragusi as well, what he was hiding.

Joe translated. Siragusi folded his hands, resting them on his chest, underneath his beard. He seemed to reflect. Could he trust this unknown man, this foreigner?

He interrogated Joe with his eyes. Joe understood the mute question and lowered his eyes. He answered personally for the good faith of his friend. "Marcel, kill Chuck Bonanza? No — it's preposterous."

2

Marcel Ribot arrived at the bus station in Las Vegas completely exhausted. He didn't even bother to glance at his new surroundings before climbing into the Greyhound which would take him as far as Goodsprings, fifty miles south, at the junction of the Springs and Providence mountains.

After six days of uninterrupted travel on the Continental Trailways bus, his experience was broad enough for him to maintain that all the bus stations in the United States were alike. He had seen the countryside change, but so gradually that it couldn't entertain him with the happy surprises that, in his opinion, only France could offer. There had been endless roads bordered by endless plains, towns which never ended, immense suburbs, forests without clearings, and unvarying mountains. Occasionally, after a long sleep or an uncomfortable night which had crossed a couple of hundred miles, the surprise of a different setting would come, but then he would be obliged to contemplate it for an entire day. Marcel had allowed himself to be inundated by space, distance, and speed. Strangely enough, a numb fear which grew in him as he approached his unknown destination acted as an opiate — soothing and infinitely agreeable.

He had slept a lot, half senseless, and his dreams had met up with other plains, other mountains, other deserts; those of another time of his life — of his youth.

* * *

Marcel found the machine marked "Goodsprings." He took out his billfold — a leather wallet with two pockets, one for coins and one for bills, fitted with a metal clasp — and inserted the necessary two dollars and five cents into the slot. The machine gave a dry cough and spat out his ticket. A few steps to the left, Marcel operated another machine, producing a flashing light, a buzz, a gurgle and a paper cup of Coca-Cola. Another button, another slot: Marcel opened a flap and pulled out a sandwich (two slices of bread, tomato, lettuce, egg, mayonnaise).

Armed with his meal and his ticket, Marcel boarded the bus. For the first time in his life, Marcel heartily thanked the Americans for having invented vending machines, those marvelous servants who understand foreign visitors so well and ask no questions of those who want, above all, to pass unnoticed. Up until then, he had considered these machines as mechanical monsters, money-eaters and, too often, frauds. Now he knew that without these automatic machines he never would have been able to undertake this terrible journey from the East to the West Coast, to come to the place where he was going to deal out death.

He sat in an isolated corner. The coach was three-quarters empty, and no one seemed to pay attention to the old man, weighed down by his bag and the long, flat case that he carried under his arm, while his right hand clutched a club sandwich and a cup of Coca-Cola.

The bus rapidly gobbled up the first twenty-five miles, leaving behind the gambling empire whose immense signs flickered brilliantly. These were the flames that drew the moths who came to burn their wings, carried away by their foolish dreams. Marcel didn't look back. One day, perhaps, he would return to Las Vegas.

Carrying his two bags, Marcel went into the toilets in the Goodsprings station. He put the suitcase flat on the seat (first taking the precaution to wipe it carefully), and then laid the long case on top of it. He took out his set of keys and opened the four locks. Then he took the rifle out of its case. He put the parts together, screwed on the silencer that he himself had fashioned, loaded the rifle, and carefully flushed the toilet. He closed the long case without locking it and leaned it against the wall covered with obscene drawings, which he understood, and scribbling, which he didn't understand, but which was probably just as obscene. He opened his suitcase, bundled up his clothes, and placed them in the lid. Then he unfolded the blanket at the bottom of the suitcase. He picked up the rifle, rolled it in the blanket, and placed it diagonally in the suitcase. Finally he stuffed his clothes into the empty rifle case. He snapped the four locks closed and walked out calmly. On the way out, he washed his hands meticulously and adjusted his red and green striped tie. After sliding the gun case into an automatic locker, he left whistling "Carolina," and headed towards Pescora Flows, where Chuck Bonanza lived in his villa. Marcel was ready, he had time, the night belonged to him.

He slept among the rocks, rolled up in his blanket, holding his rifle tightly against him. It was very cold and strange creatures prowled around him. It reminded him of the good old days, the bivouacs without campfires in the Haute Cambrousse. His rheumatism bothered him a little, and he watched the sunrise with the feeling of relief known only to insomniacs, the sick, soldiers, and all those who fear that the sun might disappear for good, swallowed up by the night.

He found the strange house clinging to the side of the mountain, and noticed a door at ground level that gave access to the garden . . . a curious garden, in fact. It was hollowed out of the slope like a slice cut from a cake. A pleasant arrangement of shrubs and exotic plants surrounded a swimming pool. In the middle of the pool stood a poor reproduction of a stone fountain whose jets of water were probably lost on the shrubs and plants before they could be absorbed by the thirsty soil. Between the pool and the roofed terrace, running the length of the very white villa, slatted chairs and a table under a large red umbrella occupied the main open space. Ribot immediately realized that this was the area best suited to his purpose.

It must have been nine o'clock, and the sun's rays had begun to beat down. Marcel had taken off his jacket and rolled up his sleeves. Stoically (he had known other vigils), he watched the villa steadily, awaiting the sounds of awakening life.

The first of these was the clanging of pots, and then the yapping of a dog (Blitz? Giocchi? . . . Marcel shuddered in spite of himself), and finally, cries and laughter carried by the wind echoed up the mountain. Marcel lifted himself slowly to peer through the rock crevice. A tall, dark, and slim woman dressed in a pale green robe, wearing mirrored sunglasses, was setting the lacquered table with the makings of a substantial breakfast. Despite the distance, and thanks to his legendary keen eyesight, the clear visibility enabled Marcel to observe all the details. He noticed a tiny Chihuahua at the woman's feet and at the same time saw that she was wearing pink slippers with pom-poms.

"Chuck, please bring out the coffee pot, wouldja honey?" she called out with a sudden brassiness that made Marcel jump. "Polly! Be nice! Go play," she cried, this time to the dog.

Chuck arrived, stripped to the waist, wearing only a pair of tan cotton slacks. He was carrying the coffee pot. Polly, the dog, didn't show the slightest sign of obedience and continued to frisk about the feet of his mistress, making each of her moves perilous. (Finally, he received the deserved kick from the pink slipper which brought a small smile, almost a grin, to Marcel's face.)

Chuck put the coffee pot on the table. Marcel hardly recognized him. Had he not heard the name being called, he certainly would have taken much longer to recognize Charlie Adams — now Chuck Bonanza — whom he had known in the old days. Chuck appeared to have grown younger. He carried himself well. The suntan, the thick blond hair, the supple, athletic walk in no way betrayed the fact that he was almost seventy years old. Marcel understood why Chuck had a wife of thirty and a daughter of sixteen; it was at the same time the reason for and the consequence of his desire and his ability to appear much younger than he was. Marcel felt a deep hatred for him.

Never letting the couple out of his sight, Marcel slid the barrel of the rifle onto the rock and, without moving an inch, lined his sights on them.

It was essential that the killing take place at the edge of the pool. Switching his gaze from the rifle sights, with one hand nestling the barrel and the other on the butt, he looked towards the calm and happy couple enjoying their breakfast and the miniscule dog lying at their feet.

Chuck and his wife had almost finished their breakfast (they hadn't left the table for a moment), when a young, blonde girl came out of the house and walked gaily towards them. Marcel was able to contemplate the figure at ease. First the hair: it was long, a deep blonde, almost the color of her father's. (Ribot didn't doubt for a single second that this was Chuck's daughter, although he would have guessed her to be twenty and not sixteen — perhaps Siragusi's information was out-dated?) Then her legs, as long, but thinner and more supple than her mother's (or step-mother's?). She wore a short terry cloth robe of an immaculate white. Marcel could clearly distinguish the movement of her puckered lips as she kissed her parents. Then, in spite of her mother's shrill protests, the young girl took off her robe and walked to the swimming pool. She appeared quite naked in the soft light of the exotic garden. Marcel was stupefied. He had never known the pleasure of contemplating so young and lovely a girl, outside of movies or magazines. Such beauty had only existed in his dreams. He admired her with more than admiration — he was amazed at the graceful figure, perfectly smooth, unspoiled by fat or boniness. The slight contour of her stomach and her perfect breasts stirred Marcel beyond all limits; at that moment he knew that he was an old man, and he wanted to give it all up.

But the dog set off in pursuit of his young mistress, growling fiercely and joyfully at the same time. He caught up with her at the exact point where Ribot had drawn an imaginary line separating the world of the living from that of the dead.

The bullet penetrated the right side, just below the breast, and mushroomed on impact without disintegrating. A shock wave passed through the entire body. The young girl, her arms stretched backwards, ready to dive, slipped into the pool amidst a shower of spray — and oblivion. Ribot saw her go down, inert, then slowly float back up in the midst of bloody swirls.

Chuck and his wife laughingly lit their first cigarettes of the day. They had noticed nothing.

* * *

Ribot walked down to Goodsprings whistling. The happy tune betrayed — less than the satisfaction of finally accomplishing a difficult mission — the annoyance that he felt at not having been able to fire again, the "insurance" bullet. He had almost fired a second shot at that lovely body floating in the water, but hesitated, realizing that the bullet might be slowed down by the water as it left the body, and be recovered intact without any difficulty. He hoped that the girl was in fact dead and wondered whether she was a virgin. He hoped that this was not the case and regretted that he, himself, had not been able to carry out that painful and necessary task, like the executioners of ancient Rome.

As he approached the first houses of the town — low, white wooden houses — he heard police sirens coming towards him, so he took the first road to his left. Quite calmly, he arrived at the bus station, transferred the rifle in the toilets, and purchased a double Coca-Cola and two packaged sandwiches from the vending machines, as well as a ticket to Las Vegas. From there, he would take the Continental Trailways bus back to New York.

He climbed into the silver-gray coach and the door closed behind him. Almost all the seats were taken and he was obliged to go to the back of the bus before finding a place to sit. Under the aluminum and plastic dome, the heat was torrid. A cloud of dust rose around the bus as it took off, and Marcel, looking backwards, saw the town disappear as if glued down by the haze. Never again, he though, will I return to Goodsprings.

After a few miles, the air-conditioning rapidly lowered the temperature.

3

The first envelope contained a bill, the following two contained calling cards on which a few lines of sympathy had been scribbled, and the fourth contained a playing card.

A single playing card.

The Queen of Spades. Pallas: red, blue, yellow and black, crowned with the elaborate pointed circlet, holding a tulip in her hand.

Xavier noticed all the details for the first time: the curve of the little finger, the pushed up breasts, the Greek profile, the ermine-trimmed sleeves, and the head-dress of fatal spades.

The center of the card had been perforated, perfectly punctured, by one of those little gadgets used to punch holes in sheets of paper for filing.

Xavier turned the card over. There was no inscription, just the usual interlaced floral and geometric designs. He examined the envelope, posted in Paris the previous day, rue de la Reine-Blanche, in the 13th district . . . no other indications, except the carefully printed address, Monsieur Jacques Bertol, 12 rue des Vieilles Tanneries, 78550, Houdan. A curious riddle.

"Florence, come and see this."

Florence came out of the next room. She was wearing the black outfit of a widow in mourning, but her eyes were laughing.

"Look what I found in the mail."

Florence finished buttoning up her jacket.

"I really don't know . . . the Queen of Spades . . . Probably a bad joke. There's no more classic symbol of death. Your father had nothing but friends, you know."

"Yes, but still it's strange, this card with the hole in the center . . . without any explanation. Do you think that my father would have known what it's all about?"

"How do you expect me to know? It's bound to be from some crazy person, and probably doesn't mean anything at all."

Xavier scowled. He put the card back in its envelope and slipped it into his pocket. In any event, the little mystery no longer had any importance. Jacques Bertol had died a few days before because of a heart attack and was being buried that very day. Whatever its significance, the odd message had arrived too late.

However, a similar envelope arrived the next day, mailed from the same post office. It contained a Four of Spades. Xavier and Florence felt that the threat was becoming more exact. But it too was a waste. The mysterious sender didn't seem to realize that his correspondent was dead.

When, the following day, they received the Three of Spades, it wasn't difficult for them to imagine that a count-down had begun. Without any distinct fear, they felt the stirrings of an inexplicable menace.

Xavier had always felt the deepest contempt — for what so-called logical minds termed "the irrational" — in other words, all that which science is not able to understand — an unyielding attitude which places horoscopes, miracles at Lourdes, flying saucers, premonitions, and all other demonstrations of popular belief in the same category. For what reason could a simple playing card be a Messenger of Death? Literature, of course, was filled with romance of this sort, but then aren't all writers eternally naive?

Now he understood that evil forces could well lurk behind these symbols — and that, as a simple man, he could dread the symptom as much as what is signified.

There remained two days before the sender of the cards would reveal himself (Xavier was convinced that this would happen) — and these two days would pass slowly. He even thought of running away. For one thing, the emotional strain after the sudden (if not entirely unexpected) death of his father deserved a few days of rest. Business would not suffer, and the villa at La Baule was only an hour's flight away. Florence would certainly not be unhappy with an unexpected break. He hesitated . . .

Finally curiosity, as well as the refusal to accept what might pass for cowardice, forced him to stay. He arranged, nevertheless, for Florence to be away from the house for a few days. It was cruel to expose her to the violence which perhaps lay hidden behind this vague threat.

He thought of the evil charm of the Queen of Spades. In spite of himself, he was caught by the spell. He also thought that his life was taking an interesting turn, in fact, an unhoped-for fear that gnawed at him was not entirely unpleasant.

* * *

Two of Spades.

Ace of Spaces.

Nothing.

He had spent the two previous days looking through his father's study, searching in vain for a clue of some sort. His address book, diary, carefully filed correspondence, drawers, blotting pad — all the traditional sources for clues — had revealed nothing.

He thought of going to the police, but the image of presenting the cards to an amused inspector, and explaining that his father (who had been buried six days earlier) was being threatened with death took away any desire to inform the police. This incoherent story would probably be attributed to a state of shock following his father's death. He was therefore obliged to face the enemy alone.

He forced himself to remain calm. After all, nothing had been addressed to him personally; he should have nothing to fear.

But there are situations where reason does not suffice, and this he was learning the hard way. Danger hovered over him. He felt it.

His hands trembled as he sorted the mail. Would there be a more distinct threat? Did he risk having a letter-bomb explode in his face? Or perhaps, even worse, was the mystery going to stop here, after the sending of the five cards, and leave him pondering their meaning. Already he knew that he would never be able to look at the Queen of Spades in the same way again.

He thought about his father. Would he have understood all this? Would he have allowed the insidious fear to grow in him? Would he have fled? Or would he have waited for the danger to show itself? The latter no doubt. He hadn't been a soldier for nothing. He had known the mixture of repulsion and attraction that risk produced in a man — and how to overcome it. Xavier had only known the dangers of business, and he had reacted too superficially. Could he be any other way?

He contrived a stratagem. Perhaps one evil spell would succumb to another? He went downstairs and tacked a card to the door, announcing the death of General Jacques Bertol, and hoped that his mysterious correspondent would then understand the futility of his threats.

Then, he returned to take cover at the corner of a window, and wait.

He didn't have to wait long. Monsieur Poinsot, the family lawyer, rang at the door. Xavier found the visit annoyingly untimely, perhaps risking his rendezvous with the man (or woman?) of the Queen of Spades. He opened the door for Poinsot, impatiently.

"Yes, Monsieur? What is it?"

"I assure you, it won't take long," the elderly gentleman replied courteously. He was the stubborn type who still wore a hat and added an expensive fur collar to his overcoat every winter. "Just a formality. I have something to give you on behalf of your father."

"From my father? But I thought that the will had been left with Monsieur — "

"Yes, of course, with Monsieur Hureaux. No, it's not that, but simply a few documents that your father entrusted to me and asked me to take care of in the event of anything happening to him. I am to give them to you . . . to you alone." (He looked down the hall and beyond, to where the living room door stood open.) "You are alone, I believe?"

Xavier couldn't help smiling. He was sure that Poinsot knew that Madame Bertol had left for La Baule and that all the other family members had returned to their respective homes.

"Yes, Florence has gone away for a few days' rest . . . what with all this upheaval, the unexpected loss . . . "

"Of course, of course. I understand," Poinsot murmured with a kind of suspiciousness that Xavier found odious.

The lawyer was reputed to sniff out trouble with a keenness that verged on delight. He was probably longing to know why Xavier had allowed his wife to go away without him, why he hadn't gone to his office for two days, and why he was there alone. Xavier didn't flinch. He continued to bar the door although Poinsot clearly wanted to come in.

"What are these papers?" he asked irritably.

"Good heavens, monsieur, I have no idea. Your father spoke of confidential documents." (He lowered his voice as a stranger passed behind him. Xavier only noticed that the guy was wearing a green and red striped tie.) "Yes, confidential. May I come in?"

"Yes, certainly," Xavier replied mechanically, watching the man walking away, a little old pensioner, dressed in a Prince of Wales suit and carrying a suitcase which didn't look particularly heavy.

"Thank you. I preferred to come here, rather than inviting you to my office, as I understand that you haven't left Houdan for a few days."

"That's very kind of you. Can I offer you a drink?" Xavier asked, showing Poinsot to the most comfortable chair in the room.

"No, no, thank you. I don't drink this early in the day . . ."

"You'll excuse me for receiving you in my father's study, but . . . "

"Not at all, it's quite natural. At any rate, this won't take long."

Monsieur Poinsot gently rested a black leather attache case on his knees (a very handsome leather case, Xavier noticed). He removed a bulky envelope with three wax seals from the case."

"*Voilà.*"

Xavier took the envelope and tossed it nonchalantly onto an end table.

"You really won't have a drink?"

If Poinsot thought he was going to learn what was in the envelope, he was greatly mistaken.

"No, really, thanks."

"In that case, my dear sir, you'll excuse me, but I have to finish tidying the house." (He almost blushed at this ridiculous lie as if Poinsot would believe for a second that he had stayed home to do household chores.)

At his nod towards the door, Poinsot rose awkwardly, closing his leather briefcase.

"Uh — I think I would like a receipt . . ." he stammered.

"A receipt for what? A receipt for a sealed envelope?" Xavier asked ironically. "Did my father get a receipt acknowledging that you had received this envelope?"

"No, your father and I were old friends. This all took place in strict confidence. It would never have occurred to your father to ask me for a receipt."

"In that case, my dear sir, I'd like you to know that I share my father's trust in you, and I certainly value your kind friendship in these cruel circumstances. So . . . after you."

Without the chance to offer the least resistance, Monsieur Poinsot found himself being accompanied to the door in a most polite manner. The door closed behind him before he even had the time to understand that he had been brushed off, and that he would probably never know the contents of the mysterious envelope. He did have a vague idea, perhaps not far from the truth. It wasn't the first time he had been entrusted with this kind of mission, and nothing, apart from Xavier Bertol's odd behavior, led him to believe that General Bertol had acted any differently from his other clients. He headed slowly back towards his office, wondering whether Xavier's strange conduct could be attributed to his sorrow at his father's death, perversity, or some other reason that he was unaware of. The third possibility seemed the most likely, and he savored in advance the dark implications with which he would entertain his less than charitable circle.

Xavier returned unhurriedly to the study, in spite of the impatience gnawing at him. He had no doubts that the beige envelope contained anything but the key to the riddle that had been plaguing him for the past five days. He even briefly considered that Monsieur Poinsot, with his preying appetite, had contrived the farce of anonymous cards to prepare for the theatrical scene which was to follow. But would the lawyer have gone so far as to post the letters in Paris? The cards could just as well have been mailed from the same town without diminishing the terror of the effect. Unless it had been an extra precaution which future events would make clear. Maybe the lawyer had had the help of an accomplice in the capital, as Xavier could hardly imagine him traveling to Paris each day to post a single letter. Monsieur Poinsot's affection for his office chair was too well known, and such deviation from his sedentary ways wouldn't go unnoticed in this small town.

These were useless suppositions; Xavier had retained enough lucidity to know that they were based on his own excitement and sense of adventure. It was simply a matter of breaking the envelope's seals, and then he would understand everything.

Xavier clawed at the first seal, but without success. He tried the opposite one, but the envelope was hermetically sealed (he recognized his father, the perfectionist) and it resisted a superficial investigation. Xavier deliberately tore one of the edges, walking towards one of the windows for more light.

Before dying, perhaps he heard the curious sound of the bullet as it punctured, without breaking, the pane at the same level as his head.

* *
*

"Let's start again, at the beginning, if you don't mind," proposed Commissioner Viliard, pulling at the left side of his thin mustache. "You returned yesterday evening around 6:30 in your own car, a dark blue Autobianchi A 112. Is that correct?"

"Yes, it is. Registration 7835AZ78," Florence Bertol replied with some irritation (and perhaps a touch of irony, ill-befitting a tearful widow).

The commissioner looked curiously at the attractive young woman whom the chance of his profession had deposited before him. She couldn't have been more than thirty, maybe less. She was wearing a black suit with a very white blouse, which became her nicely. The idea occurred to him that Madame Bertol might have had a premonition of her husband's death (which certainly led to some unpleasant suppositions) in order to be able to present herself as so captivating a widow within the first hours of the investigation. Then he remembered that her father-in-law had died the week before. Madame Bertol was therefore in mourning for the second time . . . and really very prettily. The willful and steady manner that she used in answering his questions had pleased the commissioner. He had little time for the simpering widows he usually encountered under similar circumstances. Florence Bertol appeared to play a different game — unless, of course, this was her true character, which still changed little. Was it simply a matter of finding out how and why she had killed her husband?

Florence Bertol didn't flinch under the commissioner's sharp gaze. She had taken an immediate dislike to this mustached, corpulent character. He had barely taken the time to introduce himself and, having mumbled a few words of condolence which were totally lacking in warmth, installed himself in the most comfortable chair in the living room, loosened his tie, and rolled up his sleeves. His conceit was surpassed only by his vulgarity, qualities which she found not entirely surprising in a police officer. Florence found an outlet for her feelings in the arrogance with which she responded to his questions, expressing a part of the hatred that she should have reserved for Xavier's killer.

"So, you parked your car behind the house and entered the kitchen through the back door. Stop me if I'm wrong," he added, with the affability of a door-to-door salesman. "No? Good. You were worried, you say, because the house was completely darkened, and because you'd had no news from your husband for a few days. Could you be more precise?"

"Precise? I have been. Your inspector . . . what's his name again?"

"Boruti."

"That's the one. He noted that I left Houdan for La Baule on the eleventh and that, after several unanswered phone calls, I decided to return on the fifteenth. I suppose that he's made a report?"

"Yes, I've read it," admitted the commissioner without losing his composure. "But what do you mean by 'several unanswered phone calls?' "

"If you expect me to quote you the day, the exact hour and the time I waited before hanging up, you are wasting your time. I didn't keep a record. But I called from the Post Office. You can always check there."

Still, you must remember something. All this is very recent. When did you call the first time?"

"Saturday evening, shortly after I arrived in La Baule."

"And there was no reply?"

"Yes, there was. Xavier was here, of course. He was waiting for my call."

"If it isn't indiscreet, what did you say to each other?"

"Nothing much — 'Good trip, did you arrive safely, enjoy your Sunday, be careful?' "

" 'Be careful' . . . Why 'be careful?' "

"Because of the threats, of course. Don't pretend that you don't understand."

"This business of the playing cards? We'll get to that later. So you telephoned Saturday evening. And then?"

"The following day, late afternoon, Xavier called me. He had had lunch with some friends and was worried that I might have tried to call him."

" 'Worried,' really?"

"Yes, worried. It has nothing to do with being afraid. It's a common way of behaving, you know."

"Hmm. And I suppose that you didn't say much this time either?" (Florence Bertol shrugged her shoulders, which seemed to satisfy the commissioner.) "Let's go on to the next day."

"I telephoned on Monday night around nine or ten o'clock, then early the next morning, as I hadn't been able to get through."

"What do you mean, you hadn't been able to get through?"

"There was no answer. The same thing on Tuesday, all day long. In the afternoon, I decided to come home immediately, which I did."

"So here we are, at the back door. Was it locked?"

"No, the door was open, as usual. We only lock it when we go away. We use that door all the time for going from the house to the garden . . . but I've already explained all that."

Commissioner Viliard's expression was pained. Unfortunately the investigation necessitated the repetition of questions. He loosened his tie even more and undid a shirt button. Florence realized the fat man was trying to make her understand that he was very hot, and very thirsty — but she certainly didn't intend to make life any easier for this unpleasant character, and she refrained from offering him anything to drink. The police officer began to scratch his hairy chest. Florence's disgust increased.

"So you turned on the kitchen light and went immediately into the study. Right?"

"No, as you very well know. I called out to Xavier, went down the hall, into the living room, and then into the study, whose door was open."

"Why this route?"

"Because it was the most logical. You're very irritating."

"Continue."

"Well, Xavier was stretched out on the carpet at the foot of the desk, his face horribly distorted, as if the inside had been destroyed . . . it was awful. There was very little blood. You could almost have imagined that he had only fainted, if it hadn't been for the atrocious expression on his face . . . his eyes all wide open."

Viliard was forced to admire the composure of the young woman. Her voice was unfaltering and her bearing heroic. She was only the wife of the general's son, but she truly could have been the old soldier's daughter. She possessed his strong character and proud resignation.

The commissioner's convictions about her waned. The murderesses that he had encountered were, in general, given to excessive displays of grief which immediately aroused suspicion. Even if, as he suspected, Florence Bertol had killed her husband, her attitude remained a complete riddle to him. He began to think that Widow Bertol was not pretending. This thought made him ill-tempered. His fundamental and cynical mistrust was based on the old detective's adage, "find the woman," and his esteem (perhaps even his admiration) was limited to the cleverness of female criminals. He would have been profoundly disappointed to learn that Florence Bertol didn't belong to that category.

"You immediately phoned the local police station, who in turn called us. Inspector Boruti took your first statement . . . I see that your declaration corresponds perfectly with his report . . . I congratulate you. Such tallied information is rather rare."

Florence Bertol preferred to ignore the threat implied in the commissioner's last statement. He obviously suspected that she knew more than she was prepared to admit. Perhaps he even believed that she had committed the murder? She couldn't care less, and even derived a certain pleasure at his persistent innuendoes. As long as this repulsive character stayed around asking his questions, she was not alone, and this prolonged the moment when she would finally find herself face to face with her anguish. The previous night had been hell, in spite of the comforting presence of friends (the same friends who had invited Xavier to lunch last Sunday). They had been given to understand, by the police, that they were the last people to have seen the young businessman alive.

"Tell me more about this mysterious and threatening Queen of Spades," Viliard asked with his hint of sarcasm.

"It was probably a bad joke, Commissioner. It was because of that card, and the one that followed it, that my husband decided I should go away, despite my own desire to stay with him. After all, *we* weren't threatened. At least, that's what we believed."

The commissioner tried not to smile. He politely listened as she spoke, and once the dates on which each of the cards had arrived were established, he asked, "I imagine that you have kept the cards? May I see them?"

Florence looked annoyed.

"It was Xavier who kept them, as I was instructed not to touch a thing . . . perhaps your inspectors have found them?"

Viliard groaned and shouted in the direction of the hall, "Boruti?"

The clatter in the study, whose door opened into the living room, stopped.

"Yes boss."

"Have you seen a series of playing cards anywhere? Ace, two, three, four, and Queen of Spades?"

Boruti appeared at the door with all the eagerness of a probationer. He was a young man with a lightly tanned complexion, carefully combed hair, and a bright look.

The day before, he had taken the first statements with extreme kindness and courtesy — and an enthusiasm which he had forced himself to repress. Florence had understood that this was his first assignment, which his youthful appearance made perfectly believable. She hadn't minded the zeal with which he had questioned her, and later regretted that he was not in charge of the investigation. She found him infinitely more pleasant than his chief.

"No boss. I've looked everywhere. Madame told me about the cards last night."

Viliard gave him a dirty look. He hated these youngsters with their big ideas, who showed so much initiative (an initiative that wasn't asked of them). Fortunately, Viliard himself would have the last word.

"Okay, apart from that, is there anything new?"

"Yes sir, we found the bullet . . . or at least what's left of it."

"You should have told me immediately!"

"But you told us not to disturb you."

"All right, let's see it." He turned to Madame Bertol. "Will you excuse me a moment?"

Florence, surprised at the detective's sudden outburst, simply nodded her head. She then pictured Xavier's frightful multilation — the bullet penetrating his skull as if it were an over-ripe fruit, passing out the other side, and ending up in the wood or plaster of the wall. She almost screamed out loud.

"You see it's there, just next to the bracket-lamp, in the design of the wallpaper," said Boruti to his superior. "You really have to put your nose to it, it's almost unnoticeable . . . with the angle of the light, it's difficult to see."

"Nevertheless, it should have been just as visible last night."

Boruti understood his chief's meaning well enough. He turned on the lamp.

"No, look. It's much worse like this. That's why I didn't see it then," he explained.

Viliard grumbled some more and put his nose to the hole, as Boruti had suggested. The shadow cast by the light concealed the point perfectly.

"Okay, turn it off. What do you mean? This isn't a little hole. The guy must have had his skull completely shattered."

"Only on one side. In view of the position of the corpse, it's the side where the bullet passed out. You can see virtually nothing on the side where the bullet entered the skull. Just a small, perfectly round hole."

Viliard refrained from asking how Boruti had managed to know all this. He would have been treated to a full account, tinged with a little patronizing, from his subordinate.

"What caliber?" he asked, certain that Boruti wouldn't easily admit his ignorance.

"I would have to be an expert to say for sure. On the other hand, I don't think I'd be wrong to say that it was an exploding shell, in all probability fired from a hunting rifle."

Viliard had to admit that he was beaten. "But how do you know all this, Boruti?"

"By looking and weighing it all up, boss. I would even say that it was a hard core bullet, as it didn't mushroom on impact, or did very little, anyhow. If not, the wound on the left side — the messy side, that is — would have been much cleaner, and the bullet might not have even passed through. These are simple ballistics principles, and I — "

"Yes. Thank you, Boruti," the commissioner interrupted. "Do you have any idea of where the shot was fired from?"

"No doubt from the magnolia hedge down there, just opposite . . . where, in fact, he risked being seen. It's sure, however, that the gunman would have had to be in an imaginary straight line traced from him to the hole in the window pane, the victim's head, and the final point of impact."

"And why should it have been a hunting rifle?"

"Because that's the best weapon for this kind of killing. It is both accurate and powerful, capable of firing bullets at an initial high speed. It would have been necessary to fire a pistol or revolver from a shorter distance in order to obtain such a result . . . or an extra powerful caliber, Magnum 357 type, which is hardly known in France."

"Good, fine. Advise the laboratory to remove the bullet and make a report on the trajectory — and find those damn cards for me."

Viliard left Boruti in the company of another inspector named Legriffe, an excellent assistant who never said much and always did as he was told without offering fancy theories.

Viliard relished the idea of soon having to write up an administrative report on Boruti. They would see who was the smarter of the two. "By looking and weighing it all up," indeed. Did he think his chief was an idiot?

Of course, Viliard had to admit that he wasn't a very "scientific" police officer. He had joined the force during the last war to avoid combat duty, and hadn't known St. Cyr-au-Mont-d'Or or the Police Academy. He had been trained on the job and hadn't bothered to question a method that neglected thorough investigation of material evidence and contented itself with assigning guilt *a priori*. This method was totally intuitive and perfectly routine, and worked well enough, bearing in mind the simplicity of the cases that Viliard usually dealt with. Furthermore, he didn't feel that it was necessary to concern himself with duties which he considered the domain of forensic pathologists and laboratory experts. In other words, he detested the way Boruti worked. Not only did he consider these new methods unaffective, but they would have changed his personal habits.

He returned to the armchair.

Florence Bertol hadn't left her place. She sat on the extreme edge of the sofa, refusing to seek a more comfortable position as it would necessitate tugging at the hem of her skirt, and the fact of Viliard's odious presence forbade her to relax so naturally.

The commissioner opened his mouth to ask a question (or maybe to remark that he was terribly thirsty) when the front doorbell rang.

"Boruti, go and get that," he yelled in his usual fashion.

The footsteps of the young inspector echoed in the hall, then the latch of the door clicked. Viliard strained to hear the conversation.

"Excuse me if I'm interrupting. I am Monsieur Poinsot, the family lawyer and an old friend of the general . . ."

Florence got up.

"Please come in, Monsieur."

Poinsot slid through the narrow space between Boruti and the door.

"Dear Madame, allow me to offer my deepest and most sincere condolences. What has happened is truly horrible. If I had only known, I would have asked your husband to come to my office. I have no doubt, the sad priviledge of being the last person to seem him alive."

"What are you saying?" thundered the commissioner.

The two men looked at each other coldly.

"Monsieur?" the lawyer inquired with somewhat affected courtesy.

"Commissioner Viliard, Judicial Police of Versailles," muttered the detective.

Boruti watched the meeting of the weasel and the wild boar with amusement.

"Pleased to meet you, Commissioner. Actually I did want to see you."

Florence asked the two men to sit down and offered the lawyer a drink, which the commissioner readily accepted.

In spite of Viliard's impatience, Monsieur Poinsot waited for the return of the mistress of the house. Then, after the last drop had been downed, the witness to the last hour in the life of Xavier Bertol described his Monday morning visit.

"What was the purpose of this visit?" Viliard asked.

"Ah . . . I don't know whether I can tell you . . . professional confidentiality, you know. But as there has been a murder, perhaps you will understand, dear Madame, that is is difficult for me to do otherwise?"

"Please go ahead, Monsieur," she said, in a voice suddenly full of emotion.

She, like the commissioner, was burning to know what had led Poinsot to meet with Xavier so shortly before his death. In the study, Boruti and Legriffe's rumaging became more discrete, almost imperceptible. Poinsot then explained the duty that he had performed. He didn't even look surprised when the commissioner told him that the sealed envelope had, apparently, disappeared.

"And what were the contents of this mysterious envelope?" Viliard asked authoratatively, realizing that Poinsot might stand firm on this particular issue.

"Unfortunately, I don't know," Poinsot replied drily. "I thought that I mentioned that the envelope was sealed?"

"Come, come, my dear sir, don't pretend . . . don't you have even a little idea?"

Poinsot was unperturbed. He intended to keep his "little idea" to himself. Never let it be said that Monsieur Poinsot allowed the contents of an envelope which had been given to him for safe-keeping to be revealed — without his knowing what it was all about. What he thought was his own business. Viliard understood.

"In your opinion, could the contents have motivated such a crime?"

Poinsot looked slightly amused.

"Perhaps . . . I don't really know. Did the murderer even know about it? Apart from the General — may his soul rest in peace — I was the only person to know of the existence of the envelope. M. Xavier Bertol himself knew nothing until Monday."

"Unfortunately, he is no longer here to contradict you, and you remain the only living person to have known about the envelope."

"I see that it won't be long before I am placed on your list of suspects, Commissioner. I expected that. Do you honestly believe that's possible? It would have been very easy for me to have kept the envelope, without telling anyone," the lawyer simpered.

"We only have your evidence. Nothing proves that the victim was, in fact, unaware of the envelope."

Poinsot frowned. Obviously the commissioner was an imbecile; it was hardly possible to joke with him. His severe manner indicated that he took everything seriously. Well, if that's what made him happy . . . Poinsot had his own conscience to look after.

"Okay. I'd like to ask you to remain at our disposal, and not to leave the area without advising us." (He turned towards Florence.) "I'll probably stop by again this evening. I imagine that you will be here?"

Florence nodded. She could not go to see her friends until after his visit; she hoped that it would not be too late.

Viliard muttered that he would do his best and walked to the door, adjusting his tie. Boruti and Legriffe followed.

Just before closing the door, he turned around.

"Madame, may I ask an indiscreet question?"

The indiscreet question was part of the "Viliard method," and he never missed asking it, without really knowing why. Perhaps because he had seen television detectives doing the same thing. The last question asked through a chink in the door always created the necessary suspense.

Florence raised her eyebrows.

"Madame Bertol, did you love your husband?"

The usual answer would be, "Of course, Commissioner. Why such a question?"

"No reason at all," he would reply, before going off into the night (or even better, disappearing in the fog).

"I beg your pardon?"

"I asked you whether you loved your husband?"

"Your question is utterly ridiculous," she replied coldly.

The door slammed in his face.

Furious and disappointed, Viliard caught up with the two inspectors a little further on where they stood under the next doorway out of the midday sun.

The soft September light danced in the leaves of the trees.

4

The concierge at No. 101 was a little round lady, dark-haired and smiling, who greeted the tenant with a friendly nod as he walked past, before continuing her dull contemplation of the television. Only five minutes to wait before the first show of the afternoon would begin.

She listened to the sure sound of the footsteps accompanied by the creaking of the old wooden staircase. The steps began rapidly and then trailed off, as usual. Madame Girey, like all concierges, was able to recognize each of her tenants by listening to their footsteps. This talent, the result of years of practice, was limited to the confines of her little ground-floor lodge. The sounds that reached her in the elevator or the halls were not the same, because they were muffled and diffused, as those which came through her ceiling, situated directly under the first flight of stairs. In spite of very real efforts, she had never been able to understand how a single personality was not able to produce two different series of footsteps.

The footsteps died away. Madame Girey knew that from the hallway she would be able to hear a key being turned in a lock on the third floor. She waited for the sound of plumbing, the sign that would confirm that her tenant had indeed reached his apartment; faithful to habit, he always began by washing his hands. "To remove the sand," he had once explained to her (although she didn't exactly understand what he meant by that), when she had gone to deliver a large package a little after he had moved in. Madame Girey had until then been aware of this innocent idiosyncrasy — an excessive obsession with cleanliness no doubt — and afterwards, had never missed spying on her third floor tenant to verify that he always took the same precaution. It had become a sort of mania for her too — a way of assuring herself that all was well.

The pipes clattered noisily and the sound of running water reverberated through the building. Madame Girey felt reassured. She exchanged a radiant welcoming smile with the television announcer, a smile that didn't wane when the list of actors in the serial appeared on the screen.

Marcel Ribot dried his hands carefully. He was happy to be back on home ground, this pitiful, narrow room with its tiny corner kitchen and even tinier shower. It wasn't a bad place. It was all that he needed as a penniless little old pensioner leading an austere life.

He glanced around to make sure that nothing had been touched in the room: the gaudy blanket that covered the bed, the dagger of an SS officer hanging on the wall, flanked by two hand painted maracas, and a map of the world on which he had traced "his travels." Underneath the wardrobe, a pair of perfectly polished shoes and a pair of old-fashioned cloth slippers were laid out in a strict row. The curtains hung in their usual folds, and the opposite wall was covered with trophies — medals, insignias, decorations — arranged with military perfection in spite of the layers of dust which had accumulated on them.

Marcel neatly placed his suitcase on the bed. He took off his jacket and his striped tie and changed from his Prince-of-Wales trousers into an old pair of khakis. He rolled up his sleeves, put on his slippers, then proceeded to remove the lace tablecloth and pottery soup tureen from the table — items which added an unexpectedly bourgeois touch to his apartment. These common-place gestures filled him with an incxplicable but simple pleasure. Perhaps it was simply the joy of living. And living intensely.

The two locks of the suitcase clicked open. Marcel took out the well-used blanket and unrolled it slowly, taking care not to drop the empty cartridge cases. The rifle had been swathed in the folds of the fabric as if it had been a fragile bird on the verge of flying away.

Once he had laid the weapon and ammunition on the open blanket, he want back past the kitchen to check that the door was double-locked from the inside. Then he moved over to the broom closet (which in fact contained only one broom, but plenty of other items), and removed a small wooden box with a combina-tion lock. He dialed the combination: 82.623. The box opened without any difficulty.

Beneath several layers of clean cloth lay an apparatus for reloading cartridge casings, some empty cartridge cases, a box of bullets, several sets of caliber and powder measures, a can of oil, another of grease, a cleaning rod, some small brushes, and caps and a set of tiny screwdrivers . . . everything that was needed to clean a rifle and recharge cartridges — a marvelous set of gadgets for any firearm enthusiast.

Marcel picked up the two cartridge casings and prepared to clean them. He first removed the two caps. He then returned to the kitchen, ran some hot water, and added detergent to it. Once the two cases were perfectly clean, he wiped them scrupulously with a thin cloth, then arranged them among his souvenirs, with the aid of a wire thread. He stepped back to admire his handiwork. These two cartridges were the first trophies of his most recent combat: two bullets for Biaggi's dog, one for Chuck Bonanza's daughter, one for the son of General Bertol, and two for Schültznicht's mistress. That was enough. Their role was now over. However, the battle wasn't. It would simply have been dangerous to charge them a fourth time.

Satisfied, Marcel sat down at the table, having placed his favorite chair so that he could gaze at the decorated wall. From time to time he threw a kid's gleeful eye at his new trophies, as he undertook the dismantling of his gun. A few precise moves isolated the five pieces of the breech, a name for each, and plenty of memories. For a long time now Marcel had been able to assemble and dismantle his weapon in total darkness. he had always known that the soldier's life depended on the confidence that he could have in his "best friend," and he had more than once had the occasion to prove exactly how true that maxim was. He figured that he was going to have to check the trigger and the alignment of the sight. At Brückenkirchen, the first bullet had gone too far off the mark.

* * *

Schültznicht had not been easy to dig up. The trail that would one day lead Marcel Ribot to find him on the romantic banks of the Morava River had been broken up after a battle some time ago, when Sub-Lieutenant Schültznicht had been reported missing. Ribot had then ruled him off the list. He had almost forgotten his name. But, one day he learned from another old-timer at an "Amicale" meeting that Schültznicht was not dead. He had returned to his country and had assumed the name Krantz, Dieter Krantz, and was sales manager for a trading company which dealt mainly with Eastern European countries.

So, armed with this meager information (his informer having acknowledged that he knew nothing more), Marcel used all his limited financial resources to find Krantz — who should now have been about fifty years old, with his fine blond hair, girl's hair . . . and all the refinement of a debutante. Marcel hadn't forgotten the rumors surrounding the young and beautiful Schültznicht, the favorite aide-de-camp of Commandant Groetz, the one they had all called "Fräulein."

The simplest path was to resort to the "Amicale." That, however, yielded no results. Nevertheless, Marcel persevered, cross-questioning old-timers at every available opportunity, never missing a banquet, a commemorative service, a ceremony. He participated in the functions at the Arc de Triomphe with untiring effort, never refusing a glass of white wine afterwards, in an atmosphere rich with memories recalled by total strangers. Occasionally, he met up with old comrades, and always finished with the inevitable question, "And Schültznicht, you remember, Lieutenant Schültznicht of the 2nd Company. 'Fräulein' Goetz's aide-de-camp, do you know what has happened to him?" All these efforts proved fruitless. Marcel then attempted another method. He approached the Austrian Embassy on rue Fabert, which in turn directed him to a commercial association in rue des Arcades. The name Krantz was of no help whatsoever. There were thousands of Krantzes in Austria. As for the firm, he should at least know its name. He was given the names and addresses of several organizations which might be able to assist him, but he soon realized that in spite of their good intentions these friendly people asked too many questions.

He drew up lists, and soon realized that playing amateur private detective wasn't such an easy job. Still, he never felt discouraged. On the contrary, all the difficulties that he encountered instilled within him a certain *joie de vivre*. "Victory at any price" had always been his motto.

He examined the problem from all angles, and decided that the only possible solution lay in telephone directories. He easily obtained, with the industrious aid of a staff member of a French-Austrian friendship association, the address of a firm in Vienna that was the equivalent of the French "Bottin." He wrote to the firm in question, and they replied that he could consult the directory on their premises or those in most post offices. Marcel then began to save towards a visit to Innsbruck. In February the trip materialized.

For the first time in his life, he experienced the exhilarating atmosphere of a winter sports resort. He watched the happy fortunate people flying down the ski slopes for hours. He laughed at the beginners' falls and marveled at the magnificent mountains. Shivering and fascinated, he stood at the edge of the ice and watched the curling games, which remined him of the *pétanque* played in Southern France. In the evenings, he often went to see the rhythmic swirling of the ice-skaters (especially the ice-skaters in the little short skirts, whose lovely long legs filled his mind with old dreams). And to make his visit complete, he took a sleigh ride. The sleigh was drawn by a sturdy horse with bells attached to its collar. Another evening, he treated himself to a fur-clad girl. She was firm and robust, built the way they are there, and cost him more than he had ever paid for so simple a pleasure.

He spent all his mornings at the main post office, as well as a good part of the afternoons. Without quite knowing why, he had begun his search in Innsbruck, but soon discovered that it was like looking for a needle in a haystack. There were actually fewer Krantzes than he had at first imagined; however, it would take years to verify whether the D. Krantzes that he found were in fact "Dieter" or "Dietrich" or "David." He drew up long lists of D. Krantzes with addresses and telephone numbers, in case he should require them at a later stage. For the time being, he didn't intend to call any of these gentlemen.

After having spent several days making systematic lists, town by town, of all the names which corresponded to the one he was seeking, he was horrified at the number of sheets he had filled. He realized that it was virtually impossible to achieve his goal this way. Furthermore there was nothing to prove that Krantz even had a telephone or that he was listed in the directory.

Marcel then decided to try to find the name of the firm for which his "customer" worked. Once he had started to orient his research in that direction, he was amazed that he hadn't thought of it sooner. Companies trading with Eastern Europe were certainly less numerous than the "Krantzes." Marcel took his investigation to professional directories. His command of the German language enabled him to write to the Chambers of Commerce. He obtained a list of the companies corresponding to what he was looking for, with "the most important" ones specified. Altogether, there were about thirty "Gesellschaft" with more than two-thirds of them having their headquarters in Vienna. Marcel bought a Vienna telephone directory and returned to Paris, where he became a regular visitor at the phone booths in the post office on the Place Jean-d'Arc. He imposed restrictions on his way of life — he no longer spent his time at the Café Bouchard with its expensive rounds of drinks, he replaced steaks with sausage and pigs feet and, for the moment, gave up the horse races. The money that he saved in this way was immediately swallowed up by telephone calls to Austria.

At last his perseverance paid off. Dieter Krantz was in fact sales manager for a company called *International-Weyden*, only he didn't work at the headquarters, but at a subsidiary which dealt with transport to Czechoslovakia. It was situated in a little town at the border, on the banks of the Morava: Brückenkirchen. Marcel's unknown informant willingly gave him the address and telephone number of this subsidiary. Marcel hung up, feeling the very height of happiness. He had just carried off a fine victory.

He reappeared at the Café Bouchard the same evening. The drinking was monumental and the money that was left in the "telephone kitty" was spent on Thursday's racing jackpot. Marcel lost, as usual, but he consoled himself with buying an enormous T-bone which he fried in the kitchen of his small apartment with the respect and joy reserved for solemn feast-days.

* * *

Upon arriving in Brückenkirchen, Marcel Ribot wasn't even sure that he would recognize Schültznicht, alias Dieter Krantz. He had held on to the address that *International-Weyden* had given him for several months, and hadn't attempted to verify the information. Now that the offensive had begun, he was taking no risks. He took the train to Brückenkirchen a few days after his business in Houdan, and arrived on a Thursday evening. The next morning found him seated on a public bench, without even the traditional alibi and protection of a newspaper, watching the arrival of *International-Weyden* employees. He thought that he recognized Schültznicht several times among the young executives with their sure gait and fair hair, but he realized that these young Schültznichts weren't identical to the one he had known before. And it was among the middle-aged that he should now seek his man.

Schültznicht arrived at exactly ten o'clock. Marcel recognized him in spite of his excessive weight, bloated face, and thinning hair, the look of a tired bureaucrat. Watching Schültznicht walk up the steps to the building, Ribot couldn't help feeling some pity, a pity that verged on weariness, the sudden desire to give it all up and go back home . . . a sentiment similar to the one he had felt in seeing the slow and painful walk of Ernesto Biaggi in his decrepit state. Even though Schültznicht was almost twenty years younger than Ribot, life had burnt him out more rapidly.

At the top of the steps Schültznicht turned around and for a second Marcel thought that he had been recognized. But the former lieutenant of the 2nd Company's attention wasn't addressed to him but rather to the woman driving the car that had just dropped him off. Marcel wondered whether it was his wife or daughter, or if Schültznicht had a son. From the back of his mind (was it already so long ago?) came the memory of the naked, tanned body of Chuck Bonanza's daughter . . . a body whose existence had suddenly exploded and whose life had flowed away through the opening made by a bit of copper and lead . . . a body that had been flung into death unjustly, as naked as the day it had been flung into life . . . a body sacrificed for the pain of a man.

Marcel regretted that he couldn't drive. He could have then been able to follow the young woman in the BMW without any problem. He looked in vain for a taxi ("Follow that car!") but realized that in such a small town there could only be one or two and they were probably parked in front of the train station. Marcel figured that he would have to wait until evening, hoping that Schültznicht would use one of the two cars he had seen parked at the corner of the street, a few yards away from the building. He shoved his hands deeper into his pockets in the manner common to men who are alone and idle and who don't cover up their indecision by smoking a cigarette. He made his way towards the center of town.

This wasn't the exhilarating Tyrol with its open mountains, snow-covered peaks and icy streams, but the flat country between the Wienerwald and, on the other side of the river, in the other country, the "Male Karpaty" — the small Carpathians. This region was more inclined to economy and industry than tourism. The sad and pastoral town was a little lost in the immense valley whose sky was often darkened by the thick and heavy clouds which belched from the factories.

Marcel walked up the avenue leading to the center and noted the names of the streets — Babenbergstrasse, Pöltenplatz, Weltstrasse — trying to memorize them. It was one way of killing time and making poetry with words. He went into one of the quaint Viennese-type pastry shops, a vestige of another era, and ordered coffee and *linzertorte*. The girl who served him was young and fresh. Her waist was drawn into a pleated skirt, and she wore a white lace pinafore. Her stockings and blouse were also white, and she had the pink cheeks and blonde plaits of a travel brochure model. Marcel watched each of her movements with an open admiration that made the girl blush, but she continued smiling and showing off her perfect white teeth.

Time passed and Marcel resumed his wandering in the streets. Bruchenkirchenprater . . . Brotstrasse . . . Slovachystrasse . . . St. Pauliplatz . . . St.Rudolfstrasse . . . Unterplatz . . . Did he have any chance of following Schültznicht back to his home? Would the woman come back in the car? Without luck was he going to be able to do anything? He began to feel that this business had started off badly. Of course he could always carry out his mission in front of the office building, but the risk would be enormous, if not desperate. He had to discover the identity of the young woman.

He came up with the idea of sitting on the terrace of one of the cafés on the Pöltzenplatz, near most of the town's shops, watching to see whether, by chance (a logically possible chance), the young woman would come to do her marketing.

It was a good idea. He had no trouble recognizing the car, and then the young woman got out. It was a little after eleven o'clock. The girl was dark-haired with light green eyes. Her short hair framed a face whose rough beauty was almost aggressive. She walked around the car, which was parked just opposite Marcel, and took out a large denim shopping bag. She walked past, swaying her ample backside. Her large breasts were clearly visible through the opening in her black and white dotted blouse. Marcel had no further doubts as to whether she was a woman. Schültznicht had indeed changed.

Marcel left money for his drink on the marble table and calmly went off after the woman in black. In spite of himself, he was excited by her perfume. The main thing that worried him,

however, was how he was going to obtain Schültznicht's address.
He followed her towards the market, trying to overhear her
conversation without being noticed. He learned that her name was
Greta — not very original — and observed that she didn't wear a
ring, not that it had much significance. At the moment that Greta
was about to get back into her car, he decided that the only
possible course of action was to approach her with the air of an
innocent tourist, and ask whether she knew an old friend of his,
Dieter Krantz, who lived in this town, and whose address he had
mislaid. There was no reason why this shouldn't work. Only this
time he was going to be seen. Greta would certainly insist on
taking him to Krantz herself, and he would have to invent a good
excuse. Once he had the address he would promise to stop by
during the evening, which he intended to do, but the visit would
hardly be a friendly one.

He hurried towards Greta, wondering just how much distrust
this would arouse in Schültznicht. But then, why should he be
suspicious?

With his heart beating like a lovesick schoolboy, he approached
Greta and cleared his throat.

"Fräulein Wunderink!" shouted a froggy voice.

Marcel turned and saw a chubby red-haired kid tripping
ludicrously across the street.

"Josef," Greta answered with a happy smile. She left her car
door open and went to meet him.

Marcel didn't lose his composure. Almost on reflex, he took the
envelope containing the fateful card from his breast pocket,
addressed to Schültznicht, and threw it into the car. His momentum
hadn't been betrayed by the slightest hesitation.

Greta Wunderink lived at 25 Moravaringstrasse. At least that
was the information he got from the directory, in which Dieter
Krantz wasn't listed.

Marcel found out where the street was situated and checked out
of his hotel. Then he went to the station to get the schedule for the
trains to Vienna, and from there to Paris. Finally, he walked out
towards the border post and, a few yards before the customs-
block, turned left along the river. Moravaringstrasse was hardly

more than a badly paved path leading to a few isolated houses with vast gardens and flower-edged lawns. Marcel knew that he hadn't been abandoned by his lucky star after all. Number 25 was one of the last houses, separated from its neighbors by a wealth of leafy trees.

Marcel didn't stop. It was too early for Schültznicht to be home, and before he took up his position, he wanted a clear view of the surroundings and, if possible, he wanted to find a route out other than the one he had just taken in. The customs officers at the border had looked at him with only the dull interest aroused by a passer-by during a long and tedious shift. Marcel had sufficient experience in these situations to know that he hadn't really been "seen." But he didn't want to risk being noticed a second time — it might be dangerous in view of the violent events to follow.

He walked along the banks of the Morava, the edge of no-man's-land. On the other side, the defenses and the guards appeared more numerous. From time to time a dog barked. Marcel thought to himself that a lost bullet from the other side of the Iron Curtain might easily be responsible for the deed he was about to carry out. He found a small pebbled path leading back to the town through some construction sites. Further on he saw some new buildings, already inhabited. That was the path that he would later take back to the station. There would certainly be people around, and he could pass unnoticed. He went back to Greta Wunderink's, looking for a suitable ambush.

Despite the total lack of preparation, he didn't doubt his chances of success for a second. Up until then, improvisation had been his only method of acting and it hadn't worked so badly. He had neither the financial means nor the time to prepare his attacks, taking all the eventualities into consideration. This confidence in himself, and his luck, were undoubtedly the principle reasons for his success. If he didn't act that night, he would take a room in another hotel and return the next day.

That wasn't necessary.

From his vantage point among the trees, Marcel saw the BMW leave the cottage just before five o'clock and head towards the town. He expected them to return early, but the car didn't come back until 11 o'clock. Schültznicht and his mistress (could she be anything else?) had probably been to a restaurant, or with friends, to celebrate the beginning of the weekend.

Marcel had eaten some chocolate, and jumped around a little — but discreetly — to warm himself. The vision of a girl's body — naked and tanned — floating in a blood-filled swimming pool kept passing through his mind. Marcel thought that he would maybe never know the name of Chuck Bonanza's daughter. He regretted that.

He saw the car stop at the bottom of the lawn and Schültznicht and Greta got out. The target was two hundred yards away, a difficult distance at this hour of the night. Marcel had great confidence in the precision of his gun and the soundness of his aim, but he gave himself little chance of succeeding with his first shot. The veiled moonlight and dim glow of the streetlamps spread their light insufficiently. He was sorry that he hadn't been able to equip his rifle with a sighting lens for dusk light, or even better, a lens with a central lighting point for night shots. But he was obliged to do without those costly gadgets. He hoped that Schültznicht would go up the stairs first and switch on the light, thereby illuminating the lawn — and his target — satisfactorily. He would then have to adjust rapidly and fire on a moving target, which complicated the problem even further.

Marcel aimed midway down the lawn. The silence was complete. The air was cool and humid, filled with damp and woody perfumes. Schültznicht and the woman seemed to have disappeared. Marcel lowered his rifle and peered, trying to make the couple out under the low boughs of the cedars. Perhaps Schültznicht and his mistress had skirted the house and entered by another door? Suddenly he saw them appear from behind a bush, their arms tenderly entwined, walking towards him. Wasn't Schültznicht afraid? Had he laughed at the warning that Greta must surely have shown him ("Lieutenant Schültznicht, alias Dieter Krantz" . . . a Queen of Spades, an old memory in an envelope)?

Marcel felt the hatred rising in him. He forgot the cold, the damp, and the anguish, and chased the waves of unexpected pity which sometimes paralyzed him. He grasped his rifle firmly, without useless fumbling, as he had always done, even in the most perilous moments. The two lovers, holding each other closely, turned up the path towards the door. Marcel immediately saw the ideal place: a large circle of light. He couldn't miss.

Schültznicht and Greta entered the light, antechamber to death, at almost the same instant that Marcel fired his first bullet. It whistled past their heads and Schültznicht immediately threw himself down. He hadn't lost certain reflexes. Greta wasn't so fast. More than by instinct, she obeyed her lover's scream. The second bullet struck her as she threw herself to the ground. Schültznicht probably didn't realize at first that she was dead.

Marcel gathered up his things into his suitcase. He left tranquilly, staying within the protection of the bushes. Then he crossed Moravaringstrasse and walked up the path leading through the construction sites. He came across several passers-by, hurrying home from the theater or the movies.

He caught his train.

He dreamed that Schültznicht, collapsed on the corpse of his mistress, was crying.

* * *

The trigger showed no anomaly. None of the parts appeared particularly worn, the springs kept their original flexibility, as well as rigidity, the sear pivoted normally. Marcel checked all the parts; everything was in order.

Why then had his first bullet been lost in the bushes around Greta Wunderink's cottage? A terrible doubt overtook him. Was he, and not his weapon, at fault? He looked at his swollen fingers, gnarled and deformed by the beginnings of arthritis. Could these hands still respond to his reflexes and eyesight? "I'm getting old," he complained with a peevishness that covered a sense of helplessness. He furiously rolled the rifle in its blanket after loading the magazine. Starting tomorrow he would practice at the shooting range in Versailles. This certainly wasn't the moment to lose his hand.

5

The odd trio arrived at Roissy-en-France on a morning.

Attilio Siragusi, unconscious of the soft September warmth, wore a felt hat and a black overcoat. His pointed beard gave him the appearance of an old rabbi. Joe Torronto sported a predominantly red plaid jacket and startling white trousers, while Santiana, faithful to jeans and T-shirts, advertised "MacIllany's Laundry, Chinatown, Call 322-0051." To tell the truth, it would have taken more than this to shake the airport public out of its usual moody stupor.

The three men replied that they were in Paris as tourists when questioned by C.R.S. Furthermore, they weren't carrying weapons, which certainly proved that they hadn't come on "business."

They fought for a taxi, and Joe Torronto cursed Ribot for not having met them. Then he remembered, on one hand, that Marcel didn't drive, and on the other, that he hadn't informed him of their visit. And with good reason.

Upon learning that Chuck Bonanza's daughter had been killed on her father's own property, Joe almost had a heart attack. Siragusi himself had telephoned Joe at the Cactucito, and the old Mafiosa's icy tones reminded Joe of the good old days. Santiana had immediately started the Buick and the two of them set off for Poughkeepsie. Siragusi had decided to look into the affair himself.

In the "little" conference room at Siragusi's villa — the only room Torronto had ever seen, apart from the hall — a young guy was waiting, a typical Mafia "soldier." He and Joe greeted each other with restrained smiles, side-glancing at each other while they waited. Torronto hadn't forgotten that he had vouched for Marcel Ribot, and he wondered what trick of fate had plunged him up to his neck in this dirty business after so many peaceful years of running his own restaurant. He wasn't far from believing that this guy in the three-piece suit was enjoying the spectacle of watching him sweat before pumping him full of Smith and Wesson caliber

38 Special bullets, then throwing him into the Hudson with a solid strip of concrete tied to his feet, in the good old tradition. He reassured himself to the best of his abilities. After all, times had changed. Then too, Santiana wasn't far off. And Siraguisi certainly didn't want to resume his life of crime. He was old, alone, bereft. Why was he even still alive?

Attilio Siragusi's brisk entrance startled Joe Torronto. Siragusi hadn't changed, at least not physically, but he showed a dynamism which only increased Joe's edginess. What struck him most was the rejuvenated expression and lively gleam that lit his face. Instead of the fury he had expected, Joe noticed that the old man seemed to have taken a new lease on life.

"Sorry to have kept you waiting," Siragusi dryly began. "I was on the phone with Las Vegas. This is Giu Benesco, one of Chuck's boys. Giu, this is Joe Torronto of Williamsburg, an old friend, if I may say so."

Joe Torronto didn't flinch under Siragusi's steely gaze. It was too late to avoid the trouble and far better to fight it out. Besides, Joe wasn't entirely unhappy to be taking up a little healthy activity again.

"We're listening, Giu. Sit down, both of you."

They sat in the leather chairs, and Siragusi's black maid brought in drinks and cigars. Yes, the good old days were back again.

"Chuck's daughter was killed on Sunday, August 29th, by a 7mm. expansive bullet, fired at a distance of approximately ninety yards, from a rifle . . . probably a hunting gun. The bullet penetrated under the right breast and came out the left flank, between the fifth and sixth ribs. Death was instantaneous. Chuck's daughter was sixteen. The pieces of the bullet were found by a Lieutenant Posey, who led the police investigation, and were sent immediately to the State ballistic laboratory. For the time being, the analysis has come up with nothing. The place of ambush has also been found. The killer had placed a brown wool blanket on the ground in order to cover his tracks. The cartridge case hasn't been found. It seems that only one bullet was fired. Chuck and his wife saw nothing, heard nothing. They didn't even realize immediately that Lolita had been shot. They thought that

she had simply dived into the swimming pool. It was the silence
that finally attracted their attention. Chuck thinks that about
three minutes went by after Lolita dived before they realized
anything was wrong. He first called Dr. Swanson, then me, and
finally, the police. The cops were there in five minutes . . . ten
minutes after Chuck had discovered his daughter's body. As it was
obvious that the crime had just been committed, Chuck proposed
immediate roadblocks — however as he and Posey don't get
along too well, the Lieutenant smart-assed that he knew what had
to be done, and he wasn't in the habit of setting up roadblocks all
over the United States every time a crime was committed. Before
we had time to call in our 'friends' to intervene, an hour and a half
had gone by, and that certainly gave the killer enough time to get
away. The dogs traced his scent as far as the bus station. Sergeant
O'Malley, who handles this stuff, figures that the guy must have
spent a few hours there, for his scent to have settled so strongly in
the ground. Then we called Judge Henry, but as he was spending
the night with his mistress — a blonde who works at the Alex
Emporium — we wasted even more time. By the time the cops got
on the job, the guy had escaped . . . by plane, train, car, or bus?
We have no idea. We sent our boys around to visit some of our
'competition,' but no results. If Mr. Siragusi hadn't called us, we
would still be at the same dead end. That's a bad pun, excuse me."

Giu Benesco looked at Joe and Siragusi with a smile that was at
the same time slick and a little sorry.

Joe sighed deeply. He had thought that Benesco would never
stop. After all, he didn't give a damn how the Bonanza girl had
been killed. Listening to this guy was like reading a police report

He threw an irritated glance at the little Mafia technocrat. He'd
probably spent a few years of his life at some fancy university
before getting mixed up with the Las Vegas crowd. Joe gave
Siragusi a cold, hard look. Why had the old man telephoned
Bonanza in the first place?

Siragusi understood Joe Torronto's attitude perfectly.

"Sooner or later Chuck would have found out that the trouble
came from here. Besides, Chuck is an old friend of mine, and
yours too, I think. I have no reason to protect this Frenchy . . . as
you did. I hope you haven't forgotten?"

Joe sounded the depths of the mess he had gotten himself into. "What makes you think Marcel did it?"

He knew that this question wasn't very smart, but he had to judge his own position against those whom he now had to consider as enemies.

"Come on, Joe, you don't believe I'm dumb enough to imagine that your friend had nothing to do with it. What's his name again?"

"Ribot, Marcel Ribot."

Giu Benesco took out a leather covered notebook and a gold-plated pen. The other hand held a glass of bourbon whose ice cubes tinkled annoyingly. Giu put down the glass and prepared to write.

"Are you from the police?" Joe asked. "Or do you work for a newspaper?"

"No, why? . . . I'm only taking down the name. You should also give me his address and any other information that might help our investigation."

"Sure, like I just said, you're a cop."

An ugly gleam crossed Benesco's face. He turned towards Siragusi questioningly.

"Chuck has asked Giu to investigate this business. I advise you not to make any trouble, Joe."

"I'm not making trouble Attilio. This guy should put away his notebook and his eighteen-carat pen. If his brain isn't big enough to remember all the details, he shouldn't be on this job. He should be working in a grocery store or a laundry."

Giu Benesco was ruffled. He wasn't used to being treated like this and was certainly accustomed to working under different conditions, to being "handled with kid gloves," as Marcel Ribot would have said. Once again he turned nervously to Siragusi. Joe categorized this guy as a lackey, incapable of acting without instructions from a superior.

Attilio Siragusi was beginning to enjoy himself. He had rediscovered the Joe Torronto of his youth, with his bursts of caustic humor which left any enemy helplessly confused. Siragusi had always thought of Joe as a genuine noble man, and had never understood why he had preferred to stay in Europe, participating in every possible war, before returning to New York to sell chile con carne. He ignored the pleading in Benesco's look. A heavy silence followed.

"If I understand you correctly," Benesco began hollowly (and Joe wondered whether he was going to burst into tears), "you aren't going to cooperate with me . . . I'll have to report this to Chuck."

"Listen to me," Joe explained calmly. "You will give Chuck my greetings and tell him that I share his deep sorrow. I know that he loved his daughter more than most fathers. I know that his first son was killed on the beaches at Normandy, in France, and Ben was knocked off by two little punks over some poker story. As for William, the son he had by his second wife, Eleanora, he was determined to become a racing champion — and ended up killing himself in the Indianapolis 500. So you see, kid, that makes for a lot of misery in one man's life. I'm about Chuck's age. We've even been to war together. Since his eldest daughter, Marjorie, ran off with a black man, there remained only his youngest daughter, the unhoped-for baby of his third marriage. All this I know as well as you do, maybe even better. I'm an old man . . . Attilio is an old man . . . Chuck is an old man . . . and Marcel Ribot is also an old man. Now, this is what you'll tell Chuck: I intend to handle this business personally with Marcel. I'm sure that Chuck will understand and have as much confidence in me as he has in you. And for that, you don't need your notebook, understand?"

Giu Benesco looked desperately to Siragusi for help, but the old man didn't waver. His eyes were lit with irony and pride. Joe had been right. This was the way to talk.

"Chuck will probably say okay . . . " Benesco stammered. "But why humiliate me?"

Joe smiled indulgently.

"Don't hold it against me, my boy. I'm an old-timer. You'll learn that with enough humiliations you become a man. Now go and report to Chuck."

Benesco got up slowly. It was his turn for an ironic smile. "Old fool," he thought to himself, and this thought made him feel better.

"That's what Chuck pays me for. If he agrees, you won't see me again. If not, I'll have the pleasure of bringing his reply to you. Where can I find you?"

"Right here," Siragusi broke in, to Joe's great surprise. "And you can tell your boss that Joe Torronto won't be alone . . . old Attilio Siragusi will be at his side. After all, I might as well treat myself to a vacation before I die. I've never been to France before. I understand the girls are beautiful there." (He gave a small, melancholy laugh.) "You'll excuse me for not inviting you to dinner, but I'm an old bear and I no longer know how to entertain. Take a cigar before you leave."

Giu Benesco shrugged his shoulders. He left without uttering a word. The ice cubes still tinkled in the glass he had left behind.

Joe and Attilio smiled at each other. They felt twenty years younger. They hugged each other in an old mafioso embrace. A new gang had been formed.

* * *

It was rush hour, the time of the morning when suburban dwellers converge on Paris. The taxi carrying them towards the capital advanced as slowly as the other cars in the staggered and nerve-wracking lines.

"It's the same everywhere," Joe Torronto complained.

Attilio Siragusi, carefully couched in a corner with his hands resting flat on his knees, peered gloomily through the highway railings, beyond the plains of warehouses, factories and high-rise apartments, trying to catch a glimpse of what he had heard was some of the prettiest country in the world.

Santiana beamed with all the joy of a kid being taken on his first holiday.

Joe glanced sideways at his two companions and wondered whether they wouldn't prove more of a problem than help. He inwardly cursed his display of bravado in having agreed to introduce Marcel Ribot to Siragusi. Above all, he cursed that stupid business with Chuck Bonanza's address. Joe could have given it to Marcel himself. Why had his friend imagined it was necessary to make the contact through Siragusi? Ah, if only he had known. Bonanza would never have discovered that the strange little Frenchman, whom Joe had known years ago, had left New York to pay him a visit a few days before his daughter's death. And why had Siragusi taken the initiative of informing Chuck Bonanza about Marcel Ribot? The old man could probably attribute his amazing longevity to such politic maneuvers, but this time it had landed them in the shithouse.

Joe had enjoyed playing the tough old guy in front of Chuck's little fix-it man, but he was now faced with the agonizing trouble of sorting out this problem. He didn't understand what could have happened. Marcel had clearly stated that it wasn't his intention to kill Chuck, and yet that is what he had done, or almost had done . . . as he must have misfired and it was the kid, Lolita, who received the bullet destined for her father. But why hadn't he fired a second shot? He should have had enough time. Perhaps it was the emotional shock at having killed the girl unintentionally? Yes, that was certain the answer. But Marcel had never been one to lose his self-control . . . So?

Joe didn't really understand anything. He tried to avoid the questions that boiled in his mind, and which had already prevented him from sleeping during the entire flight. After all, within a few hours he would learn the truth from his friend, Marcel. What was the use of worrying?

For five days the shutters remained closed and a damp coolness penetrated the long stucco and wood house. Yet it was warm outside, and the lawn yellowed in the autumn sunshine. Among the rare passers-by, some occasionally stopped to examine the creamy front of the house in which all the misfortune had occurred. Already the more superstitious crossed to the other side of the street and hurried past "the scene of the crime," as it was now called. Monsieur Poinsot claimed — and the news quickly spread — that the "wife of the deceased," the General's daughter-in-law, had locked herself inside and didn't want to see anyone. This business was bound to end badly. From behind their curtains the neighbors watched every movement and noted every unusual noise. Nobody was quite sure whether Florence Bertol had, in fact, locked herself in the accursed house.

Yet Florence was indeed there.

Alone.

In her distress.

She hadn't yet completely realized the course her destiny had taken.

And, in her frightened solitude, Xavier came back to her in the form of a terrible reproach, a painful wound.

"Here I am, a widow and a virgin," she thought with melancholic cynicism.

She thought of their marriage, without love, without passion, without children.

With Xavier she had had to content herself with prudent caresses . . . and more often than not, these had broken off in anger and despair.

She had believed her life was hell, yet now she realized how much she missed him. She now understood that he had been her man, her husband . . . and her child . . . and she had loved him. And she ought to have loved him more.

But it was too late.

She wandered around the deserted house, seeking perfumes, smells, forgotten objects, lost moments and memories.

She found ashtrays filled with stubs, the sticky remains of whisky at the bottom of a glass, a wrinkled tie thrown over a chair, the gabardine overcoat in the entrance hall, the dirty linen in the bathroom. Crumbs, dust, and ashes — all that remained of her broken life.

She locked herself in his room (the only place she could stand to be) and fumbled under the sheets (the bed hadn't been made since that fateful night), and pulled out the manilla envelope and the five playing cards, the punctured Queen of Spades and the rest.

*   *
*

With his feet spread and his body perfectly straight, Marcel lifted his gun slowly. His left hand supported the barrel, his right hand cradled the stock, his index finger on the trigger. He turned toward the target and aimed. His body maintained the same flexible position, and when the shot was fired he didn't budge. His right hand pulled back the bolt and the empty cartridge dropped to the ground. His movements were rapid and precise — giving the impression of ease — in spite of the great effort required to reload the gun. He fired a second time. He then repeated the procedure, until the magazine was empty. Then he engaged the safety and took a few steps back. He knew that, from a distance of 150 yards, at least three bullets were in the center of the target, and the two others weren't far off. The rifle functioned perfectly . . . and so did he. The slight error at Brückenkirchen could be attributed to the darkness and nocturnal temperatures.

He suddenly felt much better. The smell of powder and the sound of the shots — the sound he missed so much when he was obliged to use the silencer — contributed to his sense of well-being. He re-loaded and fired five times in rapid succession. The bullets missed the target and were certainly lost.

This counter-performance didn't worry him. He was in excellent spirits and decided to buy himself a beer.

He dismantled his gun, placing each part in its respective pocket in the gun-case, and walked up the path towards the Clubhouse. The first dahlias were blooming. He admired the vivid shades of some and the soft pastels of others. Yes indeed, it was a beautiful day.

Marcel found a place to sit at the bar. He disliked being alone at a table. The high stools always made him feel important. He ordered a beer and watched the tiny bubbles gathering in the foam, as he reflected on his vacation, now drawing to an end. On Monday, he would go back to work at the factory. It was a simple janitor's job — the work humiliated him, but the salary added to his small pension. He realized that he would have to pursue his mission at night, or on weekends, or maybe even wait until his next vacation. But would that be possible? People were dying like flies around him . . . the ones he wanted to remind just how good a marksman he still was. If he let a year go by, his chances of success with his mission might slip away. Luc wouldn't like that.

So he was decided; he would strike at every available opportunity, in the evenings, on Saturdays, Sundays, the long weekends, "All Saints' Day," November 11th, Christmas. In fact, his mission offered the prospect of some interesting holidays.

Two men came and sat down on the bar stools next to him. They were in their early thirties and their fresh cheeks and bright eyes showed their energetic enjoyment of life.

"No question, Boruti, you're the better man. Even with my new .22 I'm not in your class. It's not funny. I'm going to change my partner before I'm ruined . . . Adrienne, it's my turn again." (Adrienne, the bartender, raised her eyes in sympathy and drew two drafts.) "Otherwise, Boruti, what's new? Still with Viliard?"

"Of course . . . and it's no picnic."

"What's he got you specializing in? I.D.'s or renewing residence permits?"

Boruti grinned: everyone in Versailles knew Commissioner Viliard, at least everyone who had any dealings with the police. Hefner was a building contractor who frequently had to work out problems with the cops over the immigrant labor he employed.

"That's about right. Only just now I'm on something a little more interesting."

"Oh yeah? Dare I ask what?"

"The newspapers haven't talked about it too much. It's General Bertol's son, who was knocked off at the beginning of the week. So far, we don't know who did it. I'm handling the case."

"Bravo, old buddy." Hefner whistled with exaggerated admiration. "And what's Viliard doing, in the meantime? Typing up passport applications with his fat fingers? Or have you suspended him from service?"

"You're giving me a hard time because I gave you a lesson on the range. That's bad sportsmanship. Viliard is in on the case, of course, but this time I'm working with him. Legriffe too. But I'm the one who scraped up the remains."

"Well, then. You can be proud of yourself, my boy."

Boruti ignored his friends mocking tone and stuck his nose in his glass.

On the neighboring bar stool, Marcel turned his back on the two speakers. He couldn't let his face betray the troubled interest he took in their conversation. He was discovering something that he hadn't taken into account — the cops were looking for him.

"Come on, Boruti, don't pout. Tell me about your investigation. What's your method? 'The killer always returns to the scene of the crime?' Or '*Cherchez la femme?*' — I imagine there is a woman?"

"Yes, there's a woman. And a rather attractive one at that."

"Just like the movies. Wonderful! Tell me more."

"What about my professional discretion? Do you think I have the right to tell you everything?"

"Don't be a dope."

"All right, all right. Here's what I can tell you: The guy who did it used a hunting rifle, sufficiently powerful to fire expansive bullets capable of splattering a guy before he has time to realize what's happened. We can maybe even push it and say that it was the work of a professional. It wasn't an unplanned crime, nothing that occurred on the spur of the moment."

"And the motive?"

"No idea, for the moment. The victim's wife made allusions to a mysterious threat in the form of playing cards — a Queen of Spades — that the father received a few days before the murder. But at that time the general, the victim's father, was already dead. Apparently he died of natural causes, and his son got it in his place. As for the alleged threats, we haven't found anything. And that's not all. A sealed envelope, which had just been delivered to the victim by the family lawyer, is also missing."

"And what did it contain?"

"We don't know, and the lawyer claims that he doesn't know either. Which may or may not be true. It seems pretty likely that whoever it was killed in order to get the envelope."

"Maybe it's blackmail then?"

"Maybe. For the time being, everything is a little confused. Viliard is interrogating the acquaintances of the general and his son."

"Exactly what does Viliard have to say?"

"Oh, as far as he's concerned, the woman must have done it, as usual. Only that's his personal conviction, without the slightest proof to back up his eternal theory, 'Woman is the root of all evil.' What's more, I learned this morning that the woman has an alibi. Did I tell you that she was the one who found the body? All this happened Tuesday evening. The wife claims that she was away at the time the husband was killed. We've checked; she was at La Baule until Tuesday morning and, as the experts have established that the crime was committed twenty-four or even forty-eight hours earlier — which makes Monday the day of the crime — Viliard's suspicions are unfounded. But he's stubborn. He figures that it was possible for the wife to have come back here to kill her husband on Monday, then return to La Baule to make sure she was seen on Tuesday morning before returning home. She didn't have a good enough alibi for Monday afternoon and evening, when she claims she was trying to telephone her husband. However, now she remembers having changed the oil in her car — which checks out with the mileage, and with her mechanic."

"Ha! I can just imagine Viliard's expression."

"It doesn't bother him a bit. 'She's taken everything into consideration,' " Boruti grumbled, imitating the commissioner's raspy voice. " 'She must have taken the train or a plane' — which would be difficult to check. And that's as far as we've gotten."

"And you? What do you think?"

Boruti made himself more comfortable. He was pleased to see his friend's cynicism change into a genuine interest.

"I think we're going to have quite a job getting to the bottom of this one . . . unless we come up with some new information. Unless we discover a sure motive."

"And the woman?"

"What about the woman?"

"What's she like?"

"Pretty cute. A little cold, I think. It's possible that she does know more than she admits."

Adrienne turned towards the three men.

"Another drink, gentlemen . . . and you too, Monsieur Marcel."

Boruti and Hefner looked at each other then shook their heads. They had hardly noticed the insignificant little man seated next to them.

"No thank you, I have to get going," Ribot murmured feebly.

He got down from the bar stool. His legs felt weak. He picked up his gun case and stumbled towards the door.

"Another old fart who probably won't make it through the winter," Hefner remarked dryly.

"Don't say that," Adrienne scolded. "He's one of our best marksmen. I think the beer went to his head today."

* * *

It was a long time before Marcel's thundering heart slowed down and his mind stopped somersaulting. So, then he was taken for a common murderer, a killer . . . a cheap blackmailer, a thief? He shuddered with inner rage.

Fear, a strange fear that he had never experienced before had prevented him from shouting his identity and the purpose of his mission to these two idiots, from screaming at them that it had nothing to do with senseless murder.

He took a bus home and wondered at the bizarre chance that had allowed him to eavesdrop on that conversation. But luck had always been on his side, and he shouldn't be surprised. Was it really so unlikely that a police officer looking for a little target practice and a marksmen like himself should meet in the bar of the largest shooting range in the whole of Paris? Marcel persuaded himself no. Where else would they meet, if not there?

Marcel forced himself to calm his panic, and to memorize everything that he had heard. He had learned, first, that the cops were after him — and that had stupefied him, and had given him a bit of a scare. But the danger, after all, wasn't so great, as his identity was not yet known. His advantage lay in the fact that he knew their position and they were unaware of his. Nevertheless, Marcel felt distrubed — they had identified his gun. That wasn't so important, but he thought of the single bullet that he had fired in Houdan. He had fired from a difficult angle, and the conditions hadn't really been good. That bullet must still be lodged somewhere in the room. The police had certainly found it by now. He didn't doubt that this single clue would enable them to draw several conclusions. Up until this moment, his main concern had been to avoid leaving any trace at the site of his executions, but this precaution had been more for the sake of the art of his work, a witness to his sense of order and neatness. From now on, he was going to have to act differently.

He hurried home to outline a new battle plan.

6

The Torronto-Siragusi gang checked into the Paris Hotel Sheraton. In a way, after the cross-town congestion and traffic, the Sheraton — with its thick carpeting and "mood music" — reassured them. They found themselves in an atmosphere something like the world they had just left behind. The indifference with which they were treated seemed to be a guarantee of anonymity and the license to take care of the business they had come for.

First they did what travelers all over the world do upon arriving in a hotel — a little freshening up and unpacking. Then they met in the bar and ordered drinks, although they weren't really thirsty. As they hadn't yet formulated a plan of action, the first disagreements began. Attilio wanted to go out and buy weapons — or at least a gun — immediately. Joe suggested going alone to the address that Marcel had left him. Santiana wanted to know whether they would have time to see some sights.

Joe used the fact that he was the only one who could speak French as an excuse to impose his point of view.

He was the one who had insisted they leave their guns behind, because of the strict laws governing that kind of "baggage." Even an authorized gun would have attracted too much attention, even just a hunting rifle. So he now had to agree to Siragusi's request — they would go out and buy a gun. Afterwards Attilio and Santiana could take a little tour of Paris (Santiana had already arranged it with the hotel's tourist office), while Joe would visit Marcel alone.

They took a taxi to the gun shop whose address had been given to them by the hotel. They were received cordially by a rather distinguished salesman.

"Messieurs? May I help you?"

"We would like to buy a gun," Joe explained affably.

"Certainly, Monsieur. What kind of gun?"

Joe turned to Attilio Siragusi.

"What kind of gun do you need?" he asked in English.

"Whatever. I'm not going to be using it by myself."

Joe scratched his head. In his youth he had been handy enough with a revolver, but he had long since lost his taste for firearms.

"Santiana?"

"¡Me gusta la navaja!" the Puerto Rican replied with a large smile.

That didn't help. Joe tried to remember. He knew that he had an old Smith and Wesson 39 automatic in his office at the Cactucito, and that Alonso the bartender kept a Colt Cobra in perfect working condition in an empty Tobasco Sauce carton. As far as he could remember they had never been used in the restaurant.

"Do you have a Smith and Wesson pistol or a Colt revolver?" he asked off-hand.

The distinguished gentleman smiled with some amusement.

"The regulations concerning those guns are very strict. Do you have a license or permit?"

Joe asked him to repeat the sentence. He translated as best he could. The three men were stupefied.

"But we're only passing through," Joe muttered.

"I'm sorry, but unless you have a permit I can't help you."

Joe understood that it was useless to insist. He considered pulling out the traditional ten-dollar bill, but realized that in this case it wouldn't work.

"And what can we get without a permit?"

"In hand guns? A lead pistol."

Joe's translation unleashed a little laughter.

"But we didn't come to buy a toy."

"I'm sorry. Were you looking for something to defend yourself with?"

"In a way, yes."

"Well maybe an alarm pistol would help? We have some excellent models."

Joe translated and the laughter redoubled. The distinguished gentleman began to look annoyed.

"The only weapons sold freely are hunting guns, excluding .22 long rifles and sawed-off shot guns. A permit is required for all other guns, including sporting guns."

"Do you have hunting pistols?"

"I can give you their documentation. We don't sell them — that kind of hunting isn't practiced in France."

Joe was more and more perplexed. He didn't remember France as being such an underdeveloped country. How could a man without a gun be a free man?

The gun salesman went on to describe how a hunting rifle was a perfect means of defense. Joe could hardly see himself wandering around Paris with a rifle under his arm.

"You see, my friends and I have been threatened . . . here in Paris. A gun would help."

"Threatened? Good heavens. In that case, shouldn't you see the police?"

Joe realized that they would get nothing out of him. He thanked the salesman — who was visibly relieved to be rid of the infernal trio — and walked out, followed by his two wondering companions. These Frenchmen were a decidedly singular race.

Attilio muttered a few curses that were more native to New York slang than the old man's Sicilian dialect. He too had "friends" in Paris, and they would soon see whether the law preventing honest citizens from acquiring the means to protect themselves was as strict as the gun dealer had made out. After a few telephone calls and a meeting with a "nephew" in a bar on rue Blanche, he arranged an appointment for that evening at the Pigalle metro station with a "cousin" who would supply him with a Beretta M90 and MAB P15 — guns that none of them had even heard of before. The name Beretta, however, had a reassuring sound.

Joe left to find Marcel, or at least to check out the place where he lived. Attilio and Santiana went off to the rue de Rivoli to join a Vistavision tour of Paris. Joe watched them scramble into a taxi with all the joyful enthusiasm of two kids afraid of being late for a movie.

Joe's mood was different.

Marcel was his friend, and he felt apprehensive about the course of events. Why had Attilio been so insistent on procuring the guns, if not to be able to send a newspaper clipping to Chuck Bonanza describing the mysterious death of Marcel Ribot, and so to return, with a peaceful soul and easy conscience, to his goddamned fancy mansion in Poughkeepsie? The two men's outlooks were different. Siragusi had come for the sake of his reputation. (Or was it maybe the desire to have a last fling abroad? To meet a few girls? An old man's whim?) Joe, on his part, had come to save a friend's neck.

Joe felt old and alone — which, to tell the truth, he'd been feeling quite a lot lately. But more than the loneliness, it was old age that weighed on him suddenly. He couldn't endure the weariness, nor cope with these violent emotions. The anxiety that gnawed at him wasn't entirely the result of the incredible business that he found himself mixed up in. Without reason, sometimes, his heart would begin to beat violently, then suddenly stop, and he would feel a great emptiness in his chest. He had noticed that he could no longer tie his shoelaces without lifting his foot onto a chair or bed. He'd bought several pairs of loafers, but still his hand had a terrible time grasping the shoehorn. The same hand no longer dared, as before, to pat the thighs of the dancers as they shuffled by on their way to the stage at the Cactucito. The hand that might not have the strength or control to pull a trigger.

Actually Marcel, in spite of his eccentric ways and his more apparent age, possessed more energy and drive than he did. Unless, of course, he too was just trying to keep up a good front to the bitter end, to go through with his grand enterprise, to conquer . . . one last time . . . before dying.

"Come on buddy. Where do you want to go? I can't wait here all day."

Joe realized that he was standing idiotically on the edge of the sidewalk, a finger in the air. Passers-by laughed at him. The cars behind the taxi were beginning to honk their horns. He would have given anything to have been able to say, "Take me home. And make it snappy."

"Rue Chapon, please," he said to the taxi driver. He closed his eyes, letting Paris go by. From a secret corner of his heart he called up the image of a dusty little boy, leading a herd of goats, while the setting sun transformed the village on the hillside into a gold- and cinammon-colored cathedral . . . *cobre y lana* . . . *trigo y castaña* . . . his childhood.

* * *

"Marcel Ribot, C/O Mademoiselle Josyane, 70 rue Chapon, 75003 Paris." Joe Torronto knew the address that his friend had sent him, just before his visit to the United States, by heart. But who was this Josyane? A friend? A mistress? A sister? He somehow remembered Marcel saying that he lived alone. Perhaps he rented a room in an apartment?

Joe examined the letter boxes in the hall. They were as grimy and dilapidated as the exterior of the building and the spiral staircase which groped its way towards the upper floors. Most of the boxes had no markings. Some hung open on rusty hinges, and a few bore narrow strips of yellow paper or a piece of a calling card, indicating some name. Torn envelopes and fliers lay scattered on the floor.

Joe took a certain pleasure in examining one box after another. He found they reflected a kind of image of France, individualistic, disorderly, and poetically grubby. The strange smells of old wood, urine, and black soap reminded him of the barracks he had known in the old days. The paint, too — a thick coat of dark brown halfway up the walls, and sickly yellow above — belonged to a certain tradition. It was the first time since his arrival that he had rediscovered the images and odors of the past. He felt better and had the sudden impression that everything would sort itself out with Marcel. Nevertheless, neither his friend's name nor that of Mademoiselle Josyane appeared on any of the boxes.

Joe wasn't worried. He went to the concierge's lodge and knocked on the glass pane (a gesture which took him back twenty years) of the door with its dingy crochet curtain. Shortly, an old woman with a bloated face, her gray hair drawn back in a bun, wearing a linen shawl came to the door. The concierge peered at him suspiciously before asking, "What is it?" in a voice designed for an used to being rude to strangers.

"Mademoiselle Josyane, please?"

"Fifth floor, left, at the end of the hall."

Joe smiled, giving a little salute, then climbed up the staircase. Behind him, he knew, the door would close and the key would turn in the lock, and the concierge would return to the depths of her rooms where she secretly drinks a little . . .

Then the unexpected — the door on the fifth floor was opened by a large athletic-looking black man ("Am I back in New York?" he thought) who smiled affably. Joe remembered that he was, in fact, in modern-day Paris. Too bad for his dreams.

"Are you looking for someone?"

"Mademoiselle Josyane . . . or, more precisely, Monsieur Ribot — Marcel Ribot."

"Ribot? Don't know him. What's it about?"

"I'm an old friend of his. He gave me this address, care of Mlle. Josyane."

"Care of Mlle. Josyane? That would be a very temporary address." The black man sneered a little. "Go to the third floor. The name is on the door. She should be there at this time of the day."

"Thanks."

Joe turned towards the stairway.

"I hope you haven't come looking for trouble," the black man grumbled in a tone which was just threatening enough to get its point across without being too unfriendly.

Joe wondered what he meant. Could this man possibly know the purpose of his visit? Did he suspect something? What was behind this sudden mistrust?

He began to understand when two blonde dolls in thigh boots and mini-skirts — showing off their little white panties — appeared at the end of the hall. They walked past him in a cloud of heavy perfume, glancing at him with a mixture of potential interest and bored indifference. They tossed a casual hello to the black man on their way out.

"No problem, don't worry," Joe answered. "I know how to behave in the presence of ladies."

* * *

Two rusty thumbtacks held up a card marked "Josyane." Joe Torronto knocked on the door with an involuntary hesitation — once again his hand had failed him.

"Who is it?" called a rather young sounding voice.

"My name is Joe Torronto, from New York . . . the United States. I'm a friend of Marcel Ribot."

"Who?"

"Marcel Ribot!" he yelled.

A door at the other end of the hall opened and a dark suspcious eye peeped through the chink. Joe caught a glimpse of a naked thigh then the door closed quietly.

"What do you want?" the voice asked.

"It's about Marcel, of course," Joe murmured.

A key turned and the door opened. The girl had short, chestnut hair. On a table behind her Joe noticed an egg-shaped head which sported an enormous, flamboyant red wig.

"Are you Mademoiselle Josyane?" (The girl nodded.) "May I come in for a moment? It won't take long."

Not exactly happy, she stepped aside to let him pass. She wasn't very pretty and her neglected appearance didn't help much. She had one of those faces which only becomes attractive under layers of outrageous make-up. She had just taken the time to slip into a robe and a pair of old slippers. Her bed, in the opposite corner, seemed to exhale the clamminess of interrupted sleep. Joe noticed her large breasts. If he remembered correctly, that was a major criterion with Marcel.

"I'm warning you, if it's for sex don't waste your time . . ."

"No, that's not what I came for. Excuse me —"

"Oh. That's okay. Anyhow, I don't see anyone in my room except Marcel, but then it's different with him." She fumbled around on a chair under her "working clothes" — garter belt, net stockings, sexy panties and bra — and pulled out a pack of blond cigarettes, which she held out to Joe.

Joe almost refused, but realized that he had just said no to sex. Furthermore, he remembered the importance the French attached to the exchange of cigarettes. He reached out for one.

"Thanks . . . I'm sorry but I don't have a lighter."

Josyane shrugged her shoulders and pulled out a large box of kitchen matches.

"So, you're a friend of Marcel's? And an American? I'd have taken you for a dago."

She eyed him with an amusement which, Joe felt, lacked contempt, the desire to humiliate him, or to make him ill at ease. The remark had come out quite naturally.

"I'm originally Spanish," Joe corrected.

"Oh, I see . . . How is Marcel?"

"Fine, I think. At any rate he was fine the last time I saw him. He came to see me in New York in August, just about a month ago I think."

"In New York? Well what the hell do you know? To think I took him for a little nobody. Oh yeah. A letter from New York came here for him a little while ago."

"Yes, I wrote it. He had given me this address."

Joe had understood, from the beginning, that Marcel didn't live with the girl. He had simply used this prostitute as a mailbox. Joe realized sadly that, in not wanting his address known, Marcel's intentions in coming to New York weren't as honest as Joe had believed.

"That's right, Marcel asked me to do him the favor. Apparently he travels a lot and is pretty difficult to contact. He wanted to make sure he got that letter . . . So you came to see me because you don't have any other address?" Josyane said, suddenly understanding.

"Yes, that's right."

"You're out of luck, darling, because I don't know Marcel's address either."

Joe had the impression that she was telling the truth . . . but he couldn't be sure. He reflected while the girl went to put some water on to boil. From behind, her figure was extremely slim and Joe realized how enormous her breasts were, almost grotesque in proportion to her body.

"Would you like some hot chocolate?"

This time Joe refused, in spite of the hunger which was making his stomach rumble. A hot chocolate at 2:30 in the afternoon was more than he could take, even if he was an American — and had once been Spanish.

"Do you see Marcel often?"

"From time to time. When he wants to."

"How often is that?

Josyane tightened the robe which had opened to reveal white skin sprinkled with freckles.

"Maybe once a month — sometimes more, sometimes less. I've never kept a record."

Joe sensed that he was treading on uneven ground. Josyane didn't show much willingness to divulge anything else. For the moment, however, she was his only possible lead and he didn't want to jeopardize it by annoying her. He had to play his hand very carefully.

"If I were sure he'd be stopping by soon, I'd leave a note for him. It'd be a pity not to see him before I leave."

Josyane reached for the sugar and chocolate in a high cupboard and Joe admired the delicate curve of her long legs. "Too bad her face isn't better," he thought to himself.

"I couldn't tell you. He does as he likes. You can leave a note if you want."

Joe said nothing. He didn't have the least notion of writing a note for Marcel. What he wanted was to be able to find him.

The sweet smell of chocolate filled the little room, covering the stale smell of cigarettes. Joe thought he would soon have to leave. Again the idea of offering money occurred to him, but he decided to play a game that would be a bit more subtle.

"I think I'll have some chocolate after all, if the offer still holds?"

Josyane looked at him warmly. Even if this guy had awakened her to ask a lot of questions, his company wasn't entirely unpleasant and anything was better than her eternal solitude. He was polite and he had a kind of charm that made her want to be his friend. Besides, she liked older men, especially clean older men. They were usually generous, easy to please, and even more lonely than she was.

"Then, I'll make more. While I do it, it would be nice of you to run out and get a *baguette* at the bakery. Did you eat at noon?"

"No," Joe admitted. "I didn't have time."

"Good, I'll fix something for you. Will you get the bread?"

Joe agreed with a smile. He asked where the bakery was and left whistling. Walking back up rue Chapon, he felt like a twenty-year-old. The anxiety and sadness were gone. The sun shone brightly — the same sun that had shined on the little goatherder in Spain.

He bought the bread and a bunch of roses, then hurried back up the staircase. Suddenly he felt that something was wrong. A strong smell of burning chocolate filled the hallway. His heart pounding, he arrived breathless at Josyane's door. He called her name before knocking. There was no answer. He knocked violently and continued calling her name.

He was sure that Josyane had been killed over the little that she had told him . . . or before she could tell him any more.

But to his immense surprise, Josyane opened the door.

"Why the hell are you making all this noise?"

"You gave me a scare . . . I could smell something burning. And you didn't answer the door."

"The chocolate boiled over and I didn't even have time to get out of the shower before you started shouting like the devil. But there's really nothing to worry about."

"Sorry. I'm an idiot. Here, I brought you some flowers."

Josyane smiled like a happy kid. She became almost coy.

"Oh thank you. That's really sweet. Even Marcel never thought of buying me flowers . . . Hey — You look a little sick."

Joe was perspiring heavily. Was it as much a result of tearing up the stairs as his sudden emotions? He couldn't breathe normally and his face had turned gray. The pain in his chest hurt him.

"It's nothing. I should have taken the time to eat something."

Josyane covered the unmade bed with a quilt.

"Lie down. I'm going to make you a fried egg."

Joe let her help him to the bed but refused at first to lie down. Yet the dizziness got worse and he had to.

"It's the Queen of Spades courting me again," he thought. "One of these days she's going to manage to get me into her bed." He fumbled in his pockets for his pills. Josyane understood and brought him a glass of water. But the hand kept clutching uselessly at the pocket, and Joe was gripped with rage at his helplessness.

"Calm down, honey, I'll do it." Josyane's delicate white hand —
a hand whose business was caressing — found the pills.

"How many?"

"Two."

"*Voilà!*"

"Thank you."

In the pan, the forgotten butter began to sputter and hiss.

"It's burning again," Joe remarked.

Josyane broke the eggs into the pan. Joe felt better already.
Every simple gesture that Josyane made, every word they exchanged,
seemed to do him good. Once again he wished he could forget the
purpose of his trip.

When the eggs were cooked, and cheese, wine, and bread placed
on the table, and Joe had confirmed that he felt better, they sat
down and ate in silence. The bouquet of roses stood between them
and they gave little thought to the strange fate that had brought
them together.

Joe remarked that he had never eaten such good fried eggs.

Josyane said that she had never seen such beautiful roses.

They laughed together in this moment of stolen happiness.

"I must find Marcel, and you're the only person who can help
me," Joe finally continued.

"Marcel? Ah, yes. But I've already told you everything I know,
which isn't much. Too bad for Marcel. You'll see him another
time."

"Be nice, make an effort. You see him pretty regularly. You
must know him well enough if he trusts you with his mail, and you
agreed to look after it for him?"

Josyane handed him the piece of bread she had just buttered
and prepared another. She sighed.

"Marcel isn't so different from the others, and I wonder why I
agreed to let him come here. Maybe because he was sad and old
and reminded me of my father. That must be it. I remember the
first night. I wasn't in such good shape myself. We were shoved
together at the counter of the Tac-au-Tac, a bar that's not too far
from here. There was the usual talk; we had a few drinks together.
That night I just wasn't into doing my thing, so I let Marcel bring
me home. Then we had a last drink and Marcel stayed. We slept

together. He hugged me a little — I think that's all he wanted that
night. And so . . . he snored all night long." (She began to nibble
on a piece of bread and Joe had to listen very closely to hear what
she was saying.) "I didn't see him for a long time — that's always
the case with these guys — and then one day he came to say hello,
and to tell me that he hadn't forgotten me. He even brought me a
gift — a piece of silk. He said it came from Tonkin. Look, there it
is, I use it as a table cloth." (Joe had already noticed the piece of
silk; he had brought similar ones back from Indochina.) "Of
course he wanted to screw. He managed quite well, except he had
a problem coming, that was tough." (Joe thought sadly that he
could have done no better himself.) "He always paid me well. In
the beginning I didn't want his money, but he insisted. He didn't
want me to have any trouble with my pimp. Every time he comes
here, he gives me two or three hundred . . . even when it's for
nothing. Sometimes he brings me a little present."

"And you really don't know when he'll be back?"

"No idea. When he wants to. If he comes back . . . these guys
always end up disappearing someday. You never know if they got
sick of you, or found something better, or if they crawled in a hole
and died. One even died in my bed, right there where you were
lying."

Josyane bit her lip and looked contrite.

"Shit, that was a stupid thing to say."

"Don't worry, I'm better now. And I won't die in your bed. Let's
forget it. Instead, tell me more about the bar you mentioned a little
while ago."

"The Tac-au-Tac? It's two blocks over."

"Yes, that's it, the Tac-au-Tac. Does Marcel go there often?"

"Maybe. Anyhow I don't go there any more, not since I had a
fight with the owner."

"Well, okay. I'm not going to bother you any longer. If Marcel
should happen to come by one of these days, could you call me at
the Sheraton — room 2027? Don't forget the name, Joe
Torronto. But don't say a word to Marcel. We'll give him a
surprise. And if you like, we'll go out and celebrate, the three of
us."

"Why not? That would be fun."

Josyane noted the hotel name and number on a piece of newspaper. Joe was already at the door.

"So, see you soon, maybe, and thanks for the lunch."

"Sure, and thanks again for the flowers."

Back on the street, Joe found himself full of the same happy spirits he had felt an hour earlier. He almost could have believed he was in love.

This sudden burst of elations didn't, however, prevent him from realizing that he was being followed.

He continued up rue Chapon as far as rue Beaubourg, then turned in the direction of the metro station *Arts et Metiers*. The street was crowded with people, and Joe realized that this would only benefit his follower. He thought that he might be able to shake his tail in the underground hallways of the metro, but what was easy in New York wasn't necessarily easy in Paris. On the contrary, it gave the other even more of an advantage; his follower ended up in a better position.

Joe, therefore, decided that the best approach was to confront his shadow, and he did an abrupt about-face. The person following him was no amateur himself. He had paused to wait anonymously in the crowd.

Joe covered a few yards in the opposite direction and turned sharply. He eyes flashed over the waves of pedestrians, but he sensed that his man wasn't among them. He changed his rhythm and moved along at an idling pace. He remembered an afternoon before the war — it must have been January, as he recalled the skaters in Central Park — when he had played this shadow game with a guy who worked for one of the big bosses of Bugs Moran's gang. The guy's name was Dan Calloway and later, under different circumstances, they had worked together. That day Joe had finally shaken him off, but only after changing taxis four times and the subway at least half a dozen. They had both caught pneumonia and had celebrated the event years later with a monumental binge.

Joe wondered whether this guy would be as smart as Calloway, and he wondered whether he himself could still keep up the pace.

In spite of his nonchalant air, Joe was busy noting every face that walked past. He didn't overtake anyone and scrutinized the backs ahead of him. Finally he found his man: a huge guy in a charcoal raincoat, the kind employed by odd-job agencies, who glanced over his shoulder from time to time and changed his rhythm every now and then. This was undoubtedly the man. He had been smart enough to keep going, in spite of the first about-face, convinced that some second maneuver of the same sort would lead him back to his "mark." Joe felt reassured. They were playing hide-and-seek with equal strength.

Joe watched for an empty taxi. It was a difficult move as he didn't want the guy ahead of him to guess his intentions.

It happened quickly. Joe motioned briefly, decisively, and the taxi pulled up at his side. The guy in the gray raincoat hadn't had time to notice. The taxi was immediately swallowed up in traffic and sped off down towards rue Rambuteau, away from *Arts et Metiers*.

Joe turned around, hoping to catch a vexed expression on the face of his follower, but the guy had already disappeared.

"Where are we going?" asked the taxi driver.

"Rue Michel le Comte."

"But that's right here. You're making a fool of me."

"Keep quiet and you'll have twenty francs for your trouble."

Although he didn't much care for being spoken to in that tone, the taxi driver considered twenty francs a good enough reason to shut up. He dropped Joe off at the Tac-au-Tac bar and went to look for customers who were a little more polite, even if they were less generous.

7

At night, Versailles becomes a small country town. The streets are deserted early, and the residents shut themselves in behind the shutters of their "Grand Century" homes. The shadows passing in the ancient neighborhoods can almost assume the rare privilege of belonging as much to the past as to the present. Who could tell whether this woman, draped in the folds of the long and black wool cape, might not be condemned to eternally roam — the victim of some unholy spell — the empty streets surrounding the most beautiful palace in the world, this lavish quarter, once the home of painters, sculptors, musicians, royal cooks . . . and the purveyors of poison?

Watching the woman coming towards him, Inspector Boruti wondered whether she might not suddenly disappear, or if her face — so softly shimmering in the uncertain light — might not change abruptly into a ghastly and sneering skull. Wasn't this Death herself coming to take him by the hand and lead him to the bottom of the night and an irresistible and ever-lasting embrace? For a brief instant (now that he thought about it, very brief would be sufficient), he wanted to experience that ancient, ancestral terror that forced believers to cross themselves and non-believers to tremble.

But an automobile appeared on the street, its headlights exorcising the obscure vision and reducing it to its trivial and very earthly proportions. Before she had crossed the street, Boruti had recognized Madame Florence Bertol.

"Good evening, Inspector."

"Good evening, Madame."

Boruti felt himself blush. He hoped that the night would mask his discomfort. Since the beginning of this investigation he had been extremely susceptible to the charm of the young widow. And this evening she looked particularly lovely.

"The nights are getting chillier, aren't they?" he offered.

"A little, yes . . . Do you have any news for me?"

"Unfortunately no, Madame. There's nothing new."

"Too bad . . . Well, nice seeing you. Good night."

"Good night."

She wrapped her cape around her and went off toward the end of the avenue. Boruti watched her as she once again became a phantom in the night. He suddenly realized that his shift was over and that his home was in the direction that she was walking. He hurried to catch her fleeing silhouette.

"Ah, it's you, Inspector. You frightened me. I heard someone rushing up behind me."

"Excuse me, but I thought . . . I'm going in your direction, and I thought we could walk together."

She accepted with a timid smile. Boruti felt himself blushing again.

They walked along in silence. Boruti thought how lucky he was to have encountered this lovely . . . what should he call her? . . . client . . . charge?

He never imagined for a moment that he had just fallen into a trap.

"Is there a taxi stand around here somewhere?" Florence asked.

"Yes, but it's a good way ahead yet."

"My car is in the garage, and I had promised to spend the day with my husband's uncle. I didn't want to put him off. The family is already sensitive, not to mention suspicious. They insisted that I stay for dinner, and I didn't dare tell them that I didn't have a car, otherwise I would have been there for the night."

She gave her noble laugh, touched with shades of both pain and reserve.

"And you want to find a taxi to Houdan, at this time of night?"

"Don't you think I'll be able to get one now?"

"I'm afraid not — unless you're very lucky."

"I've never been very lucky." (She suddenly looked so frail and sad that Boruti longed to take her in his arms.) "If I don't find one, then I'll have to sleep at the police station. That should please Commissioner Viliard."

She gave her strange laugh again, and Boruti felt a little ill at ease.

"Let's go have a look then."

They walked on in silence. He reflected on the subtle and captivating perfume which traditionally surrounds widows. Perhaps this same perfume acted as a mask to hide the scars left by the passage of death. He must be close to the truth. Men are attracted to women in black because they sense the underlying drama, the monstrous secrets, the sorrows to be consoled . . . the perfume of death is certainly a perfume of adventure.

In spite of the subtle romance of his reflections, Boruti wasn't far off the intended track. Florence, soft and timid, already sensed the vibrating of the web into which she had lured the young detective.

There were no taxis at the stand when they arrived.

"You see, I knew what I was talking about," Boruti said.

"But one is bound to show up sooner or later," Florence insisted with mounting concern.

She stood on the edge of the sidewalk, searching in all directions, while Boruti gazed at her.

"The best thing would be for me to take you home," he offered with his most appealing smile.

Florence seemed to be surprised. She glanced shyly at the inspector.

"Do you have a car?"

"Just around the corner. Can you wait for five minutes?"

"Please don't go out of your way for me. I'm sure a taxi will come eventually . . ."

Boruti realized that he didn't want to be dismissed. He insisted.

"It's no problem at all. It won't take long. I'll be back immediately."

"No, don't leave me. I'll walk with you!" Florence said in a tone that bordered on panic, almost as if she were suddenly afraid to be alone in the night.

"Okay, come on then," Boruti allowed, feeling very strong and very protective.

They continued their walk through the sleeping town.

Boruti explained to Florence that he was only living in Versailles temporarily, and that he had managed to find a little studio apartment that suited his simple life for the time being. He missed his native South of France and hoped to be stationed there some day, once his period of probation was completed. He didn't use his car every day; he prefered to walk and keep fit. The Bertol case was his first big job, and he was anxious to get to the bottom of it.

He somewhat awkwardly excused himself for discussing her husband's death in so professional and enthusiastic a manner.

"Please don't worry. I understand your situation. After all, it's your business," she pardoned him with her mysterious smile.

Boruti opened the door of the Peugeot 204 for Florence. In spite of its being so late, and having spent a day wallowing in paperwork, he felt on top of the world — a state which he of course attributed to the brisk walk.

During the drive to Houdan, Boruti spoke of his studies, his childhood, his mother, and the pleasure he intended to take in his profession.

Florence sat wrapped in her cape, listening to his rambling with wide-eyed attention. Behind this feigned appearance she congratulated herself on the good luck she'd had in bringing off her plan so easily. She had telephoned the police station to find out whether Inspector Boruti would be there all evening — and since they had told her that he would, she had decided on instinct to use this opportunity, instead of waiting for another. She intended to find out everything that she needed to know from Boruti.

"Park in the driveway behind the house," she suggested as Boruti was pulling up in front of the home.

The inspector was obviously surprised.

"But won't you come in for a drink?" she asked with a smile.

Boruti thought immediately of Commissioner Viliard. If he ever found out, Boruti would be reprimanded for taking "initiatives," or even worse, he would be accused of leading some personal game outside of the investigation.

Boruti chased the image of the strict old father-figure from his mind. There was no harm in seeing Florence Bertol home. After all, Viliard had insisted often enough that the young inspector should be on duty "twenty-four hours a day." Perhaps he might even make some valuable discoveries in his search for "Truth and Justice."

He parked behind the house and followed Florence, whose perfume had invaded all his senses throughout the trip.

It had been at the end of a similar drive that Florence Bertol had discovered her husband's corpse. Boruti looked toward the magnolias on the other side of the lawn. That was where the killer had hidden while waiting for the right moment. Was he still lurking there? Boruti convinced himself that his professional function protected him from such risks, and that Florence too benefited from his presence. Again he felt very strong.

Florence put on soft lighting and invited him to sit on the couch. He remembered that during the earlier interrogations he and Viliard had been obliged to sit in an armchair, while Florence Bertol had always chosen the couch as her personal domain. Was this an invitation?

"Will you have whisky? Vodka? Beer? Fruit juice or a cup of coffee?"

Boruti hesitated. He didn't want any alcohol, and asking for juice or coffee seemed rather feeble.

"I'm going to make coffee for myself, if you'd like some," she continued.

"Good, coffee it is then."

Florence went off to the kitchen and Boruti moved into a more comfortable position. He had gotten to know the house so well that he almost felt at home there. He admired the obvious luxury of the carpeting, the furniture, and the curtains. He himself had never known such a richness of decor, and he felt that, for the brief minutes that it would take him to drink his coffee, he was living in a world far beyond his means.

"These are lovely things," Florence remarked, noticing the inspector's admiring gaze.

"Yes, you have a beautiful home; your taste is exquisite."

"Oh, I had nothing to do with it. All the furniture came from my inlaws. And as far as what is mine, I always followed Xavier's advice to the letter."

She placed the coffee tray on a low table and sat down next to Boruti, who suddenly felt a little nervous. What exactly did this woman want from him?

She poured his coffee and offered him sugar with a gesture of sweet complicity. He decided that she was trying to attract him without being too provocative. Maybe.

"Inspector, I'd like to know what you think about my husband's death?"

Boruti felt relieved. He hadn't been far from expecting a proposition of an entirely different nature. Under the circumstances, he preferred to exhibit the talents of this profession rather than in other fields where he would feel less certain of success.

"What do I think about your husband's death?"

"Yes . . . I mean the circumstances and, especially, the motive."

Boruti slowly stirred his coffee, drank a mouthful, then put the cup back on the saucer.

"Considering the actual evidence that we have in hand, it seems impossible to establish a motive."

"What about the threats and the envelope that Monsieur Poinsot brought?"

"That's all too vague. We only know about the threats and the envelope through your testimony and Poinsot's. We can't actually call them 'material evidence.' "

"But assuming that both Monsieur Poinsot and I have told the truth? Doesn't that bring you to some sort of conclusion?"

Boruti looked pensive. He was trying to add some weight to his words and to guard himself from saying too much.

"In that case, the first hypothesis that would come to mind is blackmail."

"Blackmail? Against whom?" asked Florence, opening her large eyes even wider.

"The general, of course . . . since the threats you told us about were addressed to him."

"But the general was already dead."

"Yes, but the blackmailer didn't know that. He first sent his reminder, the Queen of Spades, then when nothing happened, he sent the four other cards as a kind of countdown. Finally, on the last day, he acted."

"How did he act?"

Boruti frowned thoughtfully again and took another sip of coffee.

"That's where things get complicated. Try to follow this." (Little by little he abandoned his air of feigned reserve and let his real passion take over.) "A blackmailer's usual tactic is to threaten to reveal certain compromising pieces of information unless he is paid. If the person being blackmailed refuses or ceases to pay, the blackmailer divulges what he knows. But he doesn't go as far as killing his golden goose. Do you follow? So far, we cannot understand why the blackmailer came to your home with the premeditated intention of killing someone. Do you agree? Imagine our man — he blackmails the general. Everything goes along fine for him until the payments stop suddenly. What does he do? He sends reminders, like we just said, and then he decides to come and see what's happening for himself. He's pretty sly, and as he knows that all blackmailers run the risk of being knocked off by their 'customers,' he comes armed. Furthermore, he knows his gun. And it's a gun that doesn't require a permit, one that has probably never been used to shoot a person, probably a hunting rifle. He comes to the house and there the drama explodes . . . but at that point, we're in the dark. What could have happened?"

"The guy simply killed Xavier to recover the envelope!" Florence offered, beginning to share Boruti's excitement.

"It's logical enough, of course. The general might have left the papers describing the blackmail in the hands of the lawyer, with the instructions that they be turned over to the son. Maybe the documents even identify the blackmailer. In that case, it would certainly be in the blackmailer's interest to recover the envelope. This also means that he would have to have been aware of its existence."

"And is that so impossible?"

"Impossible? No — let's say improbable — unless the general had told him about it, to counter-balance his demands. In that case, the blackmailer would have had to have been on the lookout for the general's eventual death . . . which makes it difficult to understand why he would have sent the cards to the general after he had died. The theory that the blackmailer was unaware of the envelope is more realistic. Otherwise, the two blackmails would have negated each other."

"Except in the event of death! Then the one remaining would be directly threatened, and would take any risk to recover the envelope."

"That's true, but then why send the playing cards?"

"To intimidate."

"Intimidate whom? And what's the point?"

"To intimidate the heirs, in case they do know something. A sort of precaution."

"But you told me that the threats were addressed to your father-in-law."

"They were."

"Then your theory doesn't apply."

"Yes it does. Now you try to follow me." (She treated him to a little friendly sarcasm.) "The blackmailer knew of the existence of the envelope. He knew the general had just died. What were his intentions?"

"To recover the envelope, of course." (Boruti was obviously annoyed to have her cutting in on his territory.)

"Good! So far we agree. From whom do you imagine that he expects to recover the envelope? From the heirs? But he doesn't know whether the heirs have received the infamous envelope yet. So he decides to try a little intimidation before he does anything else. So he sends the cards, purely to create some mystery and fear. In other words, he is making his threat without taking too great a risk himself."

"But for God's sake it wasn't to the heirs, it wasn't to you that the cards were sent."

"Try to understand," she insisted. (Boruti now looked very sullen.) "He *knows* that the general is dead and therefore he *knows* that the heirs will open his mail."

"I don't get the connection."

"Look, the anxiety created will be very real but rather vague at the same time, since the cards are addressed to a dead person . . . so that — and this is exactly what happened — the heirs wouldn't alert the police. I seem to be explaining myself badly. Let me try again. If the heirs already knew about the blackmail, which I don't really imagine that the blackmailer believed, it would still take some time before the will and other confidential documents were made public. The heirs would only know that there was a poisonous present waiting for them among the papers. They wouldn't know what attitude to take, nor would they have made any decisions as yet."

"And if the envelope had been taken directly to the police in the first place?" Boruti asked.

"Then my husband would still be alive and the blackmailer would be behind bars."

"Then the guy was taking an enormous risk."

"He was more or less obliged to do something . . . or rather, to do something without saying anything. Okay, I'll continue." (She was certainly aware of the inspector's annoyance and was enjoying it a little.) "When they receive the cards, the heirs decide to wait for the confrontation. This allows the blackmailer to calmly carry out his plan. Whatever it was, he's then as good as achieved it. Good! But now let's look at the second version — the heirs know nothing. They would be even less worried over the mysterious cards that don't seem to have been sent to them, but they would still be placed at a psychological disadvantage with regard to the blackmailer when he was ready to enter the picture. So much for the playing cards in this case. But, going even further, there is something else that comes out of my theory. What if the general himself was the blackmailer? Because nothing says that it wasn't simply to retrieve the papers that the general was using as blackmail that the murderer prepared his plan. Then the meaning of the cards is like I just explained, and they had nothing to do with a 'countdown,' as you said. The blackmailer was the general, and the person he was blackmailing was the killer, who was just trying to get back the evidence of the blackmail. And all this is a very traditional situation in this kind of story."

Boruti gazed at Florence, stupefied. The sweet little woman who had seemed so lost in the world was suddenly revealing an astonishing capacity for reasoning and observation. He remembered that Viliard had been the first to guess that a stronger character and a sharper mind lay beneath her delicate exterior.

"Beware of this sugar-coated candy," he had said with his usual courtesy. "She is certainly more hard-headed than you think."

Boruti had smiled and attributed the remark to the Commissioner's incorrigible misogyny.

Now he saw how wrong he had been.

"Bravo," he congratulated, with a rather weak smile. "You'll soon be able to lead this investigation yourself."

Florence answered with an ambiguous smile.

"Would you like another cup of coffee?" she asked, turning her green cat's eyes on him.

"No, thank you," Boruti answered. He was beginning to feel ill at ease.

"Then let me offer you some wonderful old plum brandy. It was the only alcohol that the general ever drank."

The image of Florence Bertol lacing the general's plum brandy with a little poison leaped into Boruti's mind. In fact, how had the general died?

"What did he die of?"

"I beg your pardon?"

"I mean the general . . ."

"Oh. Thrombosis."

"Did he suffer much?"

"Yes and no. He had been ill for months. Will you have some brandy?"

Boruti couldn't refuse this time. He nodded yes. He decided to gulp down the plum brandy and get himself home to bed. With everything that Florence Bertol had just told him, he would have plenty to dream about.

"I hope that I'm not boring you by talking so much about all this?" Florence asked, suddenly a little troubled.

"Not in the least. It certainly concerns me as much as it does you," he answered with just a tinge of annoyance.

"Well then, let's get back to my blackmailer. We were up to the moment where he arrived at the house in the hopes of getting back the envelope. Why do you think he chose that particular evening?"

Boruti knew that he had to give some sort of answer.

"Maybe just by chance? You can never overlook the role that chance plays in any situation."

Florence was contemplative.

"Chance? Okay, maybe . . . but let's rule it out for the moment. Let's say that the killer knew that he was going to come on that evening. So my question still is exactly why that evening?"

"Because it corresponds to zero-hour of the countdown."

"Yes, it was the day after the last card had been sent."

"Then, in a way, the cards fixed the appointment."

"We could look at it like that."

"But why that evening exactly? Was it really a conscious choice, or again, was it a date fixed by chance?" Boruti asked Florence's question himself.

They thought for a moment in silence.

"In fact, there are only two possibilities," Boruti explained. "The first is that the date corresponded to the day that Poinsot brought the envelope because the killer knew that the information would be handed over to your husband on that day, or else — "

"Or else it was pure chance that he happened to come on that day," Florence interrupted.

"Exactly. Did Poinsot know that he was going to come on that day? I doubt it, especially as he stated that his intention was to take advantage of the fact that you were away, in order to see your husband alone. It's hard to imagine how anyone else could have known."

"Then the killer had decided to come that day, regardless of whether Xavier had received the envelope or not?"

"In my opinion, yes. This is perhaps what happened: the killer comes to the house that day. He knew the layout. He also knows that the back door is almost always open. He waits in the garden, or maybe behind the hedges or the magnolias, some place where he can see without being seen, and he waits . . ."

"What does he wait for?"

Boruti scratched his head, frowning.

"Yes, what does he wait for?"

"The right moment?" offered Florence.

"Yes, yes — the right moment. The opportunity to show himself and to settle the matter with the general's heir. And then the lawyer shows up. Our man watches the scene and understands that this envelope is probably what he's after. He waits a little longer, and once the lawyer is gone, he shoots, and enters the house to get the envelope, as well as the cards which were in the victim's pocket — isn't that what you said?"

"Yes, but why should he go so far as murder? He could have gotten the envelope by only threatening, since he was armed."

"He didn't want to be recognized."

"He could have worn a mask."

"Maybe he didn't have one."

"That would surprise me. A guy who could work out this story with the playing cards wouldn't be someone who might have to improvise at the last minute through a lack of preparation. Besides, I can hardly see our man waiting stupidly in the bushes for the opportunity to present itself. This is how I see it: the man or woman — "

"Why a woman?" asked Boruti.

"Why a man?"

"A hunting rifle is hardly a woman's weapon. Women usually use poison, a knife, a pistol . . ."

"If you think so. Then it was a man?"

"It's more likely."

"The man arrives at the house," she continued. "He slips in the back way, as you suggested, or through the front, which isn't impossible either. His idea is to force Xavier to hand over the papers that the general was using to blackmail him. Once again, the first hypothesis: Xavier doesn't have the envelope; he doesn't know a thing. He thinks the guy is crazy. After making his threats, the guy leaves. At this point he runs into Poinsot, and assuming that he knows that Poinsot is the family lawyer and that he might have the envelope, he gets his gun and waits for Poinsot to leave before killing Xavier. In the second case, Xavier had already received the envelope. He was aware of its contents. He poses a double threat to our man and, therefore, must be killed . . . The possible variations of all this aren't important, they wouldn't really get us much further . . . "

Florence then sighed deeply. Boruti notice that her pretty face was suddenly masked with fatigue. It was past two in the morning.

"No, none of this gets us very far at all." It was his turn to sigh. "I don't think any of it makes much sense. In the end, everything centers on the envelope, and there was nothing to really show that it was going to be delivered on that day. It certainly is pure luck that has played the biggest role in this drama. But your deductions aren't bad, all the same. Where did you learn to reason like this?"

"You know, since Xavier's death I've done nothing but ruminate over this whole affair, looking at all the possibilties again and again, almost like in a detective story. I've already asked myself all the questions that we've been going over tonight. I wanted to know what you were thinking about it all . . . and I was tired of being so alone."

Boruti shook his head, trying to sift the true from the false.

Something in Florence's attitude disturbed him. Maybe Viliard was right after all. She did seem capable of having committed the crime. She was sufficiently self-possessed and a master of cold reasoning, as she had just demonstrated with her complicated theories. But was that really likely?

"You see, Madame," (it was the first time he had called her that all evening), "as long as we can't find the envelope and the playing cards, we are acting on pure guesswork. It's only in detective stories that the key to the puzzle comes out of simple reasoning. In real life we need material proof, and all the rest is nonsense. I'm afraid that your husband's death will only swell the list of unsolved and unpunished crimes, since we have neither a concrete motive nor any idea about his aggressor's identity."

"So you think that the envelope and the cards might help you find the solution?"

"It's possible."

"But you already have the corpse and the bullet that was fired. Surely your laboratory can draw some conclusions?"

Boruti looked at Florence Bertol with some amusement.

"Yes, they have come to some conclusions. Your husband died of a bullet wound and the bullet is now in our possession."

"Is that all? I thought you could judge the make of the weapon? They say that a gun is like a fingerprint — no two are alike."

"Exactly, but we need a second fingerprint in order to have a basis for comparison. A single bullet fired from a commonly used gun reveals nothing. Had there been two bullets we might have been able to come to some conclusions. But with only one we know nothing."

"In that case, it shouldn't be forbidden to play the deduction game."

"No, but I think that we've played enough for this evening. The plum brandy was excellent."

He walked to the door, accompanied by Florence.

She waited until his headlights had disappeared before returning to her huge, empty house. The smells of coffee and brandy mingled with her own perfume. She collected the cups and glasses, and congratulated herself on the perfect success of her plan. Thanks to Boruti, she now knew the exact position of the police, and she also knew that she had oriented the young inspector's thoughts in the desired direction. She felt quite confident that Boruti would begin cross-questioning all of the general's friends and acquaintances to see whom he might have been blackmailing and vice versa. Viliard had already begun his investigation in that direction, and he would certainly be delighted to see the probationer following his own intuitions. She would be able to go on with her own investigation unhampered — after all, she possessed the cards and she knew the contents of the envelope.

She went up to bed feeling the immense satisfaction that rises from a sense of superiority.

8

Marcel Ribot leaned on his windowsill, wondering how he could best handle the problem. His eyes unconsciously followed a kid kicking a ball around on the square, and further on, the motioning of his friends, who urged him to join them.

It took him two hours to make up his mind. Finally he gave up the idea of a handwritten letter — a solution he would have preferred for its honesty — and also abandoned the idea of buying a typewriter (even a secondhand one would have been just too expensive), and decided to use the old trick of cutting letters out of a newspaper. This method seemed somewhat dishonest and totally cowardly, but he had to protect himself while he justified his actions. Too bad for his pride.

He took a pile of old newspapers from his arsenal-cupboard and sharpened a pair of scissors. Then he looked for two sheets of paper, one large enough to construct his letter and another to make a rough draft. He realized that he didn't have any glue and went out to buy some, giving Madame Girey a military salute as he went by. On his way back he met his friend Durel, and they discussed the chances of the horses they had backed. Then he bought a pack of *Bastos* cigarettes and gulped down a beer before returning to his apartment.

Night had fallen before he figured that his draft was satisfactory. He had spent as much time trying to find the right words as finding clean sheets of paper. His message had to be a good one — it should make them understand who he really was.

It took him a few more hours to be finally happy with his efforts, and to cut out the letters in equal sizes. At last he felt all the pride of having completed his task successfully. He leaned on his elbows and read:

To the Gentlemen of the Police,

I have the pleasure of informing you that I am not what you beleive me to be.

I am neither a killer nor a murdrer.

I am not a blackmailer like you think.

I have promised that certian people will pay for their crimes and I'll fulfill my mission to the bitter end and in spite of the fact that you beleive I am a murdrer I am acting in the cause of Justise.

I am not a theif and I didn't take the envelope and playing cards.

I'm sorry about the General's son but I didn't know that he had died.

It's too bad about all this, but justise must be done and I'll continue in spite of all obstacles, as I always have.

Don't try to find me because you will find nothing and you will only interfere with the completion of my mission.

I'm sorry that I cannot sign my name, but that would be dangerous, not for me but for my mission

Respectfully,
The Man of Houdan.

That was perfect. It was exactly everything that needed to be said. Not a single word had to be changed. There were probably a few spelling errors here and there but that didn't change the meaning. What was essential was to say just enough, without saying too much.

He folded the sheet, being careful not to dislodge the letters, before slipping it into the envelope that he had prepared.

"To the Gentlemen of the Versailles Police."

Then he had the idea of composing another letter, a letter addressed to this woman whom the police seemed to suspect. Of course he had now exonerated her, but perhaps he should apologize for having jeopardized her innocence? He began to cut out letters.

> Madame Bertol,
>
> I am genuinely sorry for having caused you these problems.
>
> It isn't my fault that the police suspected that you fired the shot while I, in fact, did it. My mission forced me to do it.
>
> I have adviced the police that it was me and that I didn't take the envelope, nor the playing cards. I am not a theif.
>
> I am sorry about your husband but I didn't know the General was dead.
>
> It's a pity about all this and I apologise.
>
> I'm taking the precaution of not signing my name.
>
> Yours respectfully,
> The one who sent the playing cards.

Marcel suddenly felt much better, almost relieved, by these two confessions. He was sure that from then on he wouldn't be regarded as an ordinary killer. He would mail the letters first thing tomorrow morning, at the rue de la Reine-Blanche post office.

Rue de la Reine-Blanche? Was he being careful enough? Until then, he had taken the precaution of posting his mail from another quarter, but that had been more for the sake of a little walk than a measure of personal protection. Should he be more careful? Perhaps now he should post his mail from the other side of Paris? Yes, he should be more careful, particularly in regard to the police. On the other hand, this didn't especially apply to his contact with those directly or indirectly involved in his mission. He shouldn't show any cowardice (as he was obliged to do with the police) in his dealings with them. In fact, they should be given every opportunity to retaliate . . . if they ever found him. He therefore decided to mail Madame Bertol's letter from the rue de la Reine-Blanche post office and the one addressed to the police from the other side of the city. He tried to think of the quarters he knew well and enjoyed visiting. He never moved about in the city without careful consideration. As far as he was concerned, the streets of Paris that he didn't know might just as well not even exist.

He first thought of Belleville and Menilmontant, where he had grown up and experienced his first adventures, his first loves, and his first scrapes . . . the old part of the city where his mother had died, alone and forgotten, and from which he had taken his Legionnaire's name. But those streets were filled with memories that he now preferred to avoid.

Then his thoughts turned to Josyane, to the rue Chapon and the other prostitute-lined streets that he had always loved to wander . . . rue Blondel, rue Sainte Apolline, rue de Palestro. These memories suddenly kindled a vague desire, a desire that he hadn't experienced since the beginning of his mission. That was where he would go. Several reasons urged him. He would mail his letter from that quarter, and then try to see Josyane, although, of course, now was one of the busiest times of her day. Maybe he'd find one of the other girls that he knew there.

He put the two envelopes in his pocket, quickly made himself a sandwich, and then went out.

He would walk to rue de la Reine-Blanche, and then take a taxi to Gobelins.

As he passed Madame Girey's lodge he could hear the talk-show host's voice blaring from the television set.

Joe had learned nothing new at the Tac-au-Tac. Marcel Ribot's name was unknown and the mention of Josyane's didn't seem to please anyone. After giving as precise a description as possible, he finally established that the "gentleman in question" wasn't a regular, that his visits were frequently interrupted by long absences, and that nobody knew when he would be back. Joe slowly finished a glass of mediocre Beaujolais before leaving, feeling annoyed but not entirely discouraged. He went off towards the metro Pigalle, where he had an appointment with Siragusi and Santiana to take delivery of the guns.

He arrived well in advance of the appointment, which had been arranged for eleven o'clock. This gave him time to enjoy the Paris that he had known . . . Pigalle Place Blanche, Boulevard de Clichy and Place Clichy. He observed that these places had hardly changed since the war. Pornography was still everywhere, more impudent than in the old days . . . and a modern office building had replaced the old Gaumont Palace. Still he had the impression that this quarter was virtually unaltered — even more so than rue Chapon, where he had sensed, without really seeing, the immense excavation and reconstruction going on behind the painted signboards and fences.

His striking outfit, along with his bemused expression, earned him numerous winks, enticing offers, and invitations into hotels and night clubs. "Come on *chéri*. French love? Bottomless? Non-stop, you'll love it . . . " All the ritual and poetic language that was frozen in his memory awakened old dreams and desires.

Joe refused with a smile. He was happy simply wandering around his old haunts. Once or twice he felt the urge to enter a club and see whether what was inside matched the pictures outside . . . but he was afraid to discover that the crude and raw copulating would be much the same as it was on 7th Avenue. Paris had succumbed to the wave of bad taste that enforced the same stereotyped shows all over the world. Joe thought nostalgically of the old days when sequins, feathers, and rhinestones dazzled the eyes, and the final unveiling of a pair of breasts caused the G.I.s to roar with delight. Those days were long gone. The dream was over, and nowadays, the spectacles were watched with a mixture of dull and depressed silence. Even El Cactucito hadn't proved an exception to the rule.

Joe made his way to the Pigalle metro at about ten-thirty. There were so many people around that he could hardly move, and the cars jammed in the traffic honked angrily — enjoying the pleasure of being authorized to shatter the peace for a few brief minutes. Joe was amused. Then he began to realize from the expression of the characters around him that something was wrong.

"What's up?" he asked the guy next to him.

"A 'Punch Operation' — our dear Minister 'Ponia' having some fun, I guess."

Joe nodded; he didn't understand a thing from this explanation. He was carried along by the crowd and suddenly noticed the blockade of police cars, officers, motorcycles, and even a television team.

"Are they making a movie?" he asked another neighbor.

The guy looked at him in amusement.

"Sure, they're putting together a little act. But it's not a movie. The TV crew is covering it for the news. Maybe the general public will feel nice and reassured when they see this tomorrow."

Joe still didn't understand. He saw the people around him pulling out their ID's. On his right, the drivers of cars were showing their papers and opening their trunks for police officers who were armed with automatic pistols. Ahead of him guys were being searched. Joe noticed one of them discreetly drop a piece of folded paper no larger than a pack of razor blades. He had seen this move often enough during the police raids on his own establishment — and suddenly understood what was going on. He saw the guy show his papers, then disappear into the crowd beyond. Joe couldn't help but smile. It was the same all over the world . . . the crook got away while a farmer from the country explained in exasperation for the twentieth time that he had left his identity card at the Hotel Saint-Jacques.

Joe found himself pushed towards a plainclothesman, to whom he presented his passport.

"How long is your stay in Paris?" the cop asked in uncertain English, as is often the case when the French are obliged to use a language other than their own.

"Until I run out of money," Joe bantered in French.

"Your French is pretty good." The cop blushed a little and reverted to his own language.

"Yeah," Joe admitted indifferently. He didn't especially feel like telling his life story to a cop.

"I'll have to ask you to follow me," the cop said dryly.

Joe knew that there were universal ways of coming up with a suspect. The French added several touches of their own, including not only finding a foreigner able to speak the native language, but far worse finding a foreigner capable of speaking perfect French. The latter circumstance was infinitely more suspicious.

Joe reflected on this as he was led away to a police van adorned with wire-mesh windows. He felt sure that if he'd had the good sense to reply to their questions in the language that had been used to interrogate him he might have been left alone.

They made him sit down opposite a police officer. Several temporary tables had been set up for the interrogation, and from time to time shouted denials turned the heads of the suspects as well as the questioners. Joe watched a guy walk past. He looked exhausted and his wrists were in handcuffs. Was he going to leave the same way after the questioning? He was suddenly sure that his intention to acquire guns illegally was written all over his face.

Nevertheless, the officer who questioned him treated him with the utmost courtesy. This time Joe was indeed obliged to tell the story of his life. They verified that his statements corresponded to the facts given on his passport and asked how he came to speak such good French. After listening to the reasons that he supplied, and taking his age into consideration, he was released, amid apologetic smiles. Joe left with his head held high and made his way through the police blockade which marked the boundary of the "free territory" for those who had triumphed. He glanced behind and his irony curdled as he saw the doors of a police van slam behind Siragusi and Santiana.

"Shit, those are my friends," he yelled to the police officer who had just let him through the blockade.

"Somehow I think that they are being taken away," the officer commented with an amused smile.

"But there's no reason . . . You must stop them. Let me through."

The cop wasn't smiling any more.

"Move along. This is enough of a mess as it is. Otherwise you'll be taken away too."

Joe thought of the guns. He wondered whether Attilio and Santiana had been caught after delivery or before. He realized the importance of keeping his cool.

"Where are they being taken to?"

"To the *dépôt*."

"What do you mean, the *dépôt*?"

"That's where suspicious characters are taken before they are either released or thrown in jail," the officer replied.

"But my friends don't speak French. They're Americans, like me. They'll never be able to make themselves understood."

"Don't worry, there are interpreters. What did you think?"

"Yes, but I should help them. It's the first time they've been to Paris. They must be completely lost."

"You can always go to the local police station," the officer suggested, his tone of voice indicating that he wasn't much disposed to continuing the conversation.

Joe did manage to get the address of the police station that they were being taken to before disappearing in the crowd himself. He walked for some distance, getting away from the police blockade and the danger of another interrogation. He went into a bar where he tossed down a cognac before telephoning Siragusi's contact, Benedetti.

"Hello, Benedetti? This is Joe Torronto, Attilio's friend. There have been a few problems — " (His heart was hammering, afraid that the guns might already have been handed over.)

"Don't worry, Mister, we know that the heat's on over there. We'll hand you the gift later on."

"Good, I'd appreciate it. Attilio and my chauffeur have been taken away by the cops."

"That's bad news. Anything serious?"

"I don't know. We had arranged to meet at the metro station, and I arrived just in time to see them being carted off. I'll try and sort it out . . . "

"If you have any big problems, let me know, and I'll put you in touch with our lawyers. Anything else?"

"No, nothing . . . thanks . . . *Salut*."

"*Salut*."

Joe hung up, conscious of feeling an immense relief. All this couldn't be too serious. He looked for the number of the police station.

"Emergency Police, may I help you?" said the voice on the line.

"Hello? Is this the rue Ballu police station?"

"No sir, at this time of night the local stations don't answer any more. All calls are channeled to this emergency service, and we take care of things from here if there's any need. What's your problem?"

Joe had a very crude idea about how he wanted to answer and almost hung up. Then he realized that this person might still be able to help him.

"There's been a police raid at Pigalle. I'm an American citizen and two of my friends have been taken into custody. They don't speak French at all. I want to help them."

"Are you sure they're at the rue Ballu station?"

"That's what a police officer told me."

"Okay. What are their names?"

"Attilio Siragusi," (he spelled out the letters one by one), "and Desiderio . . . " (he tried to remember Santiana's last name) " . . . uh . . . Columbutchi, I think. That's the name on his passport, but everyone calls him Santiana."

"Santiana? The musician?"

"What musician?"

"There's a musician with the same name. Hold the line please."

Joe held on. He waited for a long minute.

"Hello? Yes, your friends have been detained because they didn't have any identification."

"What can I do then?"

"Go to the station with their passports, or at least with your own. That should be enough. Are you staying in a hotel?"

"Yes, the Sheraton."

"Okay, our men can check with the hotel. If your friends have been booked, they should be released right away. It would be better for you to wait for them there."

"Fine. Thank you very much."

"At your service."

Joe hung up and left immediately for the rue Ballu police station. It was only two steps away and he was happy to find that nothing serious had happened to his friends.

* *
*

Attilio and Santiana had been picked up as they came out of the metro station. Attilio, whose dealings with the police had always been conducted on the highest levels, immediately incurred the wrath of an officer with a disdainful attitude. As for Santiana, always faithful to his political notions, he had refused to talk "yankee" and had only aggravated the situation by speaking Spanish. His long hair and very dark skin immediately rendered him suspect, and he had had to whimper like a child to avoid being separated from Siragusi.

By the time Joe arrived at the police station, none of the interpreters had been able to extract a word of sense from either Attilio or Santiana. A police officer whose badge indicated that he spoke Spanish had tried to interrogate Santiana, but gave up after wrestling for a short while with the New York Puerto Rican jargon. He had, however, established that the two men had forgotten their passports at the Hotel Sheraton. Attilio and Santiana were then relegated to a corner of the room.

Joe had little difficulty in arranging their release. He offered his passport as a guarantee, and his particulars were once again noted in a large black book. They asked him the same questions, which he answered politely. After having received one last reprimand, the three of them felt the relief of the cool night air, mixed with the damp smell of the street and the sweet taste of freedom.

Two telephone messages waited for them at the hotel. The first, which had arrived in the late afternoon, simply stated: "Traffic jam expected this evening. The two friends you are expecting will arrive later. I'll call back." It was signed "B."

Joe and Attilio felt doubly reassured. Not only had Benedetti avoided falling into the trap, but he had been warned several hours ahead of the "Punch Operation" — which proved that the organization's network in France was on a par with its counterpart in the United States. Attilio congratulated his French connections.

The second message had only arrived an hour before their return. It was addressed to Mr. Torronto and said "Saw Marcel this evening. He is having lunch with me tomorrow. Kisses. Josyane."

"What's this all about?" asked Attilio. He was in a bad mood, as much a result of fatigue from too long a day as from the episode with the French police.

Joe hesitated. How much should he tell Attilio? He knew that they were after the same goal, but he had more or less decided to play his own game, trying to give Marcel the time to get away. On the ride back to the hotel from the police station, he had carefully avoided the details of his meeting with Josyane and had simply stated that the address had been false and that the person living there didn't know Marcel's whereabouts. However, he had been obliged to read the telephone message under Attilio's questioning eyes, and this changed certain aspects of his problem.

"I left my name and phone number at Ribot's former address. They told me that they see him around there from time to time."

Attilio looked suspicious. All three walked towards the elevator.

"Who is 'they'?"

"The girl who knew Ribot."

"Ah. You didn't tell us that the girl knew Ribot."

"Well, she . . . she knew him without knowing him. Marcel isn't a regular customer . . . that's all. Do you understand?"

"A whore?"

"Yes, a whore." (Santiana, blank and unmoved, as if the conversation didn't concern him, pushed the elevator button.) "I told her to call me if she ran into Marcel. She hadn't seen him for more than a month."

"And she just happened to see him tonight?"

"Uh, yes, tonight . . . "

"And you don't think that's unusual?"

"Unusual? Why unusual? Neither usual nor unusual."

"Joe, it's becoming obvious that you're really nothing but an old soldier recycled to your greasy spoon. You go to the guy's place, you meet a whore there, she tells you that she hardly knows Marcel Ribot, that he doesn't live there, and that he's a customer that she only sees from time to time, and that she hasn't seen him for more than a month . . . and then she telephones you to say that, wonder of wonders, she has just bumped into Marcel. And you don't think anything of it? Well I don't know too much about frijoles and tortillas, but I think that this particular kitchen stinks. Let me see that message."

Joe took the crumpled paper from his pocket and held it out with a tired hand. Attilio almost grabbed it from him. Joe translated.

"Well, well," sneered Siragusi. "A nice intimate little lunch tomorrow. I suppose you intend to be there? Even if only for a few more 'kisses'?"

Joe shrugged his shoulders, ignoring the innuendo. He was too exhausted to argue.

"That's not necessarily an invitation, Marcel is the one who's invited, not me."

"Let's not play with words. The girl is trying to get you there."

"Sure. I asked her to contact me if Marcel showed up."

"And your Marcel? Do you think he's going to sit around sipping a cocktail while he waits for you?"

"The girl doesn't know why I'm looking for Marcel. I told her that I was an old friend passing through town and I wanted to surprise him. She promised not to say anything to Marcel and to let me know on the sly."

"*Oh la la,*" Siragusi offered, imitating the French. "This smells even worse."

Joe thought that perhaps Attilio was right. Nothing proved that Josyane wasn't playing a double hand as well.

"So what do you propose?" Joe asked.

"We'll see tomorrow. You think about it, and we'll discuss your views. Sleep well, anyhow."

Joe didn't miss the irony; he knew that he wouldn't sleep very well. He realized that Siragusi wasn't fooled by his little scheme. In spite of the old Mafioso's reserve, which often verged on abruptness, he showed surprising lucidity, followed by unexpected bursts of energy. He had just proved his prowess, and Joe realized that he had been wrong in considering his distinguished companion a burden. From then on he would have to confide in him more. Joe regretted not having mentioned the guy who had followed him. But then, maybe he had been wrong and he hadn't been followed after all.

He decided to take a couple of sleeping pills before going to bed.

9

As the first ray of sunshine that entered Marcel's room reached the foot of his bed, he threw back the covers and got up. It was Sunday and eight o'clock in the morning.

For Marcel, it was also the last day of vacation . . . and yet this day, which should have been filled with regretful brooding over the return to work, promised to be a happy one. He was going to see Josyane, and hopefully, he would have lunch and spend the afternoon with her. Maybe he would spend the evening as well . . . and who knows, perhaps the night too. A night without being alone before going back to work. He deserved it. He had never felt quite as lonely as during his vacation, a vacation which had hardly been relaxing, and which certainly had been very eventful. Luc should be pleased to know that he wasn't the only one to have drawn the Queen of Spades.

. . . Luc. It had been the 27th of June, 1944 . . . it seemed like yesterday . . . and yet more than thirty years had passed already. The sun had shone just as it did today . . . no, not really. It had been a paler sun, less golden, more white . . . a sun that heralded the beginning of summer, a mountain sun, an Italian sun, a sun of despair, and a shameful dawn . . . the death of a man, a man no more than a boy who had been like his own son . . . Luc, who had drawn the ill-fated card . . . Luc.

Marcel washed and shaved and prepared his breakfast with the slow, deliberate motions that characterized everything he did. The solemn way that he poured his coffee, then added the milk, then a lump of sugar seemed to bring him a certain happiness, the search for perfection that had become a daily ritual with him.

He was ready to leave early. He had put on his best suit and his red and green striped tie, which he'd had to re-knot several times before he was completely satisifed with the result. Then he left. He knew that he would find Josyane in bed, her face bearing traces of last night's makeup, her body exhausted, and she would probably have forgotten yesterday's invitation. She would run her fingers through her short, curly hair and light a cigarette. Then she would ask him to go and do the shopping and when he returned she would have taken a shower and put on a pair of blue jeans. Just to please him she would wear her bra without a blouse — what more could he ask? They would spend the day together quietly, and perhaps, they would make love. For a brief time they would have the impression that they lived together . . .

As he came to the corner of rue Chapon, Marcel had a strange idea. It wasn't entirely spontaneous, but more or less inspired by the sight of a little old lady who sold flowers on the sidewalk. Flowers. He would buy Josyane a bouquet of flowers. For the first time in his life he was going to give flowers as a present. Even his mother had never had such a tribute. It had simply never occurred to him. The only flowers he had ever given had been for corpses and coffins. Giving flowers had always seemed to be a sign of weakness.

He stood in front of the stall. The florist was a plump little lady wrapped in a shawl; she smiled at him maternally. The flower-filled buckets were arranged on rows of make-shift planks.

"A pretty little bouquet, Monsieur?" she offered in a friendly voice.

Marcel fiddled with his tie. He didn't quite know how he should go about this.

"Would you like a few chrysanthemums? They're very fresh and they'll last for ages if you break the ends of their stems . . . but be careful, they shouldn't be cut with scissors or a knife."

Marcel had never known that buying flowers could be so complicated. The brightly colored flowers that the florist pushed under his nose were gorgeous, but the word "chrysanthemum" bothered him. It reminded him of the flowers he had always seen in cemeteries.

"Chrysanthemums, did you say?"

"Yes, well, they belong to the chrysanthemum family."

Marcel made a face. The flower-seller was obviously used to this reaction and didn't persist.

"How about some dahlias? Or a few iris? Tokyos — oh no, they're chrysanthemums too. And roses, but they're pretty expensive this time of year."

Expensive? That suited Marcel.

"Yes, I want some roses, a large bouquet," Marcel decided with child-like joy. "With plenty of colors!"

"How much do you want to spend?" she asked, a little less friendly.

"I don't know. How much does a big bouquet cost?"

"A small bunch of 'Porcelaine' roses costs twelve francs for ten buds, the 'Baccaras' cost six francs each, the pink ones cost five francs apiece, and the yellow ones over there cost three francs fifty each. It would be pretty with a few iris. They cost four francs each."

"Whatever you say. Make it up as if it were for you. A big bunch."

The little florist dived into the different buckets, choosing the blooms she preferred, occasionally asking Marcel's advice as she cheerfully made up the bouquet.

After having paid, Marcel left with his "big bunch" and went off to Josyane's building. He was convinced that he looked ridiculous carrying the bouquet and that everyone in the street was laughing at him.

* * *

The telephone rang several times. Then a waiter knocked noisily on the door before opening it with his master key. He put the breakfast tray down beside the bed and opened the curtains, announcing that the hour at which Monsieur had asked to be awakened was long past.

Joe Torronto opened one eye and promptly went back to sleep.

It was only after being shaken by Santiana that he finally woke up. Siragusi had been waiting downstairs for more than half an hour and wasn't in such a good mood. Joe swallowed a cup of cold coffee and took an icy shower. He began to feel better, until he remembered the events of the previous day. He dressed in a dark suit and wondered nervously what he would say to Siragusi. He felt totally confused.

Attilio was waiting at the bar. He was still wearing the suit that made him look like the director of a funeral parlor, and his expression matched perfectly. Joe rediscovered the cold look, the set jaw of the killer he had known in the old days.

"I'm sorry. I took too many sleeping pills last night."

Attilio swept away this excuse with a brisk wave of his hand. He wasn't the type of person to listen to reasons for tardiness — such discussions were only a further waste of time.

"What have you decided?"

Joe was caught off guard.

"Uh . . . nothing. Let's decide together."

"If you like, but let's not waste any time. What do you propose?"

Although he hadn't given it any further thought, Joe still hoped that he could carry out his original plan — he had to meet Marcel alone.

"Nothing much. I'll go back to Josyane's place and see Marcel."

"And what if it's a trap?"

"Why should Marcel trap me? I'm his friend."

Siragusi looked like he was going to throw up over Joe's candid belief in Marcel.

"Stick to that if you like, but don't forget that he used you to find out Bonanza's address and then went and killed the kid. I don't think that he's exactly going to welcome your little visit."

"How the hell could he know about it? The girl promised me that she wouldn't say a thing."

"Just the same, your friend Marcel must have some suspicions."

Joe was becoming agitated.

"Okay, I won't go. What do you suggest as an alternative?"

"I'll tell you what I'd do if we had guns. We would have a nice little talk with Marcel, to bring things out in the open, and the conclusion would depend on what we learned from him . . . and this evening we would take a flight back to New York. Instead of which we are going to lose even more time while you work out your little intrigue."

"What intrigue?"

"All the trouble you're taking to protect Ribot. I don't hold it against you. It's perfectly normal that you should try and save the hide of an alleged friend. But don't take me for a fool."

This confirmed Joe's opinion . . . Siragusi was no fool. Once again he found himself longing to abandon the whole mess, but he knew that it was hardly the right moment to give in and that it was in his own interest to carry on.

"Okay, so what'll we do? Will all three of us go there?"

"Even if he's armed, he doesn't stand much chance against three of us."

"The chances are that we'll frighten him and he'll disappear — permanently this time."

"Okay, you go there alone and we'll wait outside, ready to help you if necessary, or to interrupt Ribot if he tries to escape. Do you agree?"

"Okay."

They looked towards Santiana but, as the Puerto Rican was paid to agree, the project was unanimously accepted.

The three of them walked out to the taxi stand in front of the hotel.

A man in a dark gray raincoat walked a few steps behind them.

Joe Siragusi and Santiana climbed into the first taxi. The man in the gray raincoat signaled discreetly to the car which was parked further up the sidewalk.

* * *

Everything went as Marcel expected.

At least, in the beginning.

Josyane was sleeping, and Marcel had to yell several times before she opened the door. As usual, a door at the other end of the hallway opened briefly to reveal a black eye and an expanse of thigh.

Josyane looked as dreadful as she usually did when she first woke up, and she was incapable of saying a word before lighting up her first cigarette. Contrary to what he had expected, she clearly remembered the invitation she had made yesterday when she had met Marcel at the corner of rue Greneta. She ran her fingers through her hair several times and only then noticed the large bouquet of flowers. She gave a little laugh and looked at Marcel questioningly.

"They're for you," he admitted.

"That's not possible," she shrieked joyfully. "Now you're taking after your friend Joe."

Marcel's expression hardened and his blush was replaced by an almost deathly pallor.

"What did you say?"

Josyane looked nervously from Marcel's bouquet of roses to the vase of flowers on the television set. Marcel followed her gaze, then saw the other bouquet.

"I said, just like my friend Joe . . . Joe Benier, you don't know him."

"No, that's not what you said. You clearly said 'your friend Joe,' didn't you?"

Josyane wanted to laugh — after all, she hadn't meant to let the cat out of the bag — but Marcel looked threatening. She felt that it was more serious than she had imagined.

"You haven't got a friend called Joe," she said, trying to calm things down.

"So, why did you say it then?"

"You misunderstood."

"I understood quite well . . . and I do happen to have a friend named Joe, and he has spent most of his life giving flowers to women . . . red roses . . . just like those over there."

Josyane realized that it was too late to cover up.

"Okay, it must be the same one. Your friend Joe is in Paris. Joe from New York! And he's looking for you. He wanted to give you a surprise. He'll be here any minute," she explained, as lightly as possible.

"You told him that I was coming here today?"

Josyane thought that Marcel was going to kill her in his rage. His face showed all the fury of a wild animal about to charge. His hands were tightening around the flower stems, as if he were fisting a club. Under different circumstances his gestures might even have been comical.

"Yes, he asked me to. What's wrong with that?"

Marcel was torn between his feelings. It was obvious that Josyane had meant no harm, and he had reason to hold it against her. She had no idea of the real situation between him and Joe Torronto. He rapidly questioned her on exactly what had happened and tried to figure out just how much Joe knew. Josyane gave him the hotel's telephone number.

"I have to get out of here immediately. We'll probably never see each other again. I can't take any risks; my mission isn't completed yet." He looked at the flowers he was holding, then tossed them onto the bed. "It's a beautiful bouquet . . . and it probably just saved my life."

He opened the door quietly, checked the hall, and disappeared without a backward glance.

Once he reached the landing, he leaned over to make sure that the elevator wasn't being used. He slipped down the stairs quietly, giving wary looks in all directions. Since he'd left Josyane he hadn't met another soul and this only increased his apprehension. He looked out on the street. Everything seemed normal. He left quickly, keeping close to the walls.

He moved in this way in order to avoid being shot at from the rooftops, and he must have looked extraordinarily strange to the passers-by on the street, who stared at him. Some even turned to watch the little old man edging his way along the sides of the walls.

Marcel didn't even notice them. His fury over the fact that he had been caught without a gun in a "danger zone" irritated him more than the fear for his personal safety troubled him. He was ashamed of having to flee like this, but he knew that, whatever danger was lurking nearby, he would be incapable of fighting it with his bare hands. Once he got to his guns he would regain his strength, his power, his youth . . .

* * *

A short distance away Joe Torronto, Santiana, and Attilio Siragusi climbed out of a taxi. Joe went straight up to Josyane's, while Santiana and Attilio kept guard at the entrance to the building.

The man in the gray raincoat slowly got out of a Peugeot 404 which was double parked a few buildings away, and began to walk towards the two men nonchalantly.

Joe arrived at Josyane's door, more out of breath than the first time, in spite of the casual pose he had tried to adopt.

Santiana mechanically watched the taxi that had just dropped them off as it snaked its way towards rue Beaubourg. Then he jumped as he saw the car turning the corner past a little guy who seemed to be in a great hurry.

"*¡Ribot! ¡Claro que sí! Se escapa . . . ¡Hay que avisar e el Jefe!*"

"All right, all right, Santiana. You know I don't understand a word of that garbage. What are you saying?"

Santiana understood English and he also spoke it, but even in the presence of the great Attilio Siragusi he refused to speak anything but the language he had been brought up by.

"*¡Ribot . . . Ribot . . . ! ¡allí está!*" he shouted with all the rich flourishes of his native tongue.

Attilio looked in the direction that Santiana was pointing, and although he didn't recognize the fleeing figure, he earnestly hoped that it was, in fact, Ribot.

"Hurry up, boy! Go on, catch him . . . *Avanti! Adelante!*"

Santiana had understood perfectly. But he hesitated for a brief second — shouldn't he go up and warn Joe first?

"Don't worry about Joe. That's my business. Go ahead, get going."

Santiana shot off like an arrow.

The man in the gray raincoat signaled the driver of the 404 and the car pulled up alongside him.

"Ribot is over there. You see that black dude running? Well, just ahead of him, there's a little old guy . . .that's him. Now move it."

If Attilio Siragusi's eyesight wasn't as good as it used to be, his hearing was still perfect — a sense increased by the presence of danger (which is so often the case with all the senses). He had clearly heard the name "Ribot" muttered just behind him, followed by a sentence which he hadn't understood. However, the intonation was just as commanding as the order he had just fired at Santiana. He heard a car door slam, and as he turned, he saw the gray 404 roar off with the squealing of tires that reminded him of his own youth.

He understood that perhaps Ribot was being covered and that Santiana might be in danger. He instinctively sped after him.

Never let it be said that Attilio Siragusi had abandoned one of his men in trouble.

The going wasn't easy. His scarf almost strangled him; he had to stop to pick up his felt hat; and his overcoat prevented him from running. His feet seemed to be glued to the pavement, obliging him to jog more than run. Attilio Siragusi had forgotten that he was nothing more than a helpless old man. Nevertheless, in spite of his feeble resources, he was trying to save the life of a man he hardly knew and with whom he had probably only spoken a few words.

* * *

Joe finally understood that Marcel wasn't coming and Josyane's incoherent explanations offered nothing more, and only wasted his time. He was sure that the young woman was lying, that she must have seen Marcel, and that he couldn't be far away. He noticed an odd lump under the covers of the bed. He grabbed Josyane and hoisted her to her feet. He pulled back the blanket and saw Marcel's bouquet.

"What the hell is this? Marcel? He's been here and you didn't know how to keep your mouth shut," he muttered with a fury that wasn't unlike Marcel's a little earlier.

Josyane tried to think of what she could do. Somehow she always seemed to be on the losing side.

"Yes, he was here. And he told me that you wanted to kill him."

"That's not true, he didn't say that. Marcel wouldn't have thought that I wanted to kill him. Where is he?"

"I don't know. He must be pretty far by now. You can always run and try to catch up with him."

"No, he can't be that far. You haven't even had the time to hide his flowers, or put them into a vase. I'll be back."

He left, slamming the door behind him. Josyane heard his footsteps in the hall, echoing down the stairs. She got up, locked the door, and lit a cigarette.

* * *

Marcel Ribot only heard Santiana's heavy footsteps when the Puerto Rican had almost caught up with him. He turned and saw the orange flash approach. And he also saw the muzzle of the machine gun jutting through the gray car's open window. He felt death bearing down. He saw the sweat and saliva on Santiana's contorted face. Marcel knew that there was no chance of getting away. For this, his last fight, he charged straight towards the gunfire . . .

Santiana stopped when he saw Marcel rushing towards him. Marcel only saw the gaping muzzle of the gun. The two men in the car fired and Marcel staggered. For a moment he lost consciousness. When he opened his eyes, Santiana was clinging to him, jerking and dancing like a puppet — the look in his eyes was already dead and his orange shirt was soaked with a deeper color. The gray car disappeared and the few Sunday morning strollers stood petrified in their places, where the gunfire had taken them by surprise.

Marcel disengaged himself from Santiana's body which fell to the ground like a loose sack. A few of the more courageous pedestrians ran towards him.

Marcel saw that he had been slightly wounded in the right hand. Blood was running down his fingers and his first thought was that he shouldn't soil his suit. The Puerto Rican's blood had already stained his vest. Marcel made a bandage with his handkerchief. Someone asked if he felt all right and suggested that he sit down in a nearby cafe. The crowd gathered around Santiana's body and word got around that he was dead. They wanted to ask the other man, the elderly one who was wounded, whether he knew the victim. But the elderly gentleman was no longer there . . .

Forcing himself to move calmly, Marcel passed the corner of rue Beaubourg.

"Where are you going?" the flower-seller asked. She hadn't left her stall and must have had a first-class view of the whole scene.

"To find the police," Marcel muttered distractedly.

He could see that the woman didn't believe him, but the look he gave her cut short any other questions she might have wanted to ask.

He signaled the first taxi that came by and asked to be taken to the Gare de Lyon. He went to the toilets and took off his vest. By some miracle his shirt hadn't been stained. He tightened the bandage and folded the vest over his right arm. He checked in the mirror to make sure there was no blood showing and that he looked presentable. He was still sweating heavily, and his heart hadn't yet regained its normal rhythm.

He strolled out towards the banks of the Seine in the autumn sunshine.

* * *

Joe Torronto had caught up with Attilio Siragusi just as the old Mafioso fell forward. As he leaned over to help him, he heard the spattering explosion of the gunfire and the cries from the top of the street. He recognized the orange T-shirt and saw his chauffeur being jolted by the impact. He watched, quite lucid, and he saw everything: the killers in the car (one holding the machine gun, the other at the wheel), Attilio's felt hat rolling into the gutter, the stupefied pedestrians, and that final death dance on the sidewalk . . .

"Take care of him . . ." he called to a pair of lovers who were standing nearby, pointing towards Attilio's waxen face.

Without waiting for a reply, he rushed towards the group that had gathered further on. He thought of running, but it was no longer necessary. The orange jersey would never be getting up again, and behind him, Attilio Siragusi lay as straight as a felled tree in his black overcoat. As he tried to recover his breath, Joe considered what he should do next.

One glimpse confirmed that Santiana was very dead. He went back again to Siragusi, but he didn't show the least sign of life either. An emergency van pulled up and the police got out with a stretcher. There was a discussion with the young man whom Joe had instructed a few minutes earlier to look after Attilio. Markings were made in chalk and photographs were taken before Attilio's corpse was removed. Joe skirted the circle of onlookers. Cars were beginning to clog traffic and drivers were getting out to inquire about the morbid details. Joe watched all this for a few minutes and then, like a lost child, went back to Josyane's.

"My two friends have been killed," he babbled, once a somewhat wary Josyane had opened the door

He sat on the edge of the bed — the flowers were still there — and searched his mind in vain for some direction.

Josyane put out the cigarette which she had lit just after Joe had left, the cigarette that had stayed lighted long enough to cut the threads of two human lives.

"What happened?"

"I don't know. I first saw Attilio fall down in front of me, and up the street Santiana got mowed down by a machine gun fired by two guys in a car . . . Marcel?"

"What about Marcel? He ran out of here like a frightened rabbit as soon as he heard that you were coming. I'm sure that he wasn't even armed. Besides, like me, he didn't know that you had two other guys with you. Also, Marcel doesn't drive. I don't know how many times he told me that he had never had his military drivers license renewed and that now he'd lost his nerve. He regretted not being able to drive. And then, too, he only just found out you were here, so I don't see how he could suddenly come up with a car."

"He might have been cautious — maybe he had his men waiting . . . in case . . ."

"Marcel? What do you mean, 'his men'? How do you expect a little old down-and-out like Marcel to have his own 'men'? Sure, he was generous with me, but you better believe that he had to save up a few francs before he came to see me. I don't want to have anything to do with your business, and I don't know what the problem is between you and Marcel, but I do know one thing . . . Marcel was no big wheel."

She was right and Joe knew it. Even if Marcel had been suspicious, he would never have been able to get a gang together. And he wasn't the type; he wouldn't have shot anyone without knowing what this was all about.

"Yes, I know. Marcel's no big deal," he murmured with a sigh. "He's an old man, like me, and I guess he doesn't enjoy this kind of horror show any more than I do. So what the hell was it?"

"How do you expect me to know? . . . What are you going to do, anyhow?" she asked, suddenly a little hostile. "You're not going to stay here, are you? I've had enough of this crap. My Sunday is all fucked up. You should go and see the cops."

"I just left the cops. I spent most of the last night with them. Do you think they'll let me off this time? I'm the ideal suspect — the nervous witness, the unknown fellow-traveler . . . I'd never get out of it."

"But you don't have anything to worry about. You didn't do it."

Joe shrugged his shoulders. He realized that he certainly wasn't going to get the comfort and support he needed from Josyane.

"The cops don't have to know that I was there," he suggested.

"They'll find out quickly enough."

Joe screwed up his eyes.

"And who will tell them? You? Nobody else in the quarter has seen me." (He though of the young couple and the inevitable woman at the other end of Josyane's hall.) "Were you thinking of telling them?"

Josyane shivered.

"You're crazy. Do you think I want to get myself in shit with the cops? Believe me, champ, you're way off."

"Yes, well I'm glad to hear it . . . because I'm the type who's rather inclined to bear grudges. Just now I didn't think we'd be seeing each other too soon, but it could be that I'd have to look you up again . . . unless you decide that you don't know me and you've never laid eyes on me."

"You can count on me."

Joe let Josyane close the door behind him.

The young woman thought to herself that one day she would get herself strangled over some kind of bullshit like this.

10

Marcel returned to his apartment in the early afternoon. He gathered from the loud laughter coming from the lodge that Madame Girey, her daughter and son-in-law, and the usual Sunday visitors, were watching *Le Petit Rapporteur* on the television. He sidled past the letter boxes to avoid being seen in the bright sunlight streaming through the main entrance before tiptoeing up the staircase. From now on he would have to be extra careful, and his comings and goings should be even more prudent. He managed to get past the lodge without seeing the inevitable edge of the curtain being lifted, without hearing the creaking of a chair before hearing the customary "Who's there?" called out. He arrived at his own door, only having made four or five stairs groan, which was quite a feat in itself.

It took him some time to open his door with his left hand. His right hand didn't really hurt, but the tight bandage had rendered it virtually useless. He tossed his vest over a chair and looked at his wound. It wasn't serious — a simple flesh-wound running from the thumb and index finger to the wrist. The bleeding had stopped and the stiffening relaxed a little once the bandage had been removed. He cleaned the wound and put on a looser bandage. Only his thumb still felt a little sore.

Then he washed the bloodstains from his vest. He left it to dry before he would remove the remaining marks with cleaning fluid. He tried not to think about the day's events until he was more composed. Only one thing really worried him — he had almost been killed and he was afraid of dying. He had probably grappled with death a hundred times in the course of his life, and each time he'd emerged with a sense of victory. This time he was left feeling miserable and feeble . . . he tried to analyze this weakening, and concluded that his life was more precious now than ever before. He suddenly found himself fearing that he would be unable to carry on with his mission all the way through to the end.

He realized that he was very hungry. He opened a can of beef stew, and the dizziness and the gnawing fear faded. After having finished off almost an entire bottle of wine his courage came back to him. He went to the cupboard and took out a package wrapped in a felt cloth and tied up with a strap. He also took out his box of firearm apparatus. He unrolled the felt cloth on the table and then held his old regulation pistol in his hands — a MAC 50, the ultimate handgun, which had saved his life twice. The time had come for the pistol to be used again. Marcel congratulated himself on having kept three boxes of cartridges. After a scrupulous checking and cleaning, the gun would be like new. He would never move without its comforting presence again.

As he took the pistol apart, he had time to reflect more calmly on the series of events from which he'd just emerged practically unscathed. No doubt his Legionnaire's luck hadn't left him.

Who could it have been, shooting from the car window? Had they come from America with Joe? Were they locally-hired gunmen? Something like this was both anticipated and yet difficult to figure out. Although he'd almost fallen into a trap at Josyane's place and he'd impulsively chosen to flee, he didn't think for a single moment that Joe would want to kill him.

And then, what had been the point of Santiana's frantic chase? Had Santiana meant to attack him or simply intercept him? Or to protect him? Marcel had felt the first burst of gunfire missing him. The killer must then have corrected his aim, but it was Joe's chauffeur-bodyguard who collected the bullets. Marcel was sure that he himself had been the real target, not the Puerto Rican who'd been left lying on the sidewalk. He couldn't find an answer to these trying questions, and he suddenly felt weighed down by heavy forces — the cops on one hand, killers on the other. Would he live long enough to complete his mission?

He looked listlessly around the room, seeking comfort in the familiar objects. His gaze came to rest on a crumpled scrap of paper on which Josyane had written *Room 2027, Hotel Sheraton, 260-3511.*

He wrapped the pistol in its felt cloth and pulled on a sweater before going out. The blaring of the television set came distorted up the elevator shaft. Madame Girey was watching the *Monsieur Cinema* quiz show and, as he passed her lodge, he heard the announcer asking, "What was the name of Tchoukrai's film, produced in 1959, in which Valentin Ejak played the part of a young recruit?"

La Ballade du Soldat, Marcel almost said out loud.

He was addicted to war movies.

* * *

At the Café Bouchard, Marcel was met with the usual warm and friendly hellos, just as he'd been hailed by the bowlers the day before. He shook hands with his cronies, who were playing canasta. He asked the owner if he could make a local call. As he

THE FIRST-BORN OF EGYPT

crossed the billiard room he was greeted with shouts of, "How was the vacation?"; "Where've you been?"; and "We haven't seen you lately!" He closed himself in the telephone booth, whose glass door was marked "For the use of our customers only."

He tried the number several times before finally getting through. He asked for room 2027 and waited for some time. Beads of perspiration broke out on his forehead. He almost lost his nerve when Joe suddenly answered.

"Hello. Hello? Who's there?" an anxious voice demanded.

Marcel almost hung up. Joe seemed so close, and therefore he presented a danger. But he could hardly back out now.

"It's Marcel," he said, cupping his hands over the receiver in an effort to keep his voice quiet.

Silence at the other end.

"Did you kill Santiana and Siragusi?" Joe asked in a voice that was as uncertain as Marcel's.

"Siragusi? Is he here? No, I had nothing to do with it. I was almost knocked off myself — but Santiana got it instead. I thought that you'd sent hired gunmen — "

"Are you crazy?"

"Well then, what are you doing here?"

"It's the Chuck Bonanza business. What happened?"

"Don't get mixed up in that. It doesn't have anything to do with you."

"Listen, Chuck's after me now, too. This is my only chance of getting out of it . . . and maybe yours too," he added.

There was another silence.

"Are you in a tight spot?" Marcel asked.

"A little. There's every possibility that the cops will pick me up before this evening. I came back to the hotel because I don't know anywhere else to go. I could hardly go to the people I know in Paris — anyhow, not under these circumstances. They're people who come to my restaurant, people who treat me like a friend. I couldn't get them involved in this . . . You know, it's good to hear your voice."

Marcel hated any form of tenderness and so did Joe. They must be in pretty bad shape to be making this kind of confession.

Marcel understood that Joe didn't dare ask for help. He should be ashamed of having involved his friend in his business.

"We could see each other," Marcel suggested.

"Okay," Joe agreed, his voice full of renewed hope.

"You could come to my place."

"If that's all right with you . . . At any rate, I'm getting out of the hotel before tonight."

"Come by this evening, 101 rue Nationale, in the 13th. It's the third floor, on the right . . . there's no name on the door. I won't be going out . . . but I go back to work tomorrow."

"I won't inconvenience you."

"I'm just telling you in case there is some problem."

"There won't be any problems."

"You never know. See you later."

"Okay, later."

Marcel didn't hang up immediately. It was almost as if the most important things hadn't yet been said, and he knew he was going to miss Joe. He waited for the click at the other end but Joe didn't hang up either. Marcel felt as if they were going to continue their conversation stupidly. He replaced the receiver with a dry click.

A fine, fateful rain began to fall. Joe had packed everything he considered necessary in his attaché case. It wasn't much — his papers, his travelers checks, a supply of cards from El Cactucito (just in case), his bottles of pills and medicines, two packets of Kleenex, a clean shirt, a wool sweater, and a silver flask of rye whiskey. Everything that he left behind indicated that he hadn't checked out of his own accord, but had simply disappeared — his pajamas, his open tube of toothpaste, a pair of socks stuffed in a pair of slippers, his suits still hanging in the closet, his traveling bag and suitcase.

Joe left, blessing his old habit of keeping his hotel keys with him. This way the reception desk couldn't testify whether he'd been in or out. He wondered if the switchboard operator would remember connecting an outside call to Room 2027.

He decided to look for a taxi a little ways away from the hotel. This was both for the sake of precaution and the desire to walk for a bit. Wrapped in his Burburry and protected by his beret, he found the rain rather pleasant. There were few pedestrians, and once he'd gone beyond New Jimmy's discoteque, hardly any at all.

Joe walked as far as the Observatoire intersection, turning around from time to time to look for a taxi. The man who had been walking some distance behind him since he left the hotel was hunched against the rain. He was only wearing a denim jacket that looked a few sizes too small for him. Who had put this little creep on his tail? The same ones as the other day? The same ones that had done the shooting on rue Chapon?

Joe turned and faced his follower. The latter stopped awkwardly and looked a little disappointed. "This kid's just waiting for the first opportunity to go home and say I shook him off," Joe thought to himself. "That won't be easy, with the two of us standing here looking at each other, all alone on the sidewalk and neither of us knowing what to do."

He decided to challenge.

"Hey kid, come here."

The other shrugged and shook his head. Joe took a few steps toward him; the kid moved back, his hands help up defensively. Joe wanted to go after him, give him a couple of slaps and ask him who he was and who he worked for. But he remembered a similar scene in which the guy had ended up with a knife in his guts before he could find out that the kid's name was Joselito Torronto. But that was a long time ago. Youth is often capable of the most unpredictable reactions.

Joe hailed the first cab that passed. He gave Marcel's address, then turned around. The kid had put his hands back in his pockets, but as the taxi stopped at a traffic light, he jeered and flicked Joe the bird.

That was too much. Joe immediately began to worry. What caused such a look of satisfaction on the kid's face? He, Joe, should have been feeling superior and the shadower should be upset. Joe examined his taxi driver's face; he was in his fifties and seemed honest enough. Then Joe looked back again and saw the gray car following behind them. That was it; the kid had only been used as a decoy to distract his attention while the Peugeot 404 turned onto a side street and waited.

"Wait a minute, I've just remembered I have to see someone. Can you drop me at the Place d'Italie?"

"Okay, mister, whatever you say."

The taxi crossed the Gobelins intersection. Too bad, he'd have to get out at the Place d'Italie — that was the only name he could remember. The gray car was still behind them. Turning around, Joe thought that he recognized his other shadower, the man in the gray raincoat. In a way, it was comforting; it's better to have familiar enemies even if you don't know what they have against you. When the cab stopped, the gray car drew up a few yards ahead. Joe got out of the taxi and leaped into a bus which had just stopped. All around him, the relatively few passengers were inserting their tickets into an automatic machine. Joe pulled out a wad of bills.

"How many tickets do I need?" he asked the driver.

"What? For the end of the line?"

"Yes."

"Two tickets."

Joe paid for his tickets and punched them in the machine. The bus had gone around the square and was heading towards Gobelins. His strategy had failed. There were neither enough passengers nor cars on a Sunday. The 404 was still following, waiting patiently at every bus stop.

After Gobelins, the bus went back up Boulevard Port Royal, towards the Observatoire intersection. "What a fucking stupid waste of money," Joe thought to himself. He got off of the bus a few feet from the spot where just fifteen minutes ago he had taken the taxi. The Port Royal metro station seemed welcoming enough. He rushed in and bought a book of tickets. He waited on the platform for the first train. All the cars were more like the surface trains he knew in America, and not like the ones in the subway. Joe didn't realize at first that he was on the suburban Sceaux line. His immediate problem was to establish whether or not he'd been followed. In this case, the limited number of passengers made his task easier. He didn't see the man in the gray raincoat, or the kid in the denim jacket.

The metro left central Paris and emerged from underground. Joe studied a map of the line. He decided to get out at Arcueil-

Cachan, a name that seemed a little familiar. It had stopped raining. As he left the station he unbuttoned his raincoat and walked cheerfully, feeling much happier.

His happiness was shortlived; it disappeared completely when he saw the gray 404 waiting for him in the parking lot. These guys were smarter than he'd imagined. They had simply checked on the direction he'd taken and then looked out for him at every station, which had been all the easier because of the overhead railway line (it would only have taken a glance up the stairway), and there was a total absence of traffic. It was all this god-damned Sunday's fault. Escape would have been so much easier in the teeming crowds of a Saturday or, even better, a Friday night. Then he could have shaken them off at the bat of an eyelid. He began to believe that this little gang was led by Dan Calloway or one of his sons. Only Joe didn't want to play any more.

He made an about-face and went back to the platform. It was a sad, deserted platform under a cement tunnel, and the wind howled through it. Joe approached a guy in a cap — obviously an R.A.T.P. employee.

"Excuse me. How often do the trains run?"

"Which direction?"

"Paris."

"Every seventeen minutes."

"Seventeen minutes?"

"It's Sunday, you know."

"I know, fucking Sunday."

The man in the cap didn't seem to take offense at Joe's nasty tone. He didn't fix the timetables and, being on duty, he probably considered it a fucking Sunday too.

Joe knew that he risked being fingered by the two guys in the 404 if he stayed on the platform. It was surprising that they hadn't moved in on him yet. He looked out towards the parking lot; the 404 was still there. Maybe they weren't after him personally, but simply wanted to know where he was going. If Marcel was telling the truth it must be some gang that was after him, and they might be trying to uncover his whereabouts through Joe.

He waved at one of the taxis outside the station, but the driver didn't seem to notice. He lifted his arm higher, again without

success. He made a few ridiculous motions which only drew smiles
from the occupants of the 404. Finally Joe put two fingers to his
mouth and whistled loudly. The taxi drivers jumped and folded up
their newspapers. The first one to get his engine started roared up
to Joe. He wondered whether he would be luckier this time.

"Where did you want to go?" asked the young, bearded driver.

"Paris."

"What part?"

"We'll see . . . let's get going."

The young taxi driver didn't need to be asked twice. The car
leapt forward. The 404 was just behind.

"So, which way?"

"Do you want to double your takings today?" Joe proposed.

"That wouldn't take much," the driver laughed. "I haven't
earned beans today."

"How about two hundred francs then?"

"Not bad. What are we doing? Do you want a little tour of 'Paris
by Night?' "

"No, this isn't a pleasure ride. Do you see the gray car behind
us?"

"The 404? Yes."

"You'll get two hundred francs if you can — "

"If I shake him off!" the driver interrupted happily. "Do you
know how long I've been waiting for this?"

"What did you say?"

"I mean this is the first time it's happened to me. You know, in
the movies there's always a guy who jumps in a cab and says to the
driver 'Follow that car,' or 'Fifty dollars if you manage to shake
off the car behind us.' I didn't think it happened in real life. Pity
you can't pay in dollars."

"I'll pay in dollars if you like."

"All right! Funny, you don't look like one . . . I mean considering
your age . . . "

"Look like what? And thanks for the compliment about
my age."

"I didn't mean to offend you. What I meant to say is that you
sure don't look like a gangster. That's not the cops behind us is it?"

"The cops would have gotten us already. And I'm not a gangster."

"Sorry, mister. Then why are those guys after you?"

"Listen kid, you should also know from the movies that the taxi driver who asks too many questions doesn't get his fifty dollars."

"This is great." The driver shook his head grinning. "Okay, let's show them a thing or two."

The stoplight ahead turned yellow and the taxi breaked sharply. The 404 screeched to a halt and Joe prepared himself for the collision. But the taxi had already shot off again, leaving the 404 behind.

"Now we'll teach them a few tricks," the driver muttered triumphantly as he turned into the first street on the right.

"Not too many tricks like that one, please," Joe said, hanging onto the seat. "Otherwise I'm going to be sick."

"Don't worry, mister, I know what I'm doing."

Joe thought to himself that he was getting what he'd asked for. He glanced backwards in time to see the hood of the 404 coming around the corner. They must have risked going through the red light.

"This isn't so easy," the taxi driver complained.

"No, it isn't easy," Joe answered, choking a little on his words.

They began to spin around the small streets. The gray car couldn't be outdistanced.

"We're not going to get rid of them here. We'll try in the center of Paris."

"Whatever you say, it's your job."

The taxi soon arrived at Port de Gentilly on the edge of the city.

"Let's see what the outer boulevards are like."

The boulevards weren't much better. Weekenders were returning to the capital and the streets were as busy as any weekday. The cab tried to weave between the lanes but the Sunday drivers were slow and lethargic and the weaving only resulted in a great deal of cursing and horn-honking from other drivers. Once or twice they just missed causing disasters. The 404 kept at a safe distance, without taking similar risks.

"Is rue Nationale far from here?" Joe asked.

"No, it's just around the corner actually. Do you want to go there?"

"Yes, try and drop me there, but first get well ahead of the 404. I'll jump out and you keep going at the same speed. You see what I mean?"

"I get it. That way they'll think you're still with me. That's the Red Indian trick — when the guy grabs on a branch and lets his horse run on."

"That's it, the Red Indian trick."

"Okay, we'll see if we can manage that."

The taxi swerved into the right hand lane to turn onto rue Nationale. Brakes screeched, engines stalled and a mammoth traffic jam suddenly developed. Joe's backward glance confirmed that the followers were temporaily blocked off.

"This is rue Nationale — what number do you want?"

"It doesn't matter. So long as I can duck somewhere before they catch up. Here is your fifty dollars."

"No shit, real dollars? I thought you were kidding. Wow . . . thank you. I'll keep one for a souvenir. Hold on . . . I'll stop here . . . and good luck with your gig."

The car slammed on its brakes and Joe jumped out.

A woman who was waiting for a taxi hardly had the time to climb in before the bearded driver took off, throwing his unexpected passenger violently backwards. The woman pulled herself together with dignity and proceeded to take down the taxi's registration.

Joe flattened himself against the wall of an entrance way and only a few seconds passed before he saw the 404 drive past. The rain had started again and night was falling.

Joe waited in the hall a few minutes, then went out on the street to look for number 101. It wasn't far away. He went up the steps to the third floor, following Marcel's instructions. He knocked several times, but there was no reply. He thought of calling out his name, but he remembered the other hallway and the door that had opened stealthily, revealing a black eye and an expanse of thigh.

From now on he shouldn't attract any attention. He knocked a last time and then went downstairs.

What had happened? Marcel had clearly said that he wasn't going out. Maybe he'd only gone to do some shopping. But then why hadn't he left a message on the door, however brief it might have been?

Joe met the concierge at the bottom of the staircase. He greeted her politely and went out into the street. It was quite dark now and he didn't know where to go. The quarter was hardly animated and the buildings looked sinister.

Joe walked to the corner where a sign "Bar-Tabac" seemed to attract lost wanderers. As he drew closer he noticed that a group had gathered on the left-hand sidewalk, opposite the bar. At the same moment he heard a police siren and shuddered. The sound seemed to die away and then returned — suddenly the police van swung around the corner and stopped a few yards away from where Joe was standing.

"Another old bum who's drunk himself silly," someone said behind Joe.

"Or maybe's been fighting with his buddies?"

Joe let the two men pass him, then crossed the street in their wake.

The police had little difficulty in breaking up the small crowd of onlookers that had gathered around the crumpled form lying on the sidewalk. A stretcher was brought out and Joe relived seeing Attilio's body being taken away that morning. The two police officers lifted the corpse, and a little trickle of blood ran into the gutter. The scanty front row of the crowd drew back instinctively. Joe could see the face in the quietly shimmering light of the street lamp.

In spite of the time that had passed, and the extra weight, he recognized it immediately.

"Jesus, Lieutenant Schültznicht," he murmured.

A guy turned to him.

"You know him?"

"I beg your pardon? I don't understand . . ." he replied with perfect composure, in English.

The guy gave him a stupid smile and returned to his dull contemplation of the scene.

"Were there any witnesses?" an officer asked.

The onlookers began to drift away without needing further encouragement. A fat red-haired woman was the only one to come forward, claiming that she'd seen the victim "keel over without a sound, as if he'd just fallen asleep," as she came around the corner.

Joe crossed the street and went into the bar.

"Cognac, please," he ordered in a weak voice.

Under the circumstances, his reaction wasn't atypical.

11

CHICAGO ON THE SEINE, IT CONTINUES . . . Boruti couldn't help but smile. With each account, no matter how sketchy, the newspapers filled their headlines with these odious comparisons (as if crime and injustice were a new and unexpected phenomenon in France). He threw some change on the pile of papers, and the woman at the newsstand snatched it up. Boruti took a paper from the top of the stack and went back into the station.

He thought of Florence Bertol. All during Sunday he had only been able to think of her and the strange evening that they had passed together. Saturday night, which had begun with all the signs of charm and seduction, had ended in irritation and frustration, and had left him under an odd kind of spell. Florence had revealed herself as much less helpless and soft than he had at first believed. Now that he knew that he ought to distrust her, he found her even more attractive. He had wandered around Versailles all through the long Sunday, hoping a little that he would meet the long, black wool cape coming around the corner of a street, but he hadn't had any luck. He even thought of going to Houdan, but he would have had to find a pretext. He wasn't ready to let the fascination that the young woman exerted over him lead him to pine under her windows like a lost dog.

Without her company, Sunday had seemed strangely empty to him.

Boruti answered the guard's salute with a nod and entered his office. He was half an hour ahead of his official work schedule. He had the time to quietly read the paper and smoke a cigarette . . . and to think a little bit more about Florence Bertol.

CHICAGO ON THE SEINE, IT CONTINUES . . . Two Deaths on rue Chapon (3rd). Another in the 13th. Boruti rapidly glanced through the subtitles and column heads:

A Former King-Pin . . . Like Lucky Luciano . . . Suddenly, a Hail of Bullets . . . I Saw a Wounded Man Running Away . . . A Bullet Full in the Chest . . . No Sound of Gun Shots . . . Rampant Insecurity . . .

This was what he was looking for, and he made himself more comfortable for reading.

Gang wars continue to plague Paris, and this time Americans are involved. Yesterday, Sunday, around 11:15 AM on rue Chapon it was first a former Mafia chieftain from New York, Attilio Siragusi, who collapsed on the sidewalk and then, almost immediately, a round of machine gun fire broke out at the other end of the street and a young Puerto Rican fell in his turn.

A Former King-Pin

With Attilio Siragusi it is an entire era of pre-war New York Mafia that dies. Born in Sicily in 1903, Attilio Siragusi belonged to that generation of poor immigrants who, for some time after their arrival, had no other care but to shoot up and bloody the country that had generously welcomed them. More discreet, and especially more prudent, than his colleagues in crime — Johnny Torrio, Joe Adonis, Joe Anastasia and others — Siragusi generally operated behind the scenes. He knew how to skillfully avoid trouble, and the experts still wonder over the reasons that allowed him to escape the big purge of September 11th, 1931, which saw the deaths of a good forty Mafia chiefs, gunned down by Lucky Luciano's killers. Probably it was because he hadn't yet taken the place that he came to occupy afterwards, and the ties that connected him to the chieftains of "Murder Incorporated" were subordinate to the superiors of that time.

His criminal activities were never distinguished by their original-ity: trafficking in alcohol, gambling, and prostitution rings . . . the usual routine. Harassed several times by the American IRS,

Attilio Siragusi served brief prison sentences, which never hampered his "business" very much. After his two sons were gunned down by rival gangs, Siragusi retired from the scene, and for the past fifteen years has led a very quiet life. No theory has been found to explain his presence in Paris.

Like Lucky Luciano

Attilio Siragusi used to boast of being a friend of the famous Lucky Luciano. At any rate, he has known a similar death. It was actually cardiac arrest, and not a bullet wound as was first believed, that felled the old man. A witness, M. Bernard Larieux, age twenty-four, describes: "I was going to have lunch at a friend's house with my fiancée when I noticed an old man, dressed in a black overcoat and hat, walking with some difficulty along the sidewalk opposite us. Suddenly the man staggered. He fell to his knees, then he crumpled completely forward before rolling over on his back, where he lay paralyzed."

Suddenly, a Hail of Bullets

"Just as we were going to cross to the old man, a hail of bullets broke out towards the end of the street. We saw a gray car . . . a 404 I think . . . speeding around the corner of rue Beaubourg. It seemed that two men were fired on, and I saw a guy in an orange jersey fall over. The other one didn't seem to have been touched. People came running up and we crossed the street. There was another guy who seemed to know the man in the overcoat. He told us to take care of the old man, and then ran off towards the other crowd that had gathered further up. Afterwards, we didn't see him again."

I Saw a Wounded Man Running Away

Mme. Serizay, florist, had set up her stand as she does every Sunday on the corner of rues Chapon and Beaubourg. "I really didn't get a chance to see everything. The gunshots broke out so close to me that I just closed my eyes and didn't even think about getting down. I didn't see the car that people are talking about. There was a young man, a dark guy, lying on the sidewalk with blood everywhere, and another man, older, holding onto his hand. He was bleeding too. People came from everywhere and I saw the wounded man run away. I recognized him. He had bought flowers from me about a half-hour before all this, and he had seemed a little strange. I remember that he'd kept on saying 'a big bouquet, a big bouquet.' When I saw him running away, I asked him where he was going and he told me that he was going to find the police. He'd been wounded in the right hand and I saw him take a taxi. I didn't think to get the license . . ." (Continued on page 3.)

Boruti was enjoying himself. This was serious, bustling, dynamic, and exciting. It was exactly the opposite of the dull hours that he spent over his paperwork, with only petty, boring cases to handle from time to time — theft in parked cars, or pickpocketing, or forged checks — things that held no interest for him other than the chance to get out for some fresh air. The mysterious Houdan crime, which had turned his routine upside-down, now looked trite and common to him.

The bottom quarter of the front page was devoted to the death in the thirteenth district.

A Bullet Full in the Chest

A visiting Austrian, M. Dieter Krantz aged fifty, was found yesterday evening not far from the intersection of rue Nationale and rue du Chateau-des-Rentiers, in a district presently teeming with crime. M. Krantz had received a single bullet fully in the chest, and in spite of the presence of a witness, the investigation promises to be very difficult.

No Sound of Gunshots

"I didn't hear the sound of a gun going off," recounted Mlle. Beley. "The man was walking in front of me and suddenly I saw him but he was completely unconscious. I didn't notice the wound at the time. I have to say that the street was pretty dark. I went to tell the man in the bar there, who telephoned the police. I really can't tell you any more than that." (Commentary, page 3.)

Rampant Insecurity

These two crimes occurring in the middle of the street at times of the day when it would seem that everyone should be able to stroll unmolested brings us again to the problem of the rampant insecurity which is becoming the number one problem in our big cities . . . etc.

Boruti went on to page three where the report continued, and the commentary took the form of an interview with Commissioner Bertholier of the CV squad (Crime and Violence).

— *Commissioner, does the shooting on rue Chapon mark the beginning of a new era in gang wars?*

— *The term "gang wars" seems out of place here. Lately we've had to intervene in several accountings between rival gangs, but these affairs haven't — by their frequency and violence — been anything but normal, if I may use that word.*

— *Then the shooting on rue Chapon seems normal to you?*

— *That's not what I meant. But the facts in themselves, as intolerable as they are, aren't particularly unusual. I deplore this situation as much as you do. On the other hand, the personalities of the victims doesn't fail to present us with with numerous problems. It is a question, in both cases, of uncovering the tracks of foreigners totally unknown to the French police.*

— *Then according to you, the two cases would be connected?*

— *I don't say that at all. We have, on one hand, a machine-gunning, in the middle of a steet in broad daylight, sprayed from a moving car, and on the other a body found on a sidewalk at dusk, on the other side of Paris. No evidence allows us to relate these two crimes.*

— *Have you found the gray car?*

— *The witnesses agree concerning the color — gray — and the make — a Peugeot 404. However, they have given slightly varied reports on the license number. We are attempting to make verifications.*

— *Who exactly are the victims?*

— *I won't talk to you about Attilio Siragusi, who isn't really certain to be directly involved in the case. He succumbed to a cardiac-related illness, and you people probably know his past activities better than I do. The young Puerto Rican who fell under the machine-gun spray, according to his passport, resides in the United States and his profession is listed as Chauffeur-Truck Driver. We know nothing more. We are waiting for information from Interpol.*

— *And the death on rue Nationale?*

— *The same thing. He was an Austrian citizen, the commercial manager of an Austrian import-export firm, and had practically no dealings with France. He had arrived that same morning — Sunday — in Paris.*

— *Everyone is wondering about the mysterious wounded man on rue Chapon . . .*

— *Yes. There is some testimony on that subject. Certain persons claim that they saw him walking on rue Chapon several moments before the shooting. The most important witness is the florist. The man had bought flowers from her a little earlier, and immediately after the shooting, this woman saw him fleeing. He no longer had his bouquet and this leads us to believe that he must have visited someone in the meantime. We are making inquiries in the neighborhood.*

— *There is also another man — a couple of witnesses claim that he seemed to know Siragusi.*

— *Yes, but that is more a question of an impression. These witnesses also noted that the man had a very slight accent, without being able to say whether the accent was foreign or provincial.*

— *Do you think that you'll wrap this up quickly?*

— *It's impossible for me to say. The evidence and the indications that we have are too few and too sketchy. We'll just have to see . . .*

Boruti refolded the paper. His colleagues in Paris had their bread on the table all right. He promised to buy himself the first edition of *France-Soir*. Maybe there would be new developments?

He imagined that he was Commissioner Bertholier of the CV squad, and he smiled while answering the reporters' questions, in the middle of a forest of microphones, with lightbulbs flashing and television cameras scrutinizing his intent and implacable face.

Legriffe's rude interruption broke up his reverie.

"The boss wants to see you. There's news."

"News? On what? Rue Chapon?"

Legriffe gave him a funny look.

"What, rue Chapon?"

"Nothing, never mind . . . I was reading an article."

Legriffe frowned, uncomprehending. Boruti got up and followed the inspector to Commissioner Viliard's office.

"*Salut,* Boruti. Here, read this."

Boruti took the sheet of paper that was offered to him with a questioning look.

"Huh . . . huh. What gorgeous spelling," he commented, as he read.

Viliard raised his eyes to the ceiling.

"Who gives a damn about the spelling? What do you think it means?"

"Aah, anonymous letters . . ."

Viliard gave a heavy sigh and restrained himself patiently.

"Read it to me, you donkey. And try to understand."

Boruti took on a pained look. Did his chief take him for a fool? He made the effort to reread, even though he had understood perfectly the first time.

"Go on, I'm listening. This is the time to make clever deductions."

"Well, this doesn't seem to be a gag. It's probably our man."

Viliard exploded.

"Of course it's our man! He knows almost more than we do about this case. That's normal if he's the murderer. Only what's even stranger is that he seems to know what we're thinking. 'I'm not what you believe me to be . . . ' That's not off the top of the head, is it? And the worst part is that he's telling the truth. Boruti, I suddenly notice that you're very bright."

"Funny, he says it just like that . . . in plain words. It'll take some time to analyze this letter."

"It'll take time? Good, I'm going to give you the time. Take this with you and make a little analysis. I want your report before noon."

Boruti faced Viliard's furious stare (when the boss bawled like this it meant that he was in a good mood). Legriffe also seemed to be enjoying himself very much. Boruti didn't know which foot to stand on. He mechanically took up the letter and returned to his office.

Viliard was right. The letter gave the impression that the guy who had written it was trying to justify himself in their eyes, as if he was perfectly aware of the first results of their investigation. "I am not *what you believe me to be* . . . I am not a blackmailer *like you think."* These sentences seemed to refer to a real knowledge of what the police had discussed among themselves.

And then there were also these references to the envelope and the playing cards. They proved well enough that the mysterious correspondent knew what he was talking about.

Yes, this letter deserved to be analyzed in detail. Boruti put himself to work. A little before noon his report was ready. He went to knock on the commissioner's door.

"Here you are. I have several conclusions to offer and I — "

"Ah, at last. Go get Legriffe. He's in Passports," Viliard cut in with a grimacing smile.

Definitely the boss was in an excellent mood. Probably because he was happy to pick up the trail after a dull Sunday.

Legriffe "finished with his customer," then asked the ones who were waiting to excuse him for a few minutes. No one remarked that they had been waiting too long already.

"We're listening," Viliard declared, pushing back his chair and stretching out his legs.

Boruti glanced over his speech. It was imaginable, from his severe and composed expression, that he was preparing to make an extremely serious statement to a very large audience. The commissioner's ironic smile brought him back to earth.

"Okay, firstly — whoever wrote this knows what he's talking about. The precise allusions to our case sufficiently demonstrate that much. The author of this letter is then either the author of the crime or else someone who is very well-informed and who is trying, for a reason that we don't understand, to mock us by making us believe that he is the murderer."

Viliard opened his eyes wide.

"What's this nonsense? Making fun of us? Trying to pass for the murderer? What are you saying, Boruti? You're the one who's mocking us."

Boruti made a face that was contrite and irritated at the same time. Was he going to have to explain to his chief that when you want to act by reasoning, you had to push each possibility to the extreme? Even Florence Bertol knew that. The commissioner preferred to stop at the most probable, and most obvious, result and risk missing the forest for the trees.

"No, Commissioner, I'm not making jokes. Nothing in this letter formally proves that the author is the murderer. Read it again." (Viliard gave him a nasty look.) "There isn't a single new indication for us. There's nothing that we didn't already know. The person who signed himself 'The Man of Houdan' doesn't tell us how he acted, what his motive was, or his weapon, or his gripe. Everything that he says is what our little group knows — or suspects. There's the three of us, Mme. Bertol and Monsieur what's-his-name, the lawyer, who all have the necessary details for a letter like this."

"That's true," Legriffe admitted. "But then, what's the point?"

"I don't really know. I don't say that the letter wasn't written by the murderer. I'm only envisioning, in a theoretical and abstract manner, what the different possibilities are." (This was said for Viliard's benefit in an attempt to head him off.)

"But tell me, Boruti, do you have some little idea in the back of your mind?" the commissioner insisted.

"Just what I said — there is no evidence in this letter. And this spelling is too awful to be believed. It's as if the purpose of it is to distract our suspicions."

Viliard shrugged his shoulders. He had noticed a few mistakes here and there, but nothing flagrant.

"All right, go on. But admit for the moment that it is our man."

"If you like. Anyway my conclusions will end up there. First I'd like to make a comment: If the murderer is the author of the letter, how does he know *what we're thinking about him?* Because you get the impression from reading this letter that it is a question of a kind of justification, to make things clear, as if the 'Man from Houdan' had overheard a conversation and he then found himself obliged to show himself in order to establish the truth and, in a manner of speaking, preserve his reputation."

"Ah, well, that's interesting," Viliard admitted. "That brings us back to saying that the murderer is either the lawyer . . . or the woman."

The commissioner looked satisfied. At last Boruti was thinking like him. It was, by all appearances, the woman who had taken things in hand.

Boruti perfectly understood the implications. He took a certain pleasure in refuting them.

"Well actually, I find that pretty unlikely."

Viliard creased his brow.

"Unlikely, huh? Go on."

"Yes, unlikely. The personality that shows up in the letter doesn't fit with what we know of Florence Bertol's character," (Boruti blushed and wondered if it was noticeable) "or with the lawyer's character either."

"Hold on," Viliard warned, shooting a conniving smile at Legriffe (who responded with perfectly subordinate attention). "We're going to have a little sideshow — the psychology of the murderer."

Boruti preferred to ignore the remark.

"We have to look in this direction. Here are the character traits that I think are revealed by the way the letter is drawn up. First, as I already said, the individual considers himself wronged, humiliated and injured by the fact that we think that he is a killer, a murderer, a blackmailer, a thief — "

Viliard burst out laughing.

"Oh? And what does he think? That we should take him for a choirboy?"

"No, but he wants to confirm the truth; he is not a criminal but a vindicator. That comes up several times in the letter. The guy talks of his 'mission,' and the 'price that must be paid.' He says that he's acting on the side of 'Justice.' "

"Yes, I know. I read all that and I'm used to that kind of garbage. With all these guys who feel the need to write to us, it's always to say that their crime is justified and to ask us not to meddle in their affairs. Unfortunately, Boruti, we are paid to do just that, to meddle in their business."

Boruti gave a little smile which he tried not to make too sarcastic.

"But, chief, I'm not trying to defend this person. Again, I'm only trying to understand."

"Understand what? That this guy is fucking around with us?"

"Understand what kind of personality is hidden behind this letter."

"But you just said it a minute ago — the lawyer or the woman."
Boruti nearly shrugged his shoulders.

"No, chief. For the moment I'm looking for a third man."

"A third man? Well, that's another thing, isn't it? What's he like, this third man?"

"He's a vindicator. At least, that's how he sees himself. Not for a single instant, in pursuing his 'mission' as he calls it, does he see himself as a murderer. He had to make sure that we were aware of his position, to make sure that we weren't just going to skim the surface of the truth, and he had to let us know that he is acting remorselessly and things are going along as he planned them. He does indeed have every intention of carrying out his 'mission' all the way through to the end. As he is a proud and exacting man, he wants us to know that we are mistaken on his account."

"That's all very pretty, but it hardly gets us anywhere."

Boruti listened politely to his chief's remark, then continued as if nothing had been said.

"Then we can now think that, by killing Xavier Bertol, our man was pursuing some kind of revenge. It is a revenge that isn't completely satisfied yet, as the man talks of continuing his 'mission.' "

"You make this deduction," Viliard sneered, "as if we hadn't thought of it."

"Can I go on, chief?" Boruti asked calmly.

"You're really in a lousy mood today. All right, go ahead."

"Thanks. The letter shows us nothing of the reasons for this revenge, but still there is a sentence that I find curious. It's this: 'I'm sorry about the general's son, but I didn't know that he had died.' What exactly do these words mean? That the guy is sorry that the general's son was killed?"

"That's the most obvious meaning," Legriffe agreed, while the commissioner nodded his head affirmatively.

"Yes, but then that leads us to admit that the guy isn't the killer. In that case, his denials are only a word game, and his letter no longer makes any sense. Because if he really isn't involved in this case, we can't imagine why he would write to us."

"The usual crazy person's letter."

"That's hard to say, given the contents of the letter. The guy may be crazy, but that doesn't prevent what he's saying from largely proving that he is good and involved in our case."

"Boruti, you're trying to confuse us completely with your clever suppositions. You take yourself for Sherlock Holmes or Commissioner Maigret. I took you for a disciple of science and the unconditional methods of the laboratory, and you disappoint me," Viliard sneered again.

"But, chief, reasoning is a scientific method. If we scrupulously analyze the contents of this letter of course we don't come up with any proof, any material evidence, nothing palpable. It only prevents us from chancing to orient our suspicions in a cloudier way. It's at least worth the bother of trying."

"I'm not arguing against it, but let up a little on the Agatha Christie, would you?"

Boruti allowed himself the luxury of a dry look. The commissioner only scoffed the more.

"Okay, I lost you a while ago myself, but let's see what you've got . . ."

"You were saying that the author of the letter maybe wasn't the murderer," Legriffe reminded.

"Ah, yes. But let's leave that very unlikely possibility aside. It would take us too far off the track, and I see that no one believes it anyhow. Me neither, in fact. Okay, the second way of reading the sentence: the guy regrets the death of Bertol's son because the death occurred *outside of his intentions.*"

"I see what you're driving at. You mean that the guy didn't want to get rid of Bertol, but only to wound him . . . or maybe intimidate him? But things took a bad turn and . . . et cetera. The usual scene?"

"Yes and no, chief. Because all the material evidence, the trajectory, the bullet, the type of wound certainly demonstrate that the guy aimed carefully and precisely from outside the house, like someone lying in wait for his prey. But the fact that a single bullet was fired might actually mean that the guy tried to stop himself in time — either because he had only wanted to wound or intimidate, or because he suddenly realized that he had gone too far."

"Yeah," Viliard admitted, barely convinced. "And which of the two possibilities do you choose?"

"I can't help but believe that the guy who wrote the letter is indeed the person who shot Xavier Bertol. Whether or not he wanted to kill him doesn't make much difference for the moment."

"I'm glad to hear you say so."

"But I offer a third interpretation of the sentence — in my opinion it's much more interesting."

"Ah? Let's have it?"

"Okay. The guy might also have meant: 'I'm sorry about the general's son, but I didn't know that the general had died.' This kind of grammatical error is common enough, and it's in keeping with the quality of the spelling in the letter."

"And so?"

"So, that changes a lot of things. The guy doesn't at all regret that Bertol's son was killed. He regrets the death of the general . . . or rather he regrets not knowing about his death. And he throws in 'too bad about all this, but justice must be done and I'll continue in spite of all obstacles, as I always have.' "

"I'm no longer with you at all."

"But it's simple. Let's go back to the playing cards." (Viliard grimaced. He had never put much faith in that business.) "They would have been sent, according to Mme. Bertol, to the general during the few days that followed his death . . . and preceding the death of the son. If the sender was ignorant of the general's demise, we can better understand the point of the cards." (Boruti remembered the little game of deductions that he had played with Florence, and he suddenly had the impression that the young woman had been hiding something from him. Maybe she had even been making fun of him? He promised himself to think about it.) "The threats that these cards seem to represent were indeed intended for the general, and then the revenge — or the blackmail — was actually meant for him, as we originally thought."

"Then it's the general and not the son who actually should have been killed?"

"That's possible, in fact. But then why did the killer attack the general's son?"

"Out of confusion."

"Huh . . . hard to admit. We said that the mysterious killer probably must have known the layout well enough. What's more, all this seems to prove that this business was carefully planned. No one carries out a 'mission' by leaving anything to chance. Personally, I can hardly imagine how our killer could have mistaken his victim. Especially at that rather short distance."

"But if everything was so well planned, how is it that the killer didn't know about the general's death?"

"We probably can't know that at this point. In any case, it shows that our man was neither close to nor familiar with the general's life."

"Yeah, and yet you still think that it was Bertol's son that he was aiming at?"

"Yes, it's possible: Egypt's first born."

"What? What are you talking about?"

"Egypt's first born . . . a relatively classic way of taking revenge on someone — through another person."

"I see. The killer wanted to revenge himself on the general, but rather than kill him, he preferred to kill his son, in order to make the vengeance more terrible, so that the general would suffer it up until his own death," Legriffe declared enthusiastically.

"That's it," Boruti answered, happy to finally get some support. "And what the killer really seems to be regretting in his letter is that his revenge couldn't — by the fact that the general was already dead — be effective."

"Whoa there, slow down," Viliard broke in. "This is all mere supposition."

"It fits together perfectly anyway."

"Fits together with what? The way you put things, everything ends up fitting together. But it proves nothing."

"That's true, chief, it doesn't prove anything. Like I told you, this kind of deduction only interests us to the point that our suspicions can be confirmed . . . or headed in a new direction. Behind this letter is the portrait of a personality that is different from the blackmailer that we, at first, imagined."

"Sure, I admit that it isn't uninteresting," the commissioner agreed. "But for the moment all these fancy ideas don't get our investigation any closer to solid ground. Your portrait is rather fuzzy."

"Let's try to find something a little more precise," Boruti proposed with a victorious smile. (He had realized that he was going to end up by convincing them.) "I see our man as someone relatively older . . . middle aged, at least."

"What makes you say that?"

"His manner. The tone of the letter, certain words and expressions, the polite formulas that are a little bit 'old France.' And then, if he has a grudge against the general, he must have known him rather well at one time. He's probably from the same generation."

"Not necessarily," Legriffe interjected. "Whatever grudge he has doesn't necessarily imply a special kind of relationship. Age doesn't matter much in this situation. The youngest recruits often despise the old brass enough that later on they want to get their revenge."

"You just said 'later on?' Before he became a general, Bertol was a colonel, a commander, a captain . . . The more we go back down through the hierarchy, the more possibilities the general had of attracting the hate of his subordinates. We arrive nowhere like this."

"The general had been retired for almost twenty years," Viliard remarked, "and nothing that we know about this case revolves around a revenge that is connected with the military. You're still in dreamland, both of you."

"There is still this kind of deference in the letter: 'Gentlemen of the Police . . .' 'I have the honor of acquainting you . . .' Here the signs of a report addressed to official superiors. This guy surely knows all about formal functionings, and is probably military."

"Okay, if it makes you happy. We'll have to go question all of the general's former recruits."

They all three agreed on a little break and had a laugh. Legriffe passed around his pack of cigarettes, and Boruti thought that Commissioner Viliard wasn't such a bad egg after all.

"We're going to have to keep looking just the same," Viliard continued after a few drags. "So, you say a former soldier, a guy who has a sense of protocol and a taste for honor, a guy who is well organized, meticulous even, and a pretty good marksman?"

"That's about it. A guy who respects the cops and the established values."

"Like the life of his fellow men?" Viliard asked ironically.

"Yes. He's not the sort who kills for enjoyment. He doesn't stop repeating there is a 'mission' to fulfill, and justice must be done. Of course his judgment is a little deranged in the sense that all his behavior revolves around this single idea — to continue his mission as he always has."

"Yeah, he's a little cracked is what."

"He certainly has a tendency to paranoia, like most criminals and soldiers."

"No fancy words, Boruti, I beg you."

"Aah, it's better to call things by their right names. The crime as much as the letter — and the sending of the playing cards — denote paranoid behavior."

"Explain it to us. You know how I adore psy-cho-lo-gy."

"Paranoia is a mental illness whose two principal traits are, on the one hand, a constant feeling of not being in one's proper place, having been wronged, bullied, and persecuted in one way or another — it can rightly be called a persecution complex — and on the other, a false judgment from which all the crisis behavior of the sufferer stems — but with perfect logic. These signs are generally very long in developing. They rarely manifest themselves in a clear manner before their maturity, which is often very tardy. That's why our man probably isn't very young. As for the events which led him to believe that he was invested with a 'mission,' they are for the time being unknown to us. It could be as much a question of a serious fact as some dreamed-up nonsense. What counts is solely the importance that he has placed on those events. His idea of justice is no longer the same as ours and what he offers in his letter demonstrates this well. He is incensed because we haven't grasped the meaning of his mission, and he asks us to have a better opinion of him, while proposing that we leave him in peace. It's very likely, moreover, that he imagines that that's exactly what we're going to do . . ."

"I see. And if we catch him he's still going to get out of it under the pretext that he's irresponsible."

"What do you want, chief? Our job is done once we have him under lock and key," Boruti replied with a feigned despair that the commissioner didn't quite catch.

"Yeah . . . and in the meantime, he's still running free."

"Maybe he'll show up again."

"His famous 'mission'?"

"Yes, but nothing says that he'll act right away. He might even wait several years."

"That's nice."

"Now, chief, don't give in so quickly. Maybe this man is old, sick, and in a hurry to finish with his burdensome 'mission'."

"Tell me then. In fact are you saying that our man intends to settle up with some new victims?"

"That's what the letter seems to say, not me."

"Then there is a chain of revenge."

"Maybe, yes."

"Then we have to find the link that connects the general to the other victims. From there we should be able to pick up the trail of our man."

"Okay, chief, but which other victims?"

"We'll have to look. Maybe there have been some unexplained cases in France similar to ours. Legriffe, you're going to bury yourself in all the reports of . . . let's say the past six months. Look at what we have here, and also check out the Paris files. Don't forget this bit with the playing cards. It would be too beautiful if the guy had pulled the same trick twice in a row. Anyhow, we're still trying. Me, I'm going to gossip a little more with the general's friends. Then you can summon the lawyer and the widow for me. I'd like to find out if maybe their tongues aren't a little too loose. It's only through them that our killer could have learned what we're thinking about him. In my opinion, I think that we're on the right track this time. Anything else, Boruti?"

"Yes, chief. Who could have taken the envelope and the playing cards?"

The commissioner's enthusiasm disappeared with this single swipe, and Legriffe rubbed his chin, daydreaming. Boruti had a point. Up until then it had been easy to believe that the killer was also the thief, but now?

"A new unknown in our equation," Viliard grumbled.

"That seriously complicates things," Legriffe complained.

"Unless the cards never existed," declared Boruti. "The 'Man from Houdan' doesn't admit any responsibility for them."

"So?"

"But there is the envelope, for sure. Someone maybe figured that the police shouldn't see its contents?"

"Madame Bertol?"

"That would seem most obvious at the moment."

"But what would be the point?"

"I don't know, but I always had the impression that she wasn't being completely truthful," Boruti remarked, with a slight taste of betrayal in his mouth.

"Very good!" Viliard gloated, congratulating himself on seeing his inspector coming around to some intelligent thinking. "We'll pay her a little visit after lunch. Right now, gentlemen, I'm inviting."

They smiled and went to the door of the office together.

"Oh, I almost forgot. Do you have the envelope from the anonymous letter?"

"It's still on my desk. You can look at it later."

Boruti turned back just the same. The envelope was in fact on the desk, addressed only to "The Gentlemen of the Versailles Police." The letter had been mailed from Paris, in the 3rd district, rue Saint-Martin.

Boruti turned it over several times, then put it in his pocket. He hadn't learned much.

Florence had spent her Sunday tidying the house from top to bottom. She had hoped that it would help to calm her nerves, and if fortune smiled on her, she would find, if not a solution to her problem, some bits and pieces to reassure herself with, because she was taking care not to overestimate her position. The fact that she had managed to put away the envelope and the playing cards (which had given her the momentary illusion of pulling strings and ridiculing the police a little) now appeared to have been more dangerous than beneficial. She had even persuaded herself that this act — which to tell the truth had been rather poorly thought out — was no doubt the neatest way to increase the suspicions of the police in her regard.

This conviction hardened when, on Monday morning, she received a letter with an address made up of newsprint. When she noticed, in the upper right-hand corner of the envelope, that the letter had been mailed from the post office on rue de la Reine-Blanche, her heart began to beat loudly. She tore open the envelope nervously.

She was frightened by what she read, and she understood immediately that the police would be on her back. Her first thought was to flee.

But where would she go?

She had broken forever with her own family, and from now on, the Bertol relatives would only receive her under very exacting circumstances and with the utmost solemnity.

As for Xavier's friends, the idea of seeing them again seemed completely out of the question.

Finally she realized that her only chance for saving face was to continue with what she had begun and lead her game herself, as she had succeeded in doing so well with Inspector Boruti. She found herself regretting that he wasn't around, and she almost telephoned him.

But the prospect of risking a confrontration with the disagreeable Commissioner Viliard, instead of the young inspector, stopped her. She went over and over it all through the morning, emptying ashtrays that had no stubs in them and dusting the fine film that had gathered since the day before. Around noon she decided to call anyhow. She left her name and Boruti called back two hours later.

"Hello. Did you call me?" he asked.

Florence detected in the inspector's voice the emotion of a young man who hadn't forgotten the evening that they had spent together on Saturday. She felt no desire to laugh.

"Yes. I would like to see you. Is that possible?"

"We were going to come by, actually."

"Who's this 'we'?" Florence asked in a pouting voice that was meant to charm Boruti.

"The commissioner and myself. We're leaving in just a second."

"If the commissioner comes, I won't be here," she declared, like a bad-tempered little girl.

"Then we'll have to summons you," Boruti answered dryly.

"As you like. But too bad for you!" She hung up.

* * *

An hour later Boruti was there.

Alone.

Florence opened the door to him with the radiant smile of a triumphant coquette.

"It's nice of you to have come as I asked you to."

"Yeah," Boruti mumbled. "The commissioner didn't especially want to come anyway. He gets car sick."

Florence had the inspector sit in the same place as the last time, on the couch, next to her. She was wearing the same black suit and a cream-colored blouse, modestly edged with lace. Boruti guessed that she must have used a shampoo-rinse, because her hair was more blonde than ever, almost silver . . . almost too silver.

"Coffee?"

"No thank you, I've already had some."

Florence understood, from the tone of the inspector's refusal, that he was trying to establish a certain distance. Maybe it was to declare that he would no longer play the dupe and that he held a bit of a grudge against her, or perhaps it was simply to remind her that he was on duty.

"I received an anonymous letter this morning. Did you?" she asked naively, pretending not to notice Boruti's bad humor.

The inspector sensed that this was a trap and that he was going to have to make a strenuous effort not to allow the conversation to turn yet again to his disadvantage. He chose to evade the question.

"Would you show me this letter?" he quietly asked.

"Hmm. Will you show me yours?"

"I have nothing to show."

"Then you didn't get a letter?"

"I didn't say that."

"Oh, then you got one?"

"Got one what?"

"You got a letter from the killer."

"If you must know — *Yes, we got a letter!* But don't expect me to tell you its contents."

Florence gloated. An enemy who lost patience was all the more vulnerable.

"I suppose that the man who killed my husband claims not to be a thief?"

"How's that?"

"He says that he wasn't the one who took the envelope and the cards."

"Oh? He told you that?"

"Yes, and you too, no doubt. That's why you're here."

"You asked me to come."

"But you already intended to come when I called you."

"That's true; we have a few questions to ask you."

"Well, ask them."

Boruti realized that he was being played with. Asking the questions that Florence Bertol was expecting amounted to his admitting that the letter that the detectives had received did indeed correspond to her ideas about it.

"Uh, well . . . we would like to know if you have by chance found the playing cards, or maybe even the envelope that Monsieur Poinsot brought to your husband?"

"I knew that you were going to come. Not only did the letter from my husband's murderer say that he wasn't the thief, but it said that he had informed the police of it too. So you were obliged to pay me a visit. I'll show you the letter."

Florence got up. She took the letter from an end table and offered it to him, without its envelope. Boruti read rapidly.

"There's no doubt, it's the same guy. There are the same mistakes, the same expressions — but a different 'signature'. I also find the confirmation of certain suppositions that we made after receiving our letter."

"So, won't you have some coffee?"

"If you insist."

Florence disappeared into the kitchen. He heard a match lighting and the hiss of the gas. Again Boruti had the impression of being at home.

"You haven't answered my question," he called across the room.

"What question?" Florence called back from the kitchen.

"About the cards and the envelope."

"They're on the coffee table, to your right," she called again with mischievous irony.

Boruti, who had risen slightly from the couch to hear better, fell back, stupefied. He turned his head towards the table. There beside a green ceramic vase lay a large manila envelope that he had already seen without paying any attention to it.

Underneath the envelope he discovered the five playing cards, carefully lined up on the table.

"Good heavens," he exclaimed while Florence arranged the coffee tray in front of him.

"You can look at it," she offered with a smile.

Boruti took the sheaf of papers out of the envelope.

"What are these?"

"Bonds, that's all. I'm sorry, but they probably don't have anything to do with the crime."

"But, I don't understand. . . . This envelope had disappeared."

"Who could have taken it?"

"The murderer . . . or you."

"Then it was me . . . since it wasn't the murderer."

"But why?"

"I don't exactly know. On reflex. When I found Xavier's body, I immediately thought that this envelope must have some connection with his death. I took it and I went to hide it in the sheets. The bed hadn't been made. That's probably why you didn't look there."

"But why hide it? And especially why hide it from *us?*"

"I told you, I don't know. Just because."

"Because? That doesn't mean anything. You must have had a reason, some kind of idea."

"Maybe I would have given it to you, but that commissioner is so unpleasant. He suspected me right away, and he told you to nose around everywhere, as if my house were a conquered country, I guess I wanted to revenge myself a little against him and to make it good."

"But, madame, the commissioner isn't your enemy, on the contrary. He was here to find your husband's murderer, to help you."

"No," Florence dryly interrupted. "He was here to find me guilty at all costs. You know that as well as I do."

Boruti nervously drummed on the edge of the table. He had really intended to maintain the atmosphere of a strict police interrogation, but with Florence Bertol it just wasn't possible. Once again the conversation had gone off the track. He regretted having given in to the invitation to have coffee. But, hadn't he already tipped his hand by agreeing to come alone?

"Now the commissioner is going to have to charge you with impeding the official investigation by withholding evidence."

"And where would that get you? In a week you haven't found anything."

Boruti restrained himself from responding to Florence's sudden hostility. He, too, realized that a nervous enemy is the easiest to play.

"And the cards?"

"The cards! I only thought of them after I telephoned . . . I mean on the night of the crime. I had remembered that Xavier hadn't wanted to talk to the police about them for fear of looking ridiculous, or passing for some kind of nut. I found the cards in his jacket pocket, and the envelopes in one of his desk drawers. I put them all in the bed sheets, with Monsieur Poinsot's envelope. And I didn't know then that he was the one who had brought it."

"But still you did know that the cards were even more important to the investigation than Poinsot's envelope. Why did you hide them too?"

"At the time, I didn't see the difference between them. But I told you, I would have given everything to *you* right away."

"And why give them up now?"

"The anonymous letter made me think."

"And certainly it made you understand that your charade was going to be more difficult to keep up."

Florence threw Boruti an icy look that ended in a smile.

"Nothing *forced* me to give you these things."

"We would have searched a second time . . . and more seriously."

"You would have found nothing just the same."

"But in any case we would have stopped believing you."

"I don't think so. It is difficult to systematically and totally refuse to believe what someone says. Even if you knew that it was a downright lie, the doubt would still remain. Each time you'd be looking to separate the true from the false. Besides, you never really believed everything I said."

"And with good reason."

"I don't hold it against you. It's your profession."

"Congratulations, at any rate, on your psychological analysis."

"Simply good sense. I've never studied it like you have."

"Who told you that I studied psychology?"

"The commissioner told me."

"Ah, the commissioner . . ."

"You see, neither of us likes him."

"He's less unfriendly than you think."

"I'd like to believe it."

"And I'd like you to believe it. You were making fun of me the other night. What was the point?"

Florence experienced a sudden weariness. She had never known how to keep up a battle for very long. Energy, with her, only came in spurts, and long struggles were usually succeeded by assaults that overwhelmed her softness and natural impulsiveness. The strength of her character quickly gave in to the accumulation of worries.

"I didn't mean to make fun of you. I only wanted to know exactly where you were and what you were thinking about the case."

"Yes, and especially to send me off on false leads."

"That's true; I wanted to put you on a false trail."

"I'm afraid that you're going to have to furnish me with some more serious explanations. Otherwise the commissioner will take charge of this himself," Boruti threatened.

"Explanations?"

"Yes, explanations. Because, under the circumstances, you have become the number one suspect."

"Your coffee is getting cold."

Boruti threw a sugar cube into his cup with an excessive gesture. He stirred vigorously with the little spoon.

"So why?"

Florence said nothing. Boruti had the impression that she was on the verge of tears. As if she were vulnerable.

"I wanted to keep you away from me. Not you personally, but your buddies, the commissioner, the police. I wanted you to go look somewhere else."

"You're not going to tell me that it was you who killed your husband?"

"No, it wasn't me, as you very well know. I just wanted a little peace and quiet. I wanted to lead my own investigation by myself."

"What? Your investigation? What investigation?"

"The investigation into Xavier's death. I want to discover for myself who killed him."

Boruti stuck his nose in his coffee cup. Had Florence Bertol completely lost her mind? He realized that the charm that he had succumbed to was even more poisonous than he had believed. Florence no longer seemed so attractive to him.

"And how did you expect to lead this impossible investigation?"

"From what I would learn from you and from the little evidence that I had but you didn't have. But I didn't learn much from you, or from my evidence either."

"Exactly what evidence is that?"

"Oh, the cards and their envelopes."

"Good, you also have the envelopes?"

Florence returned to the end table and picked up the stack of five envelopes.

"Here you are."

"This is interesting. The addresses are printed by hand."

"So that will get you somewhere?"

"Handwriting is like a signature, a fingerprint, or a voice; it's hard to find two that are alike."

"Then maybe you can tell me who wrote them?"

"Of course not. We have to compare it."

"Like the rifle bullet. Ask everyone in France to write to you."

"Very funny. But I can already tell you one thing: an expert analysis of a few lines will certainly give us some valuable information, and maybe confirm the character that we have created around our man from the texts of the two anonymous letters." (Boruti studied the smudged stamps on each of the envelopes.) "They were all mailed from the 13th district of Paris, rue de la Reine-Blanche, unlike the anonymous letter. So then that alters the situation; maybe the correspondent isn't the same person. There's the one who cut his addresses out of the newspaper and the one who printed them by hand."

Florence wasn't so sure. She went back to the end table again to look for the envelope from her anonymous letter. It wasn't there. She finally found it on the marble shelf over the radiator in the hallway.

"Look, this envelope was sent from the same place."

"You're right." (He took the envelope from "his" anonymous letter out of his pocket.) "But the letter that we received was mailed from rue Saint-Martin, in the 13th. In spite of everything, it probably was the same man. It's strange . . . these letters were both sent on the same day. Wait a minute . . . the same time shows too."

Florence leaned on the inspector's shoulder to read better. Boruti felt his skin tingling.

"That's true," Florence agreed, maintaining the contact. "But what does it change?"

Boruti, not very well at ease — although comfortably seated — smiled.

"Yet another mystery. Probably just chance."

"What are we going to do?"

Boruti wanted to turn towards Florence, but he realized that such a move would put him two inches from the young woman's face. His embarrassment was betrayed by an odd jerk of his head, a quick glance.

"What do you mean, what are *we* going to do?"

"Well of course, to find the murderer."

"But . . . but . . . you don't still intend to involve yourself in this?" (Florence looked annoyed.) "First, you're going to have to go and make another statement . . . and I don't know how the commissioner is going to take all this."

"Should I go with you right away?" she asked with such unexpected enthusiasm that Boruti jumped.

"Uh, yes. If it's not too much trouble?"

Florence stood up in an instant and swept the coffee tray off to the kitchen.

The young woman ran to the hallway and wrapped herself in the long black wool cape that had been haunting the inspector's dreams.

"Shall we go?"

"Maybe it would be better for you to take your own car," Boruti timidly suggested, agitated by the changing emotions.

"But you know that it's in the garage."

Boruti decided not to tell her that he didn't believe her. And then, maybe for once she was telling the truth.

So they left together in the black police car. It was a long, mute ride during which they only exchanged rather wistful looks and occasionally a brief sentence, in order to explain to each other the meaning of their silence. Florence's knees showed a little through a slit in her wool cape.

12

. . . They were suddenly caught in a series of explosions. The whistling shrieks fell closer and closer to them, almost nonstop now. They were surrounded by the blasts, the fire and smoke, flying earth and shrapnel, and splintering trees. Ahead of them men screamed and fell.

"Mortar fire," Lieutenant Schültznicht remarked calmly. "We can't stay here. We'll retreat two hundred yards. Pass the word."

The order spread rapidly down the column entrenched in the shallow ditch. No one moved until the lieutenant waved the retreat.

The frequency and density of the explosions let up a little. The time was right. The men of the 6th Platoon dodged in retreat, clutching their rifles to their chests or holding their machine guns at arms length. They fell back over the territory that had been covered the same morning with such extreme caution. The silent approach had failed. The pillbox controlling the hilltop hadn't allowed itself to be taken by surprise.

In the smoky mists broken by hunched, running figures, the Sergeant-Major checked that the men in his bazooka squad had stuck to his ass, as time and again he had ordered them to do.

"God damnit, where the hell is Cartier?" he shouted at an orderly.

"Haven't seen him, Sir," the other yelled back, clinging to his two haversacks to keep them from flapping against his sides.

"Has he fallen?"

"I don't know!"

"Shit, I'll go and see. Martin, take over the retreat."

"Don't be an idiot, Sarge. That's hellfire out there."

"Shut up and do as you're told."

"Yes, Sir, at your command. *Buena suerte!*"

Sergeant-Major Héberti headed back out. He found himself in the middle of horror and death. He estimated the distance between himself and the ditch as a hundred years (. . . if it could be called a ditch, that slight mound of earth behind which a part of the 6th Platoon had imagined itself sheltered for a brief moment).

The motar shelling had almost stopped, but Héberti knew that he was far too easy a target for a good shot, especially with the additional weight of the bazooka, which would slow down his hundred-yard dash considerably. He would have preferred to get rid of the gun, but he knew that he didn't have the right to overload any of his men, hurting their chances of getting away, simply to satisfy his personal desires to discover what had happened to one of his friends.

He only needed a glance at the dead and wounded that he encountered to see that his man wasn't among them. He knew all his men by sight and recognized them in spite of their mutilations: Galchard, Ramirez, young Bercot, Onditrelli, Corporal Tonin, as well as some of the Arabs from the Moroccan artillery division that the old man had seen fit to bring in as reinforcements. He also saw some Yanks from the liaison service. Then he dived into a creek bed. So far so good.

He caught his breath in a few seconds, then took his bearings. He had gone too far to the right and was beyond the spot where he had been holed-up with his men. He cradled the bazooka in the bend of his elbows and started crawling. When he reached the edge of the mound he immediately found Cartier's body curled up in a hollow.

"Shit," he thought, "if he's hurt badly I won't be able to carry him with all this weight."

He let himself slide down toward the body. Cartier didn't seem to be wounded, and he wasn't dead; he was snoring. Six days of hard fighting and never more than two or three hours sleep a day had conquered the kid's energy. He was fast asleep, indifferent to the war and the shell-fire, a faint, childlike smile on his face.

"Luc. Luc, wake up!" Héberti shouted, almost laughing.

But fatigue had too strong a hold on the boy.

* * *

"Monsieur. Monsieur! Wake up!"

Marcel awoke with a start, holding tightly to the handle of his "bazooka."

"Monsieur, I don't want your suitcase," the voice reassured him. "I only want to clean up. If the boss knew that you spent the night here — "

Marcel sat up. His haggard face gazed stupidly at the woman with her bucket and broom. Then he saw the mirrors, the bar, the fake red leather booths, and the empty beer glass on the table.

"What time is it?"

"Almost six. The weather looks lousy. It rained all night. Did you miss your train?"

"No . . . no train . . . I just fell asleep."

"Obviously. That Luc can't ever do his job right. Mind you, it's always like this on Sunday nights. When the boss isn't here the waiters do exactly as they please, and the back room is never closed up by two, like Monsieur Mastard always insists. Even though the joint is open all night, there are certain rules, you know. But that Luc . . ."

"Luc?" Marcel asked vacantly.

"Yes, he's the waiter in charge of the back room. He's not here now, of course. Would you mind going out to the bar so I can clean up?"

Marcel got up awkwardly and picked up his suitcase. He couldn't remember whether he had paid for his beer or not, and that annoyed him. But nobody paid any attention to him as he crossed through the bar. He went out onto Boulevard de la Gare.

He entered the station and sat down in the waiting room. He was nauseated by the smell of sweat, soot, and stale tobacco. He regretted not having had the courage to ask for a cup of coffee back in the bar, but he'd felt guilty about having spent the night illegally in the place, and almost ashamed at having been caught sleeping in such a vulnerable and humiliating position. He noticed a vending machine and walked towards it, dragging his suitcase behind him. He searched in his pocket for change and went through the same motions that he had made during his trip across America. The naked and bloody body of a teenager flashed through his mind and he nearly vomited. The lukewarm coffee helped a little. He also had a piece of cake (the sandwich slot was empty), and felt in his jacket pocket for his cigarettes, but they weren't there. Without realizing it, he must have finished his pack of Bastos during the night. Feeling exhausted by these simple efforts, he sank down onto a bench.

Why Schültznicht? . . . The man who'd been the hardest to find in his remote corner of Austria had been the first to track him down. No doubt he'd left too many traces. He'd questioned too many people, kicked up too much dust. A foreigner doesn't easily escape being noticed in a small country town. Also, as he knew the language, he'd talked too much and probably hadn't guarded his words. Schültznicht must have been given a good enough description for him to realize who he was dealing with and he certainly could have gotten his address from the *Képi Blanc.* Yes, that was probably how it had happened.

Coming out of the Café Bouchard after talking on the telephone with Joe, Marcel had been disturbed by the ghoulish image of a stocky figure that he'd seen reflected in the dirty mirror above the zinc bar. It was Schültznicht all right.

At first Marcel had tried to shake him off. He knew the 13th district like the back of his hand, and in spite of all the new construction which had changed the quarter almost beyond recognition, he still knew a good half-dozen complicated paths to take, discovered during the long walks of an unoccupied pensioner, "just in case." Marcel was only sorry that he didn't have his revolver with him, as he was pretty sure that Schültznicht's intentions were hardly cordial. He felt the tension of his former lieutenant's dangerous presence behind him, and he was a little afraid of what might happen in certain deserted alleys that he planned to wind through.

But Schültznicht allowed himself to be outdistanced easily. Far too easily. When he returned to his own building, Marcel again found him a few steps behind. He couldn't figure out whether Schültznicht had trailed him that carefully, or if he had just waited for him in the neighborhood. Actually there was no point in trying to lose Schültznicht if Marcel was only going to return to an address that the former lieutenant already knew.

Marcel's fear mounted each time he glanced back at his shadow. He'd had time to think during the long detour that he'd made, and his thoughts had only increased his confusion. He would have preferred being forced into action, no matter how violent. Although he had a pretty good idea, he didn't know exactly what Schültznicht wanted with him, and this uncertainty weighed on him. After going up a few steps he came down again impulsively and looked around for Schültznicht. He wanted to ask him straight out what he'd come to Paris for. After all, if Schültznicht had only wanted to kill him, he could have done so with the heartlessness and discretion that Marcel had shown in Brückenkirchen.

Schültznicht had stopped on the sidewalk on the opposite side of the street. He was waiting and watching, and Marcel felt that he was as uncertain as he himself, and that he hadn't yet made up his mind as to what he was going to do. They stared at each other. It was almost night and the darkness blurred their expressions. Marcel could hardly see Schültznicht's steely blue eyes, and he wasn't able to read their intent. Only his pose betrayed hesitation, expectation, and a certain weariness.

The street stood empty between them, a silent border.

"He's the one I should have killed," Marcel thought to himself. And his feelings were mixed with as much hatred as pity. Schültznicht was fat. Schültznicht was swaying from one foot to the other, like a shy schoolboy. Schültznicht no longer knew what he should do. Schültznicht was suffering. Schültznicht was no longer called Schültznicht.

Marcel was shaking when he turned back into his building. The concierge's television was still blaring and Marcel suddenly felt like smashing it. He reached his door and entered his apartment, then quickly assembled his rifle, put two cartridges in the magazine and walked to the window. Schültznicht was slowly walking towards the intersection. Marcel noticed that the neon sign "Bar-Tabac" had been lighted over the café. He opened the window a little, a gap just wide enough for the black muzzle of the gun and the sighting that would focus on death.

He only fired once . . .

* * *

The waiting room was becoming more and more crowded with travelers, baggage wagons, and children. Marcel watched the sudden rush of bored suburban commuters flowing through the double glass doors. Then he remembered that he was expected at the factory in Vitry, where his references had earned what he called an "odd job in the maintenance department" — which meant, in fact, refilling the toilet rolls, changing deodorizers, cleaning toilet bowls with disinfectant, mopping the floors, emptying boxes of dirty sanitary pads, sometimes unblocking drains . . . He was ending his career just as he'd begun it, cleaning up shit.

The very idea that he might be late for roll-call for the first time in his life forced him to get up and move. He grabbed the suitcase that was loaded with two guns and ammunition and walked instinctively in the direction of home, not quite knowing what he was going to do.

Marcel had realized the day before that the net was tightening around him, and he had decided to flee. Schültznicht had died too close to his home; he was sure to be traced soon. He had piled the things that he considered necessary into his suitcase: his Mas-Fournier rifle and his MAC 50 revolver, extra ammunition, and the supplies to make more. He had put his vest back on, although the patches of stain-remover hadn't yet dried, and knotted his striped tie. At that moment, there had been a knock at the door and he'd been on the verge of firing a bullet at his own head. Only the reflection that his mission was not yet accomplished stopped him. He didn't answer and waited, frozen, hearing only the pounding of his heart, which he was convinced could be heard through the door.

Was it Schültznicht knocking?

But he'd seen him fall, or rather he'd first seen him upright, walking leisurely, filling his lungs with air for the last time, and then, through the thin spiral of smoke coming from the rifle, he was lying there, thrown to the ground, struck down . . . it was almost as if Schültznicht had expected it . . . or had longed for it. Between these two last positions there had been a brief moment of eternity and then his chest had burst. No, it couldn't be the Austrian at the door.

The police then? Already?

It was impossible. Unless he had been watched without knowing it by those who thought that he was nothing more than a thief, a common blackmailer, a murder like any other.

Or maybe it was the men who had tried to kill him on rue Chapon?

But then Joe had said that it wasn't . . . Joe! Of course, how could he have forgotten? He suddenly recognized his friend's voice through the door and although he would have liked to open up for him, he couldn't. From now on he couldn't trust anyone. Too bad for Joe. He'd have to manage by himself, alone. He would only be one more obstacle in the path of his mission.

Joe left, and Marcel had hardly heard his footsteps die away on the stairs when police sirens sounded in the distance. Marcel snapped the suitcase shut and went out — tragically alone himself — into the night that would bring little comfort.

When he reached Gobelins, Marcel entered a café. Going to work with a suitcase loaded with guns, unshaven and wearing his Sunday suit had suddenly seemed completely absurd to him. Furthermore, the completion of his mission had been endangered by these recent events and he would have to devote himself to it entirely from now on.

As he pushed open the door of the café he had every intention of telephoning the factory to inform them, apologetically, that he would not resume work as expected and that he wanted to extend his vacation a few days longer. But in the end he didn't make the call.

He gulped down a cup of coffee that would enable him to ask for a telephone token without feeling embarrassed. Gazing around, his eyes caught the headline of the morning paper lying on the counter: *CHICAGO ON THE SEINE, IT CONTINUES.* He quickly glanced at the front page, dumbfounded. This was the limit — now the newspapers were also interfering. He looked around nervously, convinced that he had already been recognized and that the whole of France was after him. He paid for his coffee and walked out without waiting for his change.

He had just realized that he only had a few hours left to finish his task . . . and to die.

* * *

Ruben Langmann lived in the 3rd district, rue Sentier. Marcel took the metro from the Gobelins station as far as Opéra. He changed there for the Porte des Lilas line, which would take him to the station on rue Sentier.

It was just before nine when, weighed down by his heavy suitcase and choking in his best suit, he came out of the metro feeling completely exhausted, as much a victim of his bad night as the jostling he had suffered in the metro. He saw his reflection in a store-front mirror and was shocked at his frightening appearance. If things went wrong, he didn't want to face death looking like that.

He stopped and bought a razor and a can of shaving cream, and then looked for a café sufficiently impersonal to accept a customer shaving in the toilets (an acceptance arising more from indifference than natural generosity). He found what he was looking for and was left unhindered. He thickly lathered his face and blew his nose noisily. Then he shaved with the same meticulous care and strong emotion that always characterized his behavior before the battles of the old days, when he used to go into combat groomed as if for a social reception. He flattened his crew-cut hair with his hands and tugged at the tail of his jacket and the creases of his trousers, trying to disguise the fact that they had served as pajamas.

Finally ready, he went out and bought a pack of Bicycle playing cards in order to take out the Queen of Spades, which he put in his right-hand pocket. He threw the rest of the pack into his left pocket.

Marcel arrived at rue Sentier. He walked past the building that Ruben Langmann lived in. Everything seemed calm. The clothing and hosiery shops were obstinately closed, and Marcel remembered that it was Monday. In the absence of a well-organized plan, he realized that the empty streets would not help his getaway. It was always easier to disappear in a crowd. He remembered Brückenkirchen and the reassuring pleasure he had taken in mingling with passers-by on their way home from the movies. He wouldn't be so lucky here.

He continued down the street so that his entrance into the building wouldn't immediately follow an about-face, a move which might attract attention. He crossed the street, then came back, just as unassuming, from the opposite side. The bustle had increased a little and passers-by — mainly housewives — were headed towards the few markets that were open on a Monday morning. He kept walking, playing for time, then came back again, hesitatingly.

This new episode in his mission was far from pleasant. It was perhaps the worst. And yet it hadn't been with any relish that he had shot Ernesto Biaggi's dog. (What was its name again? Oh yes, Giocchi. A ridiculous name for a ridiculous dog.) And the American girl. Only that flash of spontaneous desire when she had stripped in the middle of the garden (a strange luxury in the

middle of a stony and sandy wilderness) had enabled him to aim
with vicious accuracy. At Houdan, he had killed a man. That had
been easier. At least he had thought so. But that particular man
was almost Luc's age — he could even have been Luc . . . There,
too, his heart had trembled. But his eye and his hand had done
their job unfalteringly. Then there had been Greta, Schültznicht's
girl. For the first time his hand had shaken, his sight had grown
dim. The first bullet had missed.

Now the most difficult part had come.

It was eleven thirty.

Marcel crossed the street clumsily. A car blew its horn and he
heard several cars slamming brakes behind him. He didn't bother
to return their insults. He was only sorry he couldn't have had a
swallow of whisky to bolster his failing courage. Not for a
moment, however, did he consider stopping there, retreating,
giving up, or running.

The stairway of the building reminded him of his own, or
Josyane's — in fact it was a typically Parisian stairway. A
stairway from a past era, winding, dark, narrow, and dirty. A
stairway that somehow reminded him of the smells of his
childhood. He climbed it puffing, weighted down by the suitcase,
which he was obliged to leave behind him so that it wouldn't bang
against the walls. Ruben Langmann lived on the sixth floor, the
last floor before the tiny attic rooms that used to be kept for
maids. On each landing the steps narrowed slightly and seemed to
grow steeper. Marcel had to stop three times to catch his breath
(no doubt the result of a night spent sleeping in a bar). A woman
with a shopping basket met him on the stairs and eyed him
suspiciously. With his suitcase, suit, and striped tie he probably
looked like a traveling salesman. Only his age and expression
must have saved him from being questioned about his climb to the
upper floors. ("Are you looking for someone? Can I help you?")
He gave the woman a forced smile and went on his difficult way.

Jacques Lange and Sons, Made-to-Order. The copper plate
with its letters engraved in flowing script was still screwed to the
door. Marcel remembered his surprise the first time he had come
to Ruben's place during a leave, just after the war had ended. At
first he'd thought that he had the wrong address, but after asking

around, he had learned that Ruben's father — Jacob Langmann — had tried to escape the random raids of the SS by changing his name. This trick soon became general practice in spite of its shortlived usefulness; anonymous and allegedly patriotic denunciations succeeded in sending "Jacques Lange" to a concentration camp, where he reverted to Jacob Langmann. At that time, Ruben had already joined up with the underground *France Libre* and found himself with the *Képi Blancs* of the 13th Division of the Foreign Legion, with whom he had fought under his real name. Of his entire family, only one nephew, who had been placed for safekeeping with a peasant family in Nivernais, had survived. The nephew had married and had a son of his own, so gradually the family had been reconstituted. Ruben had taken over his father's apartment and the copper plate had remained on the door — a meaningless token to those who didn't know.

Marcel wondered whether he would be lucky enough to find Langmann alone. He had roamed the neighborhood several times lately — not sticking around too long, however. He had just taken the time to check that Langmann was still living there, living alone, and to establish that his grand-nephew came every day at noon, on his way home from school, to see if his great uncle needed anything. Each time the scenario had been the same. But only one hitch would be enough for everything to change. Marcel was hoping that he wouldn't encounter such a hitch.

He listened at the door for awhile but he heard nothing. He looked at his watch: eleven thirty-five. There was no more time to hesitate. He knocked on the door resolutely, yet almost gently. No voice answered. Marcel knocked again. He heard a faint sound of grating and rubbing, and then the door opened.

Ruben Langmann's face showed neither surprise nor fear. It was a dead face. Only the eyes seemed to be alive, but during the brief instant that Langmann tried to push the door closed with his shaking hands Marcel was unable to read anything in those eyes. The hands flailed spasmodically. The wheelchair in which Langmann was sitting bumped against a radiator after Marcel gave it a firm kick. With his body rigid and paralyzed, and his hands beating the air, the old man looked like an insect pinned alive on a cork.

Marcel closed the door behind him and put his suitcase on a table covered with a plastic cloth. He pushed aside the remains of a light meal.

"Lunch doesn't look too exciting," Marcel said cynically, in a voice as shaky as Langmann's hands.

The old man didn't budge. Opening the two locks of the suitcase in a single motion, Marcel threw him an uneasy glance. The fear was now visible in Langmann's eyes, but gradually it gave way to a questioning interest. The old man had probably understood his helplessness and had resigned himself to the inevitable.

"Do you remember me, at least?" Marcel asked with a wide smile which he would have liked to have been more confident.

The old man was like marble. Marcel had the impression that the pupils of his eyes were contracting, as if Langmann were making an inner search to recollect the forgotten face.

Marcel rested the rifle that he was assembling across his open suitcase. He approached the wheelchair.

"Here, look at this. Try to remember," he said to Ruben Langmann, holding out the Queen of Spades.

The old man's hands drew grasping circles in the air and finished by taking the card, as if by mere chance. Marcel went on assembling the rifle. The two cartridges clicked into place in the magazine with a threatening clap . . . a noise that Langmann certainly remembered.

"Well, why don't you answer me?" Marcel asked nervously. "Aren't you even afraid? Don't you have the jitters . . . the shakes? Tell me! You were never short on words when you made fun of the men in your Company, when you thought that they were weakening. You haven't forgotten that, I hope? And the cup full of castor oil that you used to make them drink — the ones who had lost courage — before putting them in solitary confinement for two or three days, do you remember? Just enough time for them to wallow in their own filth as they shit every ten minutes like maniacs. Don't tell me you've forgotten all that? The best memories of your youth?"

But Langmann said nothing. Marcel approached him, his rifle in his hand. He took a chair and sat near the old man, facing the door.

"So now you prefer to keep your mouth shut? You still believe in your luck? You always were lucky. You think this time you're going to get out of it, too? I have good news for you, old friend. You're not going to be shot. It isn't you that I've come for. Would you like to know who it is? Well, if you just say hello to me I'll tell you."

Marcel leaned towards Langmann and touched his imperturbable face. He tried to read an answer in it. But Langmann's face was nothing more than dead flesh. The eyes were shining but Marcel couldn't see the fear that he expected. He pinched the old man's cheek violently. His mouth dropped open, gaping like the mouth of a dead fish. No sound came out.

"So, you're dumb. Well . . . how about that. You can't shout any more? You can't even spit at me? You can only move your hands, shaking and flapping like a coward?"

Marcel felt that he was beginning to lose his confidence. After all, Ruben Langmann was younger than he, and only this disgusting illness could have given him the appearance of a wasted old man, twenty years older than he actually was. In mocking the disease and misfortune that had overtaken his former comrade, perhaps Marcel was mocking what his own old age would be, once he could no longer use a gun and defend himself?

He felt some pity. Then the spectacle of Langmann's downfall encouraged him again. He knew that he would be luckier than Langmann. He, at least, intended to die while fighting.

He looked at his watch . . . twenty minutes to twelve.

Langmann's eyes rolled and followed Marcel's movements.

"Do you understand now? And are your guts turning? Are you getting the shakes? Do you want to throw up? Is it getting to you? The shits, maybe? Now that would make me really happy, you know, to see you shit in your pants, right there, sitting comfortably in your little chair. Just like Luc. Like Luc Cartier, you remember? . . . Of course you remember. That was even your own idea, that little bit, the last chance — the Queen of Spades. The Queen of the Grand Companies. She was waiting for all of us . . . and she's still waiting." (Marcel's expression became distant.) "You see, you should never have done that. I might have forgotten. In fact, I forgot for a long time. I forgot what I had promised Luc. Or rather I didn't really forget, I only acted like I had forgotten. And then one day someone came and reminded me of my promise: Luc's sister. She had managed to track me down, and it wasn't hard for her to persuade me to finish the mission that I had postponed for so long. She showed me a newspaper article and from that I got the first lead — Captain Bourges." (He sat the rifle on his knees, took out his wallet, and produced a newspaper clipping which he read out loud.)

" . . . Lieutenant Colonel Bertol, formerly of the 13th Division of the Foreign Legion (April 8th, 1943 to May 25th, 1956), presently in command of the 6th Regiment of the Navy, has just been promoted to the rank of Brigadier General. General Bertol's new command is not yet known. All the former members of the 13th have certainly not forgotten the high military spirit and profound human kindness of this man who, under the name Captain Bourges, took part in the Italian and French campaigns, as well as the operations in Indochina and Algeria. Captain Bourges was decorated with the military medal by Marshal Juin himself (who was then Commander-in-Chief of the French expeditionary forces), a short time after the Allies took Rome, in June 1944. Once his commission had ended in May 1956, Major Bourges requested a transfer into the Regular Army. His career, however, did not end there — as this promotion clearly indicates. May General Bertol find in this message the expression of our highest respects, as well as the sincere congratulations of the former 'Comrades of the Queen of Spades . . .'

"There you are, that's it." (He carefully replaced the yellowed paper in his wallet and flattened his hands on the stock of his rifle.) "You see, Langmann, when I read that in the copy of *Terre-Air-Mer* that Luc's sister showed me, all of the past that I had tried to forget came back to me in a second. It was terrible, like having a nightmare. It's true, Bourges always said: 'All of us, Comrades of the Queen of Spades, will find our deaths on a poker table. And the game will be War.' Do you remember how he always repeated that? And the day of Cartier's trial — if you can call that a trial — it was you who had the idea of making Luc draw his last card. The poor kid . . . He joined up at the age of seventeen, he had his two months in Saida, a few weeks in Sidi-Bel-Abbes, just enough time to get to know the 'Central Portion,' and then he was sent up to the Front. Don't you remember, once he even fell asleep in the middle of a mortar shelling? I dreamed about it again last night. I went to rescue him and got 'eight days' — which I never did by the way, as they needed every possible man so badly —and do you know why I got eight days? 'Almost caused his unit to lose the collective automatic arm of which he was in command.' Imagine, there was the Chief still thinking he was at day-camp, while the rest of us were in hell. After having informed me of my punishment, he congratulated me for having saved one of my men under enemy fire and gave me four days leave — which I never took either.

"It was several days later, you remember? Langmann, do you remember? Fucking stupid Cartier just dropped his pack and took off towards the south. He didn't get very far. It was right at the time of the breakthrough, in the Aurunci Mountains — May 1944. There were soldiers everywhere. Some guys from the 2nd brought him back to us the same night. I personally thought that the incident would be forgotten. He was just a kid, he was dead tired, that was obvious — he didn't even know why he had left or where he was going. But no, Bourges took it as a real desertion. A desertion under fire, in the face of the enemy, the worst offense of all. The kid didn't have a chance. Fortunately it was impossible to hold a regular court martial — or so we thought. Our unit was too far away. I was sure that the whole thing would blow over. We would play for time. Cartier would stay with us until the authorities decided what should be done. At the very worst, we would have to send our 'deserter' back into the ranks where things functioned a little more normally. And once there, they would be forced to wait until witnesses came forward. That left us a fair amount of time. Unfortunately, I had underestimated Bourges, Schültznicht, Biaggi . . . and, above all, Chance. That was negligent on my part, to have forgotten the element of chance. Especially for a 'Comrade of the Queen of Spades.' Because wasn't it chance that brought along General . . . de Régenville, his name was . . . with that young colonel from the American army, a guy named Adams? A guy we all knew well, in charge of liaison, an interpreter of sorts.

"We heard that the general's car had just been blown up by a landmine. His driver and his batman had both been killed; he'd lost contact with his unit, and Adams brought him to us in order to help him find his regiment and to put him up for the night. 'Put him up' — the general was certainly 'put up' all right. It was quite a party. There were cases of food and booze that had miraculously escaped the explosion. Everyone got very drunk very quickly in your little headquarters. Fatigue and especially privation had reduced our resistance. By midnight there were only a few left. In fact, only Bourges, Schültznicht, Biaggi . . . and you. And of course the Yank. Not forgetting the general, who was very stiff-necked and who didn't seem to approve at all but who, in fact, was more stinking drunk than anyone else. That was the moment when Bourges had the bright idea of a court martial . . . a court martial that was complete nonsense of course. They went and got Cartier, had a drunken discussion, and condemned him to death, just like that, between two drinks. You haven't forgotten I hope, Langmann? You were there, you were one of them. I tried hard enough to save Cartier. Luc was almost like a son, it's true. So you all laughed, called me 'mamma,' 'nanny' and a lot of other stupid-assed names. And then it was you who said, 'Seeing as the Sergeant-Major says it isn't a case of desertion and that Cartier was just sleep-walking, we'll please him by giving Cartier a fair chance. We'll let the Queen of the Grand Companies decide.' So you went and got a deck of cards, you picked out the Queen of Spades and the Queen of Hearts and you placed them, face down, in front of Cartier and said, 'Now draw. This is your last chance.'

"At that moment I thought that I was going to take my machine gun and kill the whole bunch of you. But I had already spent almost twenty years in the Legion. And even in front of superiors who were drunk out of their minds and ready to ignore regulations and kill a man with the help of guys who didn't even belong with us, even then, twenty years of obedience is hard to forget. Even to save a friend's life. The only thing I did, well, it wasn't much — I left. I left like a skunk. I went and joined the others who were trying to sleep and I told them what was happening. A while later Biaggi came to get me up. He wanted a squad of twelve men. In spite of his shouting and kicking and threatening to have every

man shot, nobody budged, nobody got up. Biaggi called us a
bunch of drunks and went back. Martin, who was pretending to
sleep next to me, said, 'You go, Sarge, he's your friend. Don't let
him die alone.' So I went.

"Luc hadn't drawn his card yet. He was howling and dribbling,
and when it started to stink everybody knew he had shit in his
pants. That made you laugh, didn't it? Do you remember? Then
Luc spat in your face and chose his card . . . the wrong one . . . the
Queen of Spades." (Marcel's hands gripped his rifle. He had lost
track of the time, lost in a trance. He was recalling the past with a
hallucinatory vividness. Langmann's hands were no longer trembling. He was not firmly clutching the wheels of his chair.)

"Then you asked me to make up a firing squad and I refused. I
went up to Luc and I said to him, 'I'll revenge this, I swear,' and I
went back to the other boys. Whatever was going to happen was
no longer our business. There were six of you up there. You took
your guns, you each loaded two bullets — that way there were
twelve — and you shot Luc Cartier, without a second thought,
like a shooting gallery at a fair, him tied to his chair . . .

"The next day Martin and I buried him. What a beginning for a
day. I would rather have never seen that day born. The general
and Adams left at dawn. The bunch of you weren't very proud of
yourselves. The boys were pretty nervous. Then the order to move
out came. The war had to go on. Lots of boys were killed in the
days that followed, but you all got out alive and nobody talked:
Legionnaires' stories are settled by Legionnaires. But first, before
we settled that story, we had to finish fighting that stinking war.
And many more were killed. Then the units were reshuffled and I
lost track of you all.

"Myself, I forgot . . . or I thought I had forgotten, like I told
you. But it all stayed here inside me, and the day that I read that
article I knew that I couldn't die without doing something about
it. I had a final mission to accomplish, probably my greatest
mission of all. Oh yes, it took time to find you all, but I succeeded,
little by little. Even Adams. Even General de Régenville . . . he's
over ninety now, and he's the last on the list. Not one of you six are
dead. It's as if you were waiting for me. Except Bourges. I only
missed him by a few days. You see, Langmann, I really think I had

a good idea . . . rather than kill you all, I waited until you were really attached to someone — your sons, your daughters, your wives, your nephews . . . or your dogs, like poor old Biaggi. I decided that by taking my revenge on them I would make you feel something like what I felt, one night in May 1944, in the Aurunci Mountains. Don't you think it was a good idea?"

A nearby clock began to chime, startling Marcel. It was noon.

Marcel checked his watch while counting the hollow ringing of the bell. Damn. Time had passed quickly. Too quickly maybe, and yet too slowly. The victim hadn't yet arrived, and Marcel hadn't interrupted his story to shoulder his rifle and fire, almost on reflex, at the first figure appearing in the doorway.

His uneasiness returned. What was he going to do? He had come to Ruben Langmann's for nothing and he would probably never be able to come again. He turned towards the former Legionnaire whose dead face was even more pale now, almost ghostly. A thick liquid flowed from his eyelids — tears, maybe?

Undecided, Marcel tapped nervously on the butt of his rifle. Like an invisible wave, he sensed the immense hope that was building up in Ruben Langmann's heart.

Suddenly rapid and noisy footsteps sounded on the stairs and Marcel stood up, half raising his rifle.

"I'm here! I'm late because two of my friends were having a fight and I wanted to watch!" a child's voice called from behind the door.

The two men did not move.

"Is it open?" the same voice asked.

It was open and the knob turned several times before the door swung forward. A silhouette leaned into the room and Marcel saw the astonished face of a twelve-year-old child at the end of the barrel. He fired.

But Ruben Langmann had already thrown himself forward, with all the strength and concentration of a last effort, still clutching the wheels of his chair. He smashed against the door at the very instant the shot was fired.

The bullet struck him in the kidneys, tore open his bowels and came out through the abdomen before continuing its path through the door that had been slammed in the boy's face. Marcel heard a cry of pain, followed by screaming. The child had undoubtedly also been hit.

This time Marcel really lost his composure. At first, astounded and still foolishly shouldering his rifle, he was overwhelmed by panic and had only one reflex — to get out. Besides, there was little choice. Ruben Langmann was dead. The child was crying on the other side of the door and a second shot would serve no useful purpose. Still, Marcel instinctively reloaded his rifle: swinging it vertically, pulling it towards him, drawing, adjusting . . . a series of gestures which he carried out in rapid succession. As he had always done. The empty cartridge was ejected with a metallic click, and rolled under the pedal of an old sewing machine. Marcel forgot all about it.

Now he hastily disassembled the barrel and stock, put the two pieces into the suitcase and hurried to the door. Ruben Langmann's body had been thrown out of the chair and was clinging to the doorframe. Marcel put down his suitcase and dragged the body out of his way. The expression on Langmann's face, his eyes still open, hadn't changed. Or rather, it had simply remained expressionless, as if he had been a puppet or a robot. What was left of him on the door was not a pretty sight.

"I'm hurt, I'm hurt, help me, I'm hurt," the child was screaming, lying across the landing.

Marcel bent over him. The wound wasn't serious. It was a clean fleshwound in the thigh.

"Don't worry, kid, you'll pull through," he said with a kind of a smile, and then the boy, who had been briefly silenced by his terror, started yelling again.

Marcel went down a few steps and found himself face to face with several curious neighbors who had come out to see what was happening, not entirely convinced by the child's dramatic screams.

"What's going on?" a woman asked sternly.

Marcel regretted not having taken the precaution of slipping his revolver into his pocket. It was of little use to him at the bottom of his suitcase.

"The child is wounded. It's not too serious. I'm going to get a doctor. What's your name?" he asked the woman, recovering his former composure.

"Uh, uh, Madame Loufrani," the woman stuttered.

"Would you look after him for a minute? He's Monsieur Langmann's grand-nephew. The poor man can't do a thing for him."

"I know, I know him."

"Thanks."

Marcel sped down the stairs, four at time. He had never known fear to push him to such an extent. At each landing more anxious faces appeared in open doorways and questioned him, either with words or looks.

"It's nothing. Madame Loufrani is taking care of it. I'm going to get the doctor," he explained each time, trying to smile.

He saw faces all around him — wide-eyed, napkins tucked under chins, jaws chewing, fingers picking at teeth, running noses, cigarettes hanging out of mouths — those faces spun dizzily past in a grotesque dance.

"Hey Mister, leave your suitcase here. You can get it later," a voice called after him.

Marcel pretended not to hear. As he reached the ground floor Madame Loufrani's sharp screams began attracting the people upstairs, an instinctive reaction which always helps a getaway.

Marcel was fortunate enough to find a taxi immediately. In a state of sheer exhaustion, he gave the driver the address of General de Régenville, 5 Boulevard Victor, opposite the Air Ministry.

13

"Well, well, well. There you are," Commissioner Viliard grumbled when Boruti appeared at the door of his office. He greeted Florence Bertol with a nod and motioned for Boruti to come closer. "What's she doing here?" he asked in a low voice.

"She came to make a new deposition. She's also received an anonymous letter, and she's confessed to a few white lies in her former story," Boruti answered quietly.

"Not very surprising, is it? Okay, take her into the next room and then come back here. There's more news."

Boruti hurried her off so quickly that Florence didn't have time to ask questions.

"So, what's up?" Boruti asked the commissioner once he'd returned.

"Legriffe is in Paris. He's come up with some stuff. It seems that some of his buddies at the Balistics Lab and the Legal-Medical Institute agreed to help him with the little job I gave him this morning. These buddies had a few interesting things to say, and it appears that our case is related to a similar one that happens to have taken place yesterday. A guy got himself killed in the 13th. Did you know about it?"

"Uh, yes, vaguely."

"Good. It seems that I'm the only one around here that doesn't know what's going on. Well, Legriffe says that you better get over there, you know more about the case than anyone else. Obviously, I count for nothing in this place. Here's the name of the guy you have to see. Now move it. Legriffe is already there."

"But, chief, I, uh . . . what's it all about?"

"Do as I say and get over there. In the meantime, I'll take care of passports and permits."

Boruti grinned and Viliard seriously decided to prepare a report on the young inspector's conduct.

Florence saw Boruti dashing by. She stood up.

"Madame?" asked the officer across the desk from her.

"I just saw the inspector go past. I need to have a word with him," she said firmly.

The policeman let her go and Florence caught up with Boruti as he was getting into his car.

"If I understand correctly, you're deserting me," she pouted. "I no longer interest you?"

"Sorry, but they're waiting for me at headquarters in Paris," Boruti said briskly. "Go see the commissioner."

"To hell with the commissioner. I'm coming with you."

Boruti's smile tightened. This woman was becoming intolerable.

"Out of the question. Let me get on with my work. I'll see you later."

Florence had to let go of the door as the car pulled out. She watched Boruti turn the corner and then ran as fast as her narrow skirt and flowing cape would allow to the street where her own car had been parked since Saturday night. She took off nervously, flooring the accelerator, and two days' worth of parking tickets fluttered from under the windshield wipers.

She caught up with his car on the freeway and followed him recklessly, convinced that the inspector wouldn't think for a moment that he was being tailed. Their bumpers were almost touching when Boruti stopped at the entrance to one of the buildings on the Quai des Orfèvres.

Florence watched him show his badge and a paper that caused the guard to wave his arms hurriedly, pointing out directions. Boruti drove off and Florence followed. She was stopped.

"I'm with Inspector Boruti. He asked me to follow him," she lied openly.

"The inspector didn't say anything to us. Do you have a permit or registration?"

"Of course not. I'm not a member of the police force. I'm the main witness in his investigation. The Houdan case, you know?"

The guard shrugged his shoulders and frowned. Apparently he didn't know.

"Okay, follow his car," he agreed.

Florence offered him a superb smile to thank him for being so easily deceived and shot off. In her rearview mirror she could see that he was watching her to make sure that she kept to her story.

She parked in the first vacant parking place she could find close to Boruti's car and saw him sprinting up the main steps. She rushed after him, looking back with a last mischevous grin in the direction of the guard.

At an intersection of the corridor Boruti turned around out of curiosity. He wondered what the guys coming towards him were staring at. He turned around to find Florence quickly approaching him.

"Good God, what the hell are you doing here?" he choked.

"I'm in pursuit of the truth. I'm sure that you're here on account of our case," she answered without flinching.

"But this is ridiculous. You followed me all the way here?"

"I had no choice. You wanted to leave me alone with that awful commissioner."

"I'll have to have you shown out," he said dryly.

"That's not very nice. I thought you liked me . . ."

Boruti was exasperated. This was no time for flirting. He looked around for help. But he was virtually a stranger here. No one paid any attention to him and the only admiring looks were directed at the attractive young lady in black.

"I assure you," he said, "it would be better for you to leave. How did you get here anyhow?"

"With my car," Florence admitted contritely.

"Great. Another lie. I thought your car was in the garage."

"If they're waiting for you, you're going to be late."

"Don't change the subject. You have to leave. Now."

"I won't leave."

"Look, enough kidding around. Get going or else — "

"You'll call the police?" Florence laughed.

Boruti shrugged and signaled to a police officer who was approaching.

"I'm warning you," Florence hissed, "if you tell that lousy cop to throw me out I'm going to scream. I'll roll on the floor. I'll say that your pass is faked and that you tried to rape me. I'll make sure that your visit here is one that you won't forget."

Boruti stared at her anxiously. He knew that she was a woman of her word.

"Sir?" the officer asked.

"Inspector Boruti, Versailles. Versailles. I'm looking for Commissioner Mainguet's office."

"I think it's on the second floor. They'll tell you up there. The elevator is to your right," he advised as he walked by.

"And I'm warning you — I've never seen you before. Now do as you like," Boruti muttered to Florence.

Florence followed him triumphantly to the elevator.

Legriffe raised his eyebrows in astonishment when he saw Florence march in behind Bourti.

"Uh . . . Commissioner, this is Inspector Boruti . . . and Madame Florence Bertol."

They shook hands and the commissioner's look questioned Boruti about the presence of the lovely widow. As Mainguet turned back to his desk, Boruti raised his eyes to the ceiling, sighing deeply but silently. Florence smiled with all her heart.

"Good. At Inspector Legriffe's suggestion I asked your chief in Versailles to send you here," explained Commissioner Mainguet. "I think we should pool our knowledge about these two separate cases which now appear to be somewhat connected. However, I don't quite understand the lady's business with us here?"

Boruti felt himself blush to the roots of his hair. This bitch had gotten him into a charming mess. Division Commissioner Mainguet was certainly not a man to be treated lightly. His manner emphasized that every minute was important and that he was in no mood to waste time with chitchat. He seemed as old as Boruti had heard, and he wondered why the commissioner hadn't retired yet. He was probably still around because of his famous reputation. The smoke from his pipe, which he puffed on with small, sucking noises, filled the room with a foul smell.

Before Boruti could come up with a satisfactory explanation, Florence intervened.

"I'm here against the inspector's will," she admitted.

Mainguet coughed out a large cloud of smoke.

"You mean 'against *your* own will.' Did the inspector force you to come?"

"No, no, I said 'against *his* will.' I absolutely insisted on coming along with him."

"I see. And may I ask what your purpose is?"

"To find out the truth."

"That's what we're all searching for."

"That's what I'm searching for too, since my husband was killed mysteriously. I want to know why. Besides, I was almost accused of the crime myself. I don't want to be manipulated any more without trying to defend myself."

Again Boruti raised his eyes to the ceiling, his whole manner indicating that he was in no way responsible for this ridiculous interruption.

But, inside, he was actually thankful to Florence for stepping in to save his own face. In a way he even admired the strength she showed by her frank confession.

Mainguet sucked nervously at his pipe.

"My dear Madame, I understand less and less of your reasons for being here, beyond the laudable sentiments that you express. Are you saying that you followed Inspector Boruti here and got yourself onto the premises of Judicial Police headquarters under false pretenses?"

"That's exactly right, Commissioner," Florence acknowledged with her loveliest smile. "I want to be right here when my husband's murderer is arrested. Do 'Law' and 'Justice' have anything against that?"

The commissioner looked embarrassed. Florence's serenity and courtesy hardly gave him an excuse to blow up, and even if he had wanted to reprimand her, her total lack of insolence prevented him. He found himself faced with a new kind of problem, and no immediate solution appeared likely. Furthermore, he was highly intrigued. Instead of the emotions of distress, hatred, or revenge that he usually encountered in the indirect victims of a murder, he sensed a fierce strength accompanied by a genuine "detective's" curiosity in Florence Bertol's attitude. It occurred to him to ask a strange question.

"Madame Bertol, did you love your husband?"

Florence hesitated a moment and then looked the commissioner straight in the eyes.

"No, I didn't love my husband in a passionate way. For me it was a marriage based on weakness . . . I know that. And some tenderness. Only now do I realize how much I miss him and how I ought to have loved him."

The commissioner rested his dead pipe in the ashtray. He took another, already filled, from his pocket.

"That is unfortunately often the case," he admitted with a kind of sadness in his voice. "It hasn't taken you long to realize it. That's certainly all the better for you. It is usually only towards the end of life that people see things in their true perspective . . . and admit to it." (He struck a match and sucked greedily on his pipe.) "I must say that this is the first time in my experience that a woman in your situation hasn't insisted that she worshiped her husband, loved him to distraction." (He turned to the two inspectors who were standing by respectfully, as befitted their subordinate rank.) "If you don't have any objections, I'm authorizing Madame Bertol to join our investigation . . . in the capacity of a privileged witness."

Legriffe and Boruti were careful not to hint at any objections. Florence thanked the commissioner by lowering her eyes. She seated herself discreetly on the chair which was offered to her. (She knew that she would only be accepted if she was prepared to remain in the background.)

"Do you know anything about the rue Nationale crime?" the commissioner asked, turning to Boruti.

"Only what I read in the newspaper this morning," the inspector answered.

"Do you see any connection between the two cases?"

"Uh . . . no. I only linked them when Commissioner Viliard told me that Legriffe was here because of the rue Nationale business. And then there's also the envelopes."

"The envelopes?"

"Yes. Before the Houdan murder, several anonymous letters had been sent to the victim, and then this morning we also received one and so did Madame Bertol. All the letters sent to Houdan had been posted in the 13th — rue de la Reine-Blanche."

"Interesting. And what did they say, apart from the one addressed to you in Versailles, which Inspector Legriffe has shown me a copy of."

"Here's the letter sent to Madame Bertol and the playing cards that had been sent in the other envelopes."

Legriffe rushed to the desk. He had been unaware of the latest developments.

Commissioner Mainguet quickly read the letter before handing it to Legriffe.

"The same man, without a doubt. But I thought that the cards hadn't been found?"

"That was true until this afternoon."

"I see. Well. All this seems to fall into place perfectly. I don't think that we're far from the conclusion of this case, if things continue at this rate."

It was Boruti's turn to be surprised. What did the commissioner mean? He didn't seem to attach much importance to the anonymous letters, or the cards either, for that matter. He didn't even seem to care how they had reappeared. (This arrangement was fine with Boruti. Florence's questionable role would come out later, and he preferred it that way.)

"Did you read the eleven o'clock edition of *France-Soir* this morning?" the commissioner asked once Legriffe had finished reading the letter.

"No, Sir."

"You should have."

"I meant to, but I didn't have the time. I went to Houdan and as soon as I got back — "

"I'm not reprimanding you," Mainguet interrupted with a fatherly smile. "It would have saved some time if you'd already been informed, that's all." (He exhaled another cloud of smoke towards the ceiling, lowering it considerably.) "Okay, I'll stick to the essentials without bothering with the extraneous details in the newspaper. Since it came out this morning, things have developed at such a rate that we'll have to see if we can get things straight as they stand now. Try to follow as closely as possible. First, do you know about the machine-gunning on rue Chapon?"

"That was also in this morning's paper."

"Okay, let's talk about that. There were three things to look for in that business: the gray 404 from which the shots were fired, the man who was wounded and got away, and finally another man who, according to some witnesses, appeared to know one of the victims — the one who, incidentally, died of a heart attack, the former American Mafioso, Attilio Siragusi. Commissioner Bertholier, the head of the Crime and Violence squad, managed to trace this guy pretty quickly. He's also an American citizen and is of Spanish origin. His name is Joe Torronto, and he lives in New York. He's registered at the Sheraton Hotel with Siragusi and the Puerto Rican who was killed on rue Chapon. We would have been completely in the dark without the help of the rue Ballu station — they had stopped these three men in a 'Punch Operation' on Saturday night. Bertholier went straight to the Sheraton, but it appears that Torronto hasn't gone back to his room. Nevertheless, his luggage and clothes are still there." (Mainguet looked from one to the other to see if they had any questions before he went on.) "Good, I'll continue. Now the car. We didn't have its exact registration and it wasn't easy to trace. The files show a gray Peugeot 404 with approximately the same license number as the witnesses reported, but we couldn't reach the owner. It was impossible to establish whether the owner was involved or if the card had been stolen. By the time we did get hold of the owner, who was traveling near Lyon, the 404 had been found abandoned close to Porte de Versailles — and we had learned nothing. That's where things stood last night."

"And the other guy?" Boruti interrupted. "The one who was wounded?"

"No idea. We thought for awhile that he might be the same man."

"The same?"

"That is, this Joe Torronto. All the witnesses gave pretty much the same description for both . . . an elderly man, about sixty (although some said older), dressed in a three-piece suit. But it does seem that there were two men after all."

"You're sure?"

"We weren't sure. But now look at what has happened today. Just after the newspaper reports came out, we had several calls from drivers who had been out on Sunday evening, saying they'd witnessed a chase between a taxi and a gray 404 from Boulevard Peripherique through Boulevard Masséna not far from rue Nationale. Some drivers whose cars had been damaged during the chase had even noted the 404's license — but no one got the taxi's number and none of the witnesses agreed about its color or make. We talked to various cab companies, and at eleven this morning, the taxi driver presented himself of his own free will. There's no doubt that the man he drove from the Arcueil-Cachan Station on the Sceaux line was Joe Torronto. What's more, the taxi driver dropped him at rue Nationale, a few yards from the spot where the Austrian was killed. The times coincide perfectly."

"So the connection between these two cases is obvious. But I still can't see what the Houdan business has to do with this," Boruti remarked.

"Be patient, Inspector, one thing at a time. We're coming to that. Inspector Legriffe, please explain to your colleague how we tied the third case to the two others."

Legriffe emerged from the thick smoke to lean on the commissioner's desk. Realizing that his gesture was too familiar, he took a step backwards, rubbing his hands together while he spoke.

"Well then. Commissioner Viliard instructed me to look through the files and at any reports that had come into our station to see whether there was anything resembling the Houdan case . . . anything that looked like an inexplicable revenge, involving the use of a hunting rifle and expansive bullets. I didn't find anything. So the boss authorized me to extend my search. I telephoned the ballistics lab. I've got an old friend there named Carouge. First I asked him to get his hands on our file and then to see whether there hadn't been anything similar recently, something that would allow us to suppose that the two might have something in common. I gave him as many details as possible on what we think happened in this case, the murderer's personality, etc. Then I called another friend who works at the Legal-Medical Institute. This time it was the type of wound that interested me. After all, not every corpse has been killed with an expansive bullet."

"If I understand correctly, Inspector Legriffe, your connections have been pulling strings for you?" the commissioner commented ironically.

"I wanted to save time, Sir. If I'd gone through official channels it would have meant a mountain of paper work, and it would have taken at least a week, maybe longer."

"Okay, okay, you did the right thing," Mainguet said, nodding, "Go on."

"Well, as soon as I'd hung up, Carouge called back. He had some interesting stuff for me . . . fresh stuff even. A guy had been shot in the 13th and the particulars were pretty much like ours. And just about an hour earlier there'd been yet another similar shooting, on rue du Sentier. Carouge thought this last one would especially interest me, as the killer had left a cartridge behind."

"Okay, I'll interrupt you, Legriffe. I know that almost immediately Legal-Medical called you back about the same case. You informed your chief, who in turn contacted us. It became obvious that we should work together on this thing. Bertholier is dealing with the shooting on rue Chapon, another team is on the rue Nationale affair, and another is on the rue du Sentier business. That's without counting you on the Houdan case. My role in all this is to coordinate the action, because we're dead sure that all these are simply different episodes of the same story. We even know the killer's name."

Boruti couldn't hold back a surprised start, and Florence rose from her chair. The commissioner's look quieted them.

"Inspector, do you know the *Képi Blanc?*"

"Uh, not exactly. Isn't it the Foreign Legion's newsletter?"

"Precisely. This morning we received a phone call from an ex-member of the Foreign Legion who works on the paper and is part of a Legionnaire's friendship association. He wanted to see us, so I had him come here."

"I was sure that this affair had something to do with the military," Boruti said triumphantly. "Is he our murderer?"

"No, it's not that simple. This man just wanted to tell us that a former lieutenant from the Legion had paid him a visit on Sunday morning — and that he thought that the Austrian 'Dieter Krantz' who was shot on rue Nationale was in fact a Lieutenant Schültznicht."

"How did he know? There weren't any photographs in the newspapers."

"No, but this guy keeps a sort of file on former Legionnaires, from what I understand, and he had given the Austrian the address of another ex-soldier who lives at 101 rue Nationale. That's exactly where Schültznicht-Krantz was gunned down."

"I see," Boruti said excitedly. "And this other guy, the one living at 101?"

"His name is Marcel Ribot . . . he was Marcel Héberti in the Legion. He's been retired since the end of the Algerian war. He works as a janitor at a factory in Vitry. He's been on vacation for the past month and he hasn't showed up for work today as scheduled. He also seems to have disappeared from his apartment.

"Did you find anything in his rooms?"

"Yes, souvenirs mainly. And then a pretty complete supply of everything for the maintenance of firearms — powder, bullets, cartridge cases, everything needed to make his own cartridges."

"Do the cartridges correspond with what we've found?"

"Yes, according to the laboratory. In fact it appears to be a very unusual type of ammunition: seven fifty-four Fournier."

"What?"

"Yes. Apparently it's a homemade version of 'war-cartridges' — 7.5 mm which can be adapted to 7 mm expansive bullets. The only gun which could have fired them is a MAS-Fournier hunting rifle. There again, it must have been an adapted MAS 36."

"And is that available commercially?"

"Absolutely. It's a hunting rifle used for deer and wild boar. Our man used it on a different kind of game, but its reliability seems to have been sufficient."

"An odd weapon, just the same."

"It's used a lot more commonly than you would imagine. And in this case, it's more a question of a transformed military weapon than a hunting rifle. Ribot probably chose it because it was most similar to the gun he'd used all his life . . . although the MAS Fournier is pretty far removed from the military weapon that it evolved from. Okay, let's get back to Ribot himself. The description given by his concierge corresponds with that of the second guy on rue Chapon."

"The guy who was wounded in the machine-gunning . . . who might actually have been the intended victim?"

"Yes. But apart from that, the woman hasn't been much help. Ribot seemed to be a peaceful old guy, always polite, extremely discreet and not much of a talker. It was always hard to tell whether he'd gone out or was just shut up in his apartment. The concierge figures that he must have been traveling some during the last few weeks, because she'd often seen him with a suitcase. He never got any mail. According to the concierge, again, he wasn't at home on Sunday. At any rate, she hadn't seen or heard him. On the other hand, she did run into a stranger in the hall of the building at the time the shooting of the Austrian is assumed to have occurred."

"And would that be Joe Torronto?"

"No doubt. Her description tallies with the taxi driver's, right down to the raincoat and beret."

"So he might even have shot Shültz-what's his-name?"

"I don't think so. Actually I don't know. All this is pretty confused. But in my opinion, it must have been Ribot, on account of the gun."

"Yes, of course. They might even be in on this together," Boruti said thoughtfully. "What about the guys in the gray 404?"

"As for them, no news, no idea. We haven't got a clue. Apparently there were two of them," the commissioner said as he placed his second pipe in the ashtray.

He opened a desk drawer and took out a third one, which also had been filled in advance, and began to light it.

"And the third case you mentioned?"

"Rue du Sentier. A Jewish guy named Langmann," muttered the commissioner while lighting his pipe. "Another former Legionnaire. Plenty of witnesses. It was indisputably Ribot. That's where we found the empty cartridge case that allowed us to identify the weapon for sure. A kid was wounded by the same bullet that had killed his great uncle — a cripple who was three-quarters paralyzed. From our first indications, it looks like things didn't go as Ribot had planned. Langmann got the bullet in his kidneys. The bullet then left his body, went through the door, wounding the boy in the leg. Nothing too serious." (The commissioner checked that his pipe was drawing well then shook out the match.) "The shot was fired point-blank, but according to the lab the shock wasn't enough to knock Langmann out of his wheelchair. They found his blood and remains on the door, as well as signs of recent impact, paint chipped by the wheelchair, almost as if Langmann had been thrown against the door."

"If the shot was that violent, maybe it actually did propel the wheelchair against the door?"

"No, I don't think so, not to the point of smashing the door."

"Okay. So what do you think?"

"Well, someone suggested that it might have happened in an attempt to get away, or call for help — or to warn the kid who, it seems, always visited his great uncle at that time of day."

"Or to protect him. Maybe Ribot intended to kill the kid?"

"That's your theory, I know. Legriffe has explained the 'first-born of Egypt' bit to me. It's not exactly out of the question. Oh, I almost forgot, we also found a Queen of Spades on the scene, which is sufficient proof that we are indeed dealing with the same person."

"So we all have to do is get our hands on him and find out the reasons behind the three crimes."

"There's also the rue Chapon shooting," Legriffe reminded.

"Well, gentlemen, that's exactly why I asked you to come here," the commissioner nodded solemnly, just as the phone rang on his desk. "Hello. Ah, Carboni . . . Yes, all right . . . Very good, old friend. No, I'll be here. That's fine. Later." (He hung up.) "Well, one of my men has just confirmed that Marcel Ribot, the Austrian, General Bertol, and Langmann all served in the same battalion during the Second World War, the famous 13th Division of the Foreign Legion. You aren't familiar with it, are you?"

Legriffe and Boruti looked at each other. It was true; they weren't familiar with it.

"And Joe Torronto, do you know whether he — ?" Boruti started to ask.

"Yes, he also belonged to the 13th Division. As for Siragusi and the Puerto Rican, they're unknown to the Legion. Maybe they served under other names. But it seems improbable in Siragusi's case, and we can scrap the Puerto Rican — he was too young."

"Just the same, we now have one common factor applying to each of these cases."

"Although it doesn't get us much further," Florence remarked, noticing that the three men seemed to have forgotten her.

"True," admitted the commissioner. "However, it remains that the main characters in this case all knew each other about thirty years ago, and Inspector Boruti's theory could be relevant."

"It's my theory too," Florence insisted, strangely disturbed.

"I don't doubt, Madame, that you have anything but a perfect understanding of this entire affair."

Florence responded to the commissioner's caustic remark with a polite smile. It was clear that her presence was only being tolerated and silence was all that was expected of her. She sat back quietly and regained her composure.

There was a knock at the door, and an officer entered with a sheet of paper in his hand.

"News from Interpol," he announced simply.

"Ah, Austria. Dieter Krantz was Sales Manager at Brücken-kirchen for an import-export company — International-Weyden. No police record. His mistress, Greta Wunderink, was killed last Friday night by a rifle bullet. Circumstances surrounding the murder unknown. Investigations are being made centering on an elderly man, sixtyish, with a French accent, who was spotted by several witnesses. The police saw Krantz on Saturday but he was missing on Sunday. Any further details will follow . . . All this seems to confirm your theory, Boruti — yours and Madame Bertol's, that is."

"Yes, I thought so," Boruti admitted without excessive modesty. "Ribot wanted to get his revenge against Krantz, and he took it out on the mistress. The same applies to Bertol's son and Langmann's nephew."

"It's pretty obvious now. And Krantz would have come to Paris to settle up with Ribot. We know what happened then."

"And Ribot is still free," Legriffe added. "What chance do we have of finding him?"

"Every chance. A general alert has been sent out, and Carboni is bringing me a photograph — unfortunately it isn't a recent one. We've drawn up a portrait, based on descriptions."

"I mean, what are the chances of finding him before he commits another murder?"

"Do you think he's going to?"

"I can't swear to it, but the anonymous letters say that he'll go on with his 'mission' to the end, and who can tell when that will be?"

"We've got to find the key to the puzzle." Boruti briskly announced. "We'll have to trace each of the ex-Legionnaires from this battalion."

"That would take too long," the commissioner replied, cutting him off. "And it's probably impossible. Most of them must be dead by now. And usually they didn't fight under their real names.

As for the addresses that we could get, they most likely wouldn't be good any more."

"Still, the guy at *Képi Blanc* had Ribot's address all right."

"Yes, but that's not the same. Ribot was a member of this club. There's nothing to prove that all the others from the 13th Division were also members. No, our only chance is to uncover the secret — maybe it isn't even a secret . . . let's call it an 'event' — that links these men to each other. Once we understand that, we might even be able to figure out who the next victim will be. That's the theory that Carboni is working with."

"Okay, and what are we working on?" Boruti asked a little impatiently.

"The Houdan case, of course," the commissioner answered calmly. "I'm waiting for you to tell me what you know. All three of you." He pointed the stem of his pipe at each of them, including Florence. "I hope you don't mind?"

14

Joe Torronto had finished his first cognac, then another. Back out on the street, he was no longer sure that the man he'd seen lying on the sidewalk had actually been Schültznicht. Thinking it over, the man had been too stocky, too corpulent, too old even to be the blond, graceful figure that he had known in the old days.

He walked about idly for a while, trying to convince himself that it couldn't have been Schültznicht. And yet he'd recognized him at first glance — the brutal reality of a nightmarish memory. How could he ever forget the icy gaze and the cruel mouth of his former lieutenant? Schültznicht had never been kind to him, nor to anyone for that matter.

Joe had first known him in the early days of the 13th, at the time of the Narvik "picnic" in June, 1940. The rumors had been that Schültznicht was the son of an Oberführer who was closely connected to Ernst Rohm, and that his entire family had been massacred in the purge known as "The Night of the Long Knives."

Schültznicht had been obliged to flee from his homeland. He enrolled in the French Foreign Legion, where he found himself in the company of former German communists (who in turn had fled from the massacre which followed the Reichstag fire), commanded by a German sergeant of Jewish origin. *Legio Patria Nostra,* the Legion is Our Country: a motto that didn't lie . . . Joe came to understand this motto himself when he left the "Espadrille Legion" after Barcelona had been taken and joined up at the Vienot barracks in Sidi-Bel-Abbes. There he met up with Reds and Phalangists, guys from the "Condor Legion," and all the others in the International Brigades. These were soldiers with neither countries nor parties, now fighting side by side when only yesterday they had been in opposing camps. They were, above all, before everything else, soldiers.

Schültznicht had been one of them. He had fought against his own country because his country had once fought against him. He didn't care about his own fate, nor anyone else's either. He'd certainly made them all suffer at Narvik.

After all, it might have been Schültznicht, considering how he'd been killed, only a few paces from the building where Marcel Ribot lived. (. . . Marcel Héberti, three times demoted.) After the events that Joe had lived through that day, nothing could really surprise him. There must be some connection between the murdering of Chuck's kid and Schültznicht's death. Joe tried to reason it out, but in vain. Then too there was the gray 404 and the deaths of Attilio and Santiana; it was all beyond his comprehension. Poor old Attilio. And faithful Santiana. Joe hadn't even had time to mourn for them. At the moment, the fear that death was closing in on him left him less concerned about the others.

He turned and went back the same way he'd come. The streets had returned to shabby, deserted calm.

Mein Rigiment, mein Heimatland,
Meine Mutter habe ich nie gekannt,
Mein Vater starb schon fruh im Feld, ja Feld
Ich bin allein, auf dieser Welt . . .

He sang softly, without realizing that the bits and pieces of memories had brought the song of the "3rd Foreign" to his mind.

A sudden pressure in the small of his back brought him back to the present. It had been ages since he had felt the butt of a pistol in his kidneys, but he immediately recognized the long-forgotten sensation.

"Don't do anything stupid. That's enough funny business. We're getting tired of your games. We're even feeling a little nervous, you know what I mean?"

Joe felt a little nervous himself. He didn't budge. A car drew up beside him; a gray Peugeot 404.

A sharp jab in the back made his mind up for him — there was no point in talking. He climbed into the back of the car. The guy with the revolver followed him.

"Haven't I seen you somewhere before?" Joe asked, recognizing the young man in jeans from the Boulevard Montparnasse.

The kid smiled sweetly. A second man climbed in next to the driver and the car pulled away. Joe had a strange sense of well-being. It was as if he'd found some company to end his insecurity and loneliness. Nothing in the world would make him return to that dark, damp street.

"What's that?" asked the man in the passenger's seat.

"My overnight bag and my medicine . . . for my heart," Joe answered, resting his attaché case on his knees.

"I see. Your hot water bottle and nose drops," the guy sneered.

"I believe that we've also had the pleasure . . . " Joe commented dryly, recognizing the odd-job man who'd followed him along rue Beaubourg. "What's your line? Sewing machine repairs or hi-fi equipment?"

"Who told you that?" the guy grumbled.

"No one. Just an idea I had."

"Funny. I thought maybe someone told you. I do a few odd jobs."

"I know you do." (The guy looked puzzled.) "So, where are we going?" Joe asked matter-of-factly.

No one answered and Joe let it drop. The car was driving along the outer boulevard, headed towards Porte d'Italie.

"You aren't armed, are you?" the odd-job man suddenly asked.

"Alas, no," Joe sighed.

Nevertheless the punk started feeling his pockets for a gun. Then he opened the attaché case.

"The old heart doesn't look too good," he said, examining the various bottles of pills.

"Are you a doctor?"

"My old man used to swallow all this garbage towards the end. That didn't stop him from keeling over in the metro one day."

Joe couldn't think of anything to say. Maybe it was death waiting for him . . . a sharp pain in the arm, then the chest; finally the suffocation, the choking, and the end. It was all very well to play the witty old gangster, but in the eyes of his kidnapers, he was only a dotard with a weak heart.

He kept his mouth shut for the rest of the ride.

They passed Porte d'Italie, then Porte d'Orleans, and Porte de Vanves. At Porte de Versailles the car swerved onto rue Vaugirard, took a left turn and stopped.

"We go on foot from here," said the odd-job man, who seemed to be the leader of the gang.

Joe didn't ask any questions. He seemed lulled by a lazy sleepiness that was almost comforting. The idea of wandering alone in the city no longer appealed to him. Now he felt too tired to even think about a getaway. That someone else was going to be making his decisions for him was just fine. Besides, at least he would find out who these men were and what they had against him. Once an enemy has been identified, he becomes infinitely less frightening.

The three of them closed around him as they walked.

"Just keep going straight ahead. And don't forget that we won't be shy if you start clowning around."

Joe walked along silently, allowing the others to lead the way.

They came to the main street, opposite the Air Ministry, and walked a little further before entering an apartment house. The elevator only held three passengers, and the kid in jeans was obliged to climb the stairs. They got out on the fourth floor. There was a brass plaque on the door reading "General Louis de Régenville." The name meant nothing to Joe.

An eye showed at the peephole after the odd-job man had rung the bell, shouting, "We're back."

The kid arrived panting just as they were going into the apartment. Joe immediately recognized the man who had opened the door.

"I'm surrounded by familiar faces," he commented in English.

"Small world, isn't it?" the man said with courtesy that matched the cut of his impeccable suit.

"Unfortunately, I think I've forgotten your name," Joe apologized.

"Benesco, Giu Benesco," the other reminded him without the slightest sign of embarrassment.

Joe squinted thoughtfully.

"Giu Benesco. I should have known. It's all so simple, so logical. But it didn't enter my mind for a second. Of course, everything has happened so quickly."

"You can't think of everything," Benesco said with such an awful American accent that his temporary "partners" hadn't even realized that he'd spoken French. "I hope you will excuse the violence that was necessitated more by circumstances than my personal will. You don't hold this little kidnapping against me?"

Joe recalled the first time he'd met Giu Benesco . . . about twelve days ago at Attilio Siragusi's place. He had tended to look down his nose at this smart-assed young man with the high-voice and interminable sentences. The guy had hardly appreciated the treatment he'd received and it wasn't likely now that he'd be very indulgent. His calm courtesy indicated a man who knew he had the upper hand. Joe couldn't resist the urge to irritate him.

"Not at all, not at all. It just means that you know how to do your job. Chuck is going to be proud of you. In fact, I'm going to tell him just how good you've been. But tell me, I thought you were more the University type, or a businessman — and not a gangster?"

Benesco's tanned face tightened.

"This is the first time that I've been involved in this . . . rather particular . . . kind of business. I work for Chuck. He makes the decisions. Don't hold it against me."

"No one's holding anything against you. You shouldn't be so sensitive."

"That's enough, Torronto. You're all alone and your little schemes won't work."

"What schemes?"

"All your attempts to save Héberti."

"Chuck didn't trust us?"

"No, Chuck didn't trust you. Was he wrong?"

"It's always wrong not to trust people."

"And occasionally it's wrong to trust people too much."

"You didn't even give me a chance to see Marcel."

"Chuck decided that there wasn't any point. He doesn't need the kind of explanations you would have come up with later. He wants to get Héberti. He knows exactly what this is all about."

"So what was the purpose of letting us make this trip then?"

"Simply so that we could get to Héberti more easily. Chuck had no idea where to find him. We wanted to be sure of our man, on account of the two names."

"What two names?"

"Ribot and Héberti, of course. Chuck knew Héberti, but not Ribot."

"Oh yeah? Chuck knew Marcel?"

"He knew him once. But let's not talk in the hallway. After you?"

Joe entered the living room. At first he didn't notice the darkened corner where an old man was propped up on several cushions. The furniture was old and the carpets smelled musty. The tables were cluttered with knickknacks, and gilt-framed pictures covered the walls and shelves.

Joe only discovered the presence of another person when the old man raised his hand and motioned for him to approach.

"General de Régenville," Benesco explained. "His English is about as good as my French. I'd rather that you introduce yourself."

"But I don't even know who he is."

"He'll certainly tell you."

Joe walked cautiously to the bed, as if the old man might already be dead.

"My respects, General. I'm Joe Torronto."

"Ah, yes, Héberti's friend. Benesco has explained," he said, looking straight ahead, almost speaking to himself. His voice was weak and monotonous. "A great sin. We committed a great sin."

"Uh, I don't quite understand, General. What do you mean?"

"It's an old story. Thirty years already. I've never forgotten the look on Héberti's face. I always felt him just behind me, and I used to say to myself that one day I'd turn around and find him there. He's taken a long time getting here."

Joe understood less and less. He turned to Benesco helplessly.

"General, *excusez-moi,* but Mr. Torronto . . . he doesn't understand . . . *ne comprend pas. Il n'était . . . pas avec Héberti . . .* he wasn't there that day. I'll explain, uh . . . *je vais expliquer.* If you don't mind?"

The general made a sign that could either have meant that he understood very little of Benesco's stammering or that he didn't really care. Giu Benesco interpreted it as an authorization to continue in English. He indicated a chair for Torronto, and the two of them faced each other across a carved oak table.

"What do you know about the connection between Chuck and Héberti?"

"Nothing. Except for this recent business. The only thing that I can figure is that Marcel had an old debt to settle with Chuck. But what it's about I have no idea."

"Didn't Marcel tell you?"

"I haven't seen Marcel since his trip to the United States."

"But you managed to find him."

"Yes. Or rather I picked up his trail. And I led you to his trail, too."

"That's right. We've been following you since you left New York. Some guy at your restaurant told us you were going to France. I took the same flight as you — only not in first class. When I got here, one of Chuck's contacts had already gotten a crew together for me."

"I see. And you've been shadowing us ever since?"

"Exactly. We needed you. We wanted to see who you were going to meet."

"You questioned Josyane after me?"

"Who?"

"Josyane. The girl who lives on rue Chapon. She knows Marcel."

"Ah yes. Rue Chapon. No, the boys didn't go to see her. They'd been instructed that only you could lead us to Héberti. It was just a question of waiting. So you see Chuck did trust you."

"Sure, trusted me enough to use me. At any rate, your boys almost got Marcel. How did they know it was him?"

"They were just behind Siragusi and the Spic when Héberti took off. That's when the Spic tried to catch him, and that's how he got hit. Things didn't work out so well."

"For everyone except Marcel. He got out okay. Tell me, do your boys speak English?"

"A little. But Siragusi and — whatever his name is — mentioned the name Ribot. That was all they needed."

"And after that? This little chase?"

"Once you returned to the hotel we didn't have to be too smart to figure out that either you were backing out or you knew where to find Héberti."

"Why do you keep saying Héberti?"

"That's what Chuck calls him. I think it was the name Ribot used in the Legion?"

"Yes, a name that stood for courage, loyalty, and honor. Marcel isn't a gangster."

"I know," Benesco said, looking a little ashamed. "But should we let him attack us without defending ourselves?"

"And why did you keep following me? You could have picked me up any time, like you just did."

"Chuck said that we should only use you as a last resort. I think he wanted to avoid putting you in the position of betraying your friend."

Joe smiled with some emotion. Yes, that would have been Chuck's idea.

"And now we've come to the last resort?"

"I'm afraid so. It won't be long before the cops are on our backs, and I don't want to take any risks. Time is too precious."

Joe sensed that the unavoidable question was coming. He wanted to stall for time.

"How did they find me again just now?"

"They came back here and we did some quick thinking. The last time they saw you was at the intersection of Boulevard Masséna and rue Nationale." (He had some trouble pronouncing the names.) "Then, at Gare d'Austerlitz, they realized that you were no longer in the taxi. Once they had gotten themselves out of that traffic jam at Masséna they caught up with the cab again at some other intersection, so they knew that it wasn't between there and Austerlitz that they'd lost you. Therefore it had to have been between the intersection and Boulevard Masséna.

"Nice work."

"So I sent these two idiots out again with the kid, who had by then returned from Montparnasse, to patrol the neighborhood. It was our last chance to find you, as somehow I don't think that you intended to go back to your hotel like a good boy."

"Right again. So, apparently, Lady Luck smiled on you."

Benesco was looking very pleased. As if he'd done everything himself.

"And now you're going to tell me where to find Héberti."

This was it. Now things would get serious.

"You know that I won't tell you."

The two men eyed each other bluntly. The general was still staring into space, and there was no way of knowing whether he was listening to them, sleeping, or thinking of other things.

"The boys can make you talk."

Joe looked at Benesco sympathetically.

"At my age, with my heart, I won't last long. And you still won't know."

"Come on, Torronto. Don't try to make believe that you're impervious to pain."

Joe wanted to smack the little playboy intellectual who was claiming to know so much about life.

"I understand a hell of a lot more about pain than you do. I'm old enough to be your father. I've fought wars in Spain, North Africa, Italy, and France. I don't think that you have anything to teach me."

"Don't lose your temper, Torronto," the unreal voice of the general interrupted. "Loud noises are very hard on me," he announced in careful English.

"Excuse me, General, but I don't like the way this young man is talking to me," Joe explained in French.

"The young man is a jerk. Colonel Adams would never have behaved like this," the General admitted, and returned to his reveries.

Turning back to Benesco, Joe said tersely, "Look, sonny, I'm going to tell you something. Keep it up like this and you'll learn nothing. On the other hand, if you would nicely explain to me what this is all about, why Marcel killed Chuck's daughter, and what the hell you're doing in this old man's apartment, I might just tell you what I know, if I think it's worth it. You're the one who likes last chances. That's my offer."

"If that's all you want . . . " Giu Benesco said, looking a little deflated. "I can tell you everything I know. It's no secret. But we'll come back to my question later."

"All right, we'll get back to your question. Go ahead, I'm listening."

"During the last war Chuck saved the general's life, at the time of the Allied invasion on Rome, and ever since the general has kept in touch, writing to Chuck, sending little presents for his daughter from time to time. But I think that there must be something else behind their friendship, some story that's not too pretty. Chuck only told me that someone was out to get him and that his daughter had been killed in his place. Before the murder, he had received a Queen of Spades in an envelope — and that seemed to disturb him pretty badly. After the crime he got out the card, which had been sent from France, and he said to me, 'You see, it was a message. I would never have believed it after all these years' — and then he went to look through his address books. You know how organized the boss can be. He kept records of everything. Finally he found what he was looking for. 'The guy who did it was probably this Héberti. He was sergeant-major of the 13th Division of the French Foreign Legion in 1940. It's not going to be easy to find him.' That's exactly what he said. And then, the next day, Siragusi telephoned to say that a Frenchman named Ribot had asked for Chuck's address. So Chuck knew that it was the same guy."

"And Marcel knew Chuck during the war? I had no idea."

"He never said anything to you about his business with Chuck?"

"No, nothing very precise. Just that he had an account to settle. I didn't even know that he had a gun with him. Actually he never really talked to me about Chuck. He asked me to arrange a meeting with Siragusi, and he asked Siragusi for Chuck's address, apparently not realizing that I could have given it to him myself. Marcel told Attilio that Chuck was an old friend that he'd lost track of, and as Chuck had often spoken of Attilio Siragusi, he thought that he would know where to find him."

"It all fits together. Chuck told me exactly the same thing. He used to deal with Héberti and other guys in the Foreign Legion. At the time, he was an officer, an interpreter in charge of coordination between the Allied Forces. He used to brag that he knew Siragusi, whose name was world-famous then. He even let on that in the United States he was known as 'Chuck Bonanza,' and not Colonel Charlie Adams. With all that to go on, it couldn't have been very difficult to find him, even after thirty years."

"And what's the general got to do with all this?" Joe asked quietly, glancing at the invalid whose gaze was still fixed in the distance.

"When I left for Paris, Chuck gave me his address and told me that no doubt the general was also involved in the business. Chuck claimed that the general would help me to understand more clearly what was going on. Unfortunately, that hasn't been the case. The old man isn't very lucid."

"And the general let you take over his apartment like this?"

"Actually, we didn't ask for his permission. Our orders are to stick to the general until things are settled with Héberti. Chuck is convinced that, sooner or later, Héberti is going to try to kill the general. If we can't go to Héberti, Héberti will come to us."

"What's at the bottom of this revenge, this ugly story that you mentioned? Do you know what it's all about?"

"I've told you everything I know."

"That's not much. You're going to kill a man without even knowing why?"

"He killed Chuck's daughter. That's reason enough."

"It's a reason, that's all. Don't you want to know the motive behind it all?"

Benesco shrugged his shoulders.

"Out of personal curiosity, maybe. But I'm not paid to be curious. If you want to know, why don't you ask the general? I'm warning you, though, you won't get much sense out of him."

"Does the general live alone?"

"A nurse takes care of him. She's in the kitchen. In perfect health," Benesco added, noticing that Torronto seemed to suspect otherwise.

"And your three goons? Are they camping here too?" (Benesco nodded.) "Where did they come from?"

"I don't exactly know. Chuck had them recruited. I can't complain about them."

"They're not real smart, you know. Especially as they're always seen in the same car."

"That car should only have been used once. But there was too much to do, and we didn't have time to pick up another one. Any other stupid questions to play for a little more time?" (Joe answered Giu Benesco's question with a broad grin.) "Well then, are you going to give me Héberti's address now?"

Joe went on smiling. Did this guy really believe that he would give him an old friend's address so that they could go sweet as you please to his home and kill him?

"It's late and I'm getting tired. Aren't you? I guess not, at your age. I could stand a bit to eat."

"This no longer amuses me, Torronto. You won't have anything to eat or drink until you talk," Benesco threatened, pleased that Joe himself had provided the means for pressure. "And don't think you're going to sleep either."

"Fine, whatever you say. Can I talk to the general?"

Joe understood that Benesco was beginning to lose patience. He went over to the old man, leaving Chuck Bonanza's lackey at the table. Benesco was probably trying to think up a way to get it all over with as soon as possible.

"General. General, can you hear me?"

"What, do you think I'm deaf? Thank God at least I can still hear."

"General, why does Héberti want to kill you? And why did he kill Colonel Adams' daughter?"

"A terrible sin. Yes indeed, a terrible sin. I knew he'd come some day. He said he would revenge him."

"Who? Who does he want to revenge?"

"The young man. The young man who drew the Queen of Spades. A terrible sin."

"Yes, that's it, the young man who drew the Queen of Spades. What was his name again?" Joe tried to help the general with his thoughts.

"A terrible sin. We have to pay for it. It's only right."

"Of course. It's only right . . . for the sin — "

"Stop repeating the same thing over and over, and let me die in peace!" the general interrupted with a sudden burst of vehemence.

Joe didn't persist. Benesco had certainly already tried to get a coherent explanation, without any success. Joe now understood why. He turned to the younger man.

"Are we going to spend the whole night staring at each other?" he asked Benesco calmly.

"That's not up to me," the other answered with obvious bad humor; the prospect disagreed with him. "I've got to find Héberti pretty quick, and you know it."

Joe had thought from the beginning that Marcel wasn't taking any chances. He'd been carrying out his plan for a long time now, and he knew what he was doing. It could only have been him who had shot Schültznicht, and by now the area must be alive with cops. Giving his address to Benesco would hardly do the gangsters any good. Still he was determined not to give in to their demands, and not to betray Marcel in any way.

Benesco stood up wearily. He opened the living room door.

"Tie the gentleman to a chair," he ordered in French to the three men standing in the hallway, smoking.

One of them tied Joe up, and then they all sat down at the table for a snack. The nurse brought the old man soup and his medicine, which he accepted ungraciously. The nurse was neither young nor pretty. A pity, Joe thought to himself. At least that might have boosted his morale.

"I should take my medicine, too," Joe said as the nurse tiptoed warily past him.

"No medicine," Benesco insisted dryly. "Nothing until you give us the address."

"Sorry, the boss says no," the nurse said with a timid smile.

The time that followed was filled with pain and anxiety. The euphoria after the two cognacs was replaced with a terrible fatigue and thirst. The day had been eventful, to say the least, and Joe had eaten nothing since the morning. His heart's rhythm became irregular and the tension in all the muscles of his body reminded him of his weakness.

In the early hours of the morning he had had the impression that he was waking from a coma. He might have slept a little, in spite of the desk light shining in his face and the rough pokes that he had suffered from the three men who had taken turns at keeping him from giving into a weariness that neither thirst nor pain could fight against. But now he was no longer tied to the chair. He was lying on the couch. The nurse asked him if he felt better, and told him that he had fainted. Benesco loomed over him.

"A guy was killed last night, not far from the spot where we picked you up."

"I know. A former Legionnaire, an Austrian."

"And no doubt you know who murdered him?"

"Probably Marcel."

"Yes, and Marcel must live around there, or I should say, used to live there, because I don't think it's worth the trouble of going to check. He's probably taken off." (Joe forced himself not to respond to the remark.) "Okay, you can have something to eat and you can sleep if you want to. We're not going to get anything out of you," Benesco added, with a kind of admiration. "We'll see if the cops are any smarter than we are. For the time being it's better to wait for things to calm down."

* * *

They waited all day.

The newspapers and the radio kept them informed of what they didn't already know. The evening papers published a picture of Marcel Ribot, alias Marcel Héberti, who had become "Public Enemy Number One" for these few brief hours. The picture had been taken at least ten years ago. It showed Marcel dressed in his uniform, his sergeant-major's stripes on his sleeve. He was wearing all his medals, including the "Red," as it was called in the Legion, that he had earned in Indo-China. His facial expression was hard, reflecting neither pride nor humility . . . the look of a soldier, a man who always finished what he started.

The caption read, "Ribot, when he was Sergeant-Major Héberti, a man trained to kill."

It was no doubt because he was feeling so very weak that Joe let two silent tears fall on the photograph.

15

Marcel entered the *Café-Bar de l'Aviation* and ordered a beer and two hard-boiled eggs. It's true, he thought . . . emotions increase the appetite. He immediately ordered another draft and a ham sandwich. Around him was the daily crowd of regulars, swelled a little by those whose favorite cafés were closed on Mondays. The customers, mostly men, were drinking coffee along with a "little drop" of apple brandy, or after-lunch cognac. The mood recalled a soldier's mess; everyone talking loud and drinking freely. Besides, behind the gray and navy blue suits of the office workers were hidden the soldiers stationed in the administrative buildings of the Air Ministry, and it was only by their patronage that the dull cafés in the Balard quarter brightened up. There were even a few young guys in uniform, emphasizing the military atmosphere.

Marcel felt perfectly at ease in this atmosphere. He ordered a coffee in his turn, and a white cognac from Burgundy, very pale in its small glass with a gold rim. Marcel turned the cone-shaped glass, catching the light in the delicate bit of gold. Customers came and went beside him — he had stayed standing at the bar — glancing at him with a smile, as if he, too, were a regular, and they didn't want to seem too proud to recognize him.

Marcel listened, as much as he could, to the conversations, savoring the sound of the military terms which he himself had once used. He felt that he belonged here, and the mediocre alcohol that he was drinking wasn't the only cause of this feeling.

The bar emptied little by little, and the men crossed the boulevard and went back to their offices. Marcel was left alone, leaning heavily on the counter.

"Is anything wrong, Monsieur?" asked the woman who seemed to be the owner.

Marcel had the impression of waking with a start, like that morning in the café near the Austerlitz train station.

"Where's Luc?" he mumbled, looking around him in alarm.

"Who? Everyone's gone, Monsieur. It's two-thirty. Everyone went back to work. Don't you work?"

Marcel looked at the woman suspiciously, as if she knew what was in his mind. But the woman was peacefully wiping a glass, smiling. She must have been about thirty and her figure, maybe a little too heavy, lacked neither softness nor a certain charm. Marcel thought that she was a little like the canteen girls from his time.

"No, not today," he answered after a while, surprising the woman. She had probably already forgotten her question.

"That reminds me, we haven't seen Mlle. Mercier," she called out.

"I think that there's a lot of company at the general's," answered the man who was clearing the tables. "I saw two strangers this morning who seemed to be going up to his apartment. And yesterday there was a lot of noise up there."

"He hasn't died, I hope," she remarked, in a voice that was neither interested nor concerned.

"Who knows," shrugged the other with the same lack of interest.

Marcel himself followed this dialogue with certain curiosity. He hadn't forgotten why he had come there.

"Are you talking about General de Régenville?" he asked without embarrassment.

"Yes," the woman answered. "Do you know him?"

"I knew him at one time. Doesn't he live just above here?"

The woman took a dry towel from above the coffee maker and began drying a new row of glasses.

"No, he lives above our apartment on the fourth floor. We're on the third."

Marcel smiled broadly.

"What I meant was he lives above the café, in the same building." (The woman returned his smile.) "But I thought that the general lived on the fifth floor?" Marcel lied.

"No, no. The general has always lived on the fourth. The Joliveaus are on the fifth. But they're not there right now. They always spend half the year in the country. They have a house in Tarn and they don't come back to Paris until November. That's the good life."

Marcel quickly analyzed the information gleaned from the conversation. There was only one apartment at each landing, and the general's was between two that were currently empty.

"I guess it's practical for you to live above here. Between the busy times you can go up to your apartment."

"Aah, don't you believe it. The time it takes to get this place in order and re-stock the supplies is just enough. Then it starts all over again. At four o'clock the customers come back for their coffee breaks, and then they come back again around six for cocktails. No, we aren't exactly spoiled. We leave the apartment early in the morning and don't go back until the night."

That was what Marcel wanted to know. He took out his wallet.

"It's always like that," he agreed sympathetically. "How much do I owe you?"

The woman held her towel and a glass in the same hand. She took up her order pad in the other.

"Are you going to see the general?" she asked. "My husband says that there's a lot of company up there right now. Do you know them?"

Marcel calmly checked her addition and refrained from responding to the woman's sudden curiosity. But his own curiosity grew stronger.

"What kind of company?"

The woman made a vague gesture. She hadn't seen anyone.

"Jacques, what do the people look like who you saw going up to the general's?"

The man sat two cases of bottles behind the bar. He was sufficiently well-built to command respect, and he had a swarthy complexion and thin mustache. He looked a little like a gypsy. He looked sharply at Marcel, and the old Legionnaire knew that his own face wouldn't soon be forgotten.

"There was a kid in Levi's, sort of a blond, and another guy who looked like a mechanic, who seemed to take himself for a big deal. I think that they had been doing some grocery shopping, because they were carrying a couple paper bags and a case of beer — or soda pop, I don't know which."

This description didn't mean much to Marcel. He hoped (or feared?) that one of the men was Joe.

"Were they speaking French?" he asked, without bothering to explain his odd question.

"Yes, I think so," the gypsy-type answered with some surprise. "Do you know them?"

"No, but I know that the general has some friends in America, from the last war. They come to see him sometimes," Marcel explained, realizing that the story that he was inventing could be true anyhow.

"Wait. Now that you mention it, one of the guys, the kid, said something like, 'this business is getting to be a pain in the ass and that American is driving me nuts' — then he saw me, and shut up. Maybe there's an American with them?"

"I think I know who it is. I'll go up and say hello," Marcel announced simply.

He took up his suitcase, left a generous tip (where he was going he wouldn't need money any more), and went out of the café to enter the apartment building.

"Do you know that guy?" the gypsy-type asked his wife.

"Never saw him before," she answered. "But he seemed to know the building."

Two soldiers came in the door which hadn't quite shut yet. One was wearing the cap and blue shirt of the Air Force and the other, the navy blue beret and khaki jacket of the Infantry. They both had the yellow arm bands of the MP on their sleeves.

"Two ice creams," they ordered casually.

* *
*

Marcel took the elevator to the fifth floor. He came out of the cage as quietly as possible and closed the iron gate without making a sound. The building was perfectly silent. Pricking his ears, he could hear the boring drone of a television, the dialogue far-off and reassuring.

He sat his suitcase on the red wool carpeting and put his ear to the door of the Joliveaus' apartment . . . not a sound. He looked around and went towards the other door, a simple wood panel painted in imitation stone, like the rest of the hall. The door opened easily and led to a narrow, winding set of stairs which Marcel decided to explore. The stairway went down on the right to the other floors, and led above to a twisting hallway where the maid's rooms and attic lofts were located. Some of the rooms were posted with the names of the people who lived in them. A radio was playing somewhere, something like the hit-parade. Marcel went forward, taking care to get familiar with the place and register as many details as possible.

Suddenly a door opened behind him and he jumped.

"Oh. Excuse me. I scared you."

She was young and pretty. A student, certainly. She had a large shoulder bag and a few books in her arms.

"That's all right. I'm looking for Monsieur Durand . . . Marcel Durand," Marcel explained, to head off any questions.

"I don't recognize the name," the girl answered with a nice smile. "But I don't know everyone. Excuse me, but I'm very late."

She skipped off, and Marcel heard the fake stone door slamming. Then the elevator disengaged, groaning and creaking heavily.

Marcel went on with his exploration. He only found a wash basin — an oval sink encased in the wall — under a fan window which gave access to the roof. Then he went back down.

On the back of the door that opened to the fifth floor he found a notice:

"The charges covering the maintenance of the elevator
are not included in the rents of the tenants on the 6th floor

and they are reminded that the use of the elevator is strictly forbidden to them."

Marcel thought that young people didn't respect anything any more. He laid his suitcase out flat on the carpet. Still guarding against the least noise, he opened it. He put the heavy revolver in his pocket. The lump that it made was too obvious and cumbersome. He found that it was wiser to slip the gun between his belt and his shirt above his kidneys. He left his jacket open and closed the suitcase, after having loaded his rifle and checking that the provisional second charge was ready as usual. Counting his revolver, that made forty-two shots available to be fired. Forty-two. That was the year of his third wound. He didn't know if he should consider the number lucky or unlucky.

He figured that he was ready. He looked at his watch — twenty minutes to four. He went down a few steps and realized that he didn't really know what he was going to do. He went back.

"Advance, attack, then withdraw," like the Legion, in good order and defending to the last cartridge. It wasn't really a plan. It was only a manner of proceeding.

And then too, he didn't know whom he was going to shoot.

De Régenville lived alone, that much he knew. The general had never married, and the string of housekeepers (for whom he had perhaps felt an affection that would have been strong enough to name them as victims) had disappeared, leaving only the old maid Mercier, a nurse with neither compassion nor tenderness.

Yes, really, whom could he shoot?

There hadn't been, in the general's life, anyone dear, and it was for that reason that Marcel hadn't come earlier, even though he feared every day that death would come to rob him of the revenge that was Luc's right.

Circumstances now obliged him to act without waiting any longer. But he still didn't know how.

He went back up to the hall above, the strange labyrinth whose odors and darkness reminded him again of the building that he himself lived in, and Langmann's, and Josyane's. The swinging door, as well as the thick red carpet and the fake stones frightened him a little on the fifth floor. Above he felt better, almost at home.

He found, at the end of one of the branches of the hallway, after a kind of unexpected fork that he hadn't yet explored, a door to a little room. A poorly lighted nook. Towards the back he made out a sink and an old-fashioned commode with a wooden seat and its water tank above with a pull-chain. He placed his suitcase along the wall and sat down mechanically, as if on some sort of chair, unconsciously reverting to an old childhood habit. When things were going badly he used to shut himself for hours in the john on rue Héberti, a john just like this one, with a real wooden seat.

Marcel thought about Luc Cartier's sister, the unknown young woman who had come to see him one day, to remind him of the promise that he had made to Luc.

How had she known?

He hadn't, at the time, thought of asking the question. That promise had been made in perfect faith, and it had seemed normal to him that Luc's sister should be aware of it. Afterwards he had often wondered who indeed might have told her of the terrible drama in the Aurunci Mountains. It certainly hadn't been Luc. Bourges, maybe? She must have known him, since she was the one who put him on the trail of the former "Companion of the Queen of Spades." And then this good idea: revenge through another person — that too had been her idea. He had boasted to Ruben Langmann, leading him to believe that he had thought of it himself. The business with the playing cards also; that had been another of her inventions. She had given him money, too, more than twenty thousand francs, for his "fees," so that "Justice could be done." With that money he had been able to go to the United States. But that, Luc's sister hadn't known . . .

Someone knocked on the door and Marcel emerged abruptly from his dreams.

"Luc . . . 'Luc, is that you?" he babbled.

"No, Monsieur, excuse me. But you've been in there for a while," called out a man's voice.

Marcel listened to the steps echoing back down the hall. He became conscious of his ridiculous position and stood up. He was feeling the stiffness in his legs. A painful fatigue weighed on his body and his mind. He only had one desire: to go home and sleep. Too bad if the cops were there. Too bad if the general got away from him this time. He would come back tomorrow, or later, when he got out of prison.

He picked up his suitcase and went back to the elevator. It was almost seven o'clock.

When his weary hand pushed open the gate on the ground floor, a cry of almost terrified surprise greeted him. He recognized the woman from the café and offered her a sad smile. But the woman backed up in faltering steps.

"What is it? Is something wrong?" Marcel asked with polite concern.

"Don't kill me, don't kill me!" screamed the woman, suddenly hysterical. "It's too late, the police are already here, my husband called them. We recognized your picture in the paper!"

Marcel took the revolver from his belt. He approached the woman to force her to come with him back upstairs, but it really was too late. The pale glow of a flasher slid past the front of the building, and Marcel saw the police car stop. He limped back into the elevator and pushed the button for the fourth floor. De Régenville would pay, after all.

The woman stayed in the hall, petrified.

With the return of danger Marcel felt himself recovering his strength, his forces, his life . . .

He had almost cracked, abandoned everything, as if finally old age and despair had conquered his determination. Now he became a soldier again.

The elevator stopped with a dry clap, like the trigger of his rifle. He could hear the shouting below. Marcel blocked the elevator by pushing the emergency button. He opened his suitcase, took out his rifle, and assembled it with quick, efficient moves, not at all affected by the imminence of combat, and put all the extra ammunition in his pocket. He could hear the noise of the troops in the stairwell. Marcel leaned over and fired two shots from his revolver at random. The troops stopped short.

"Ribot, you're through. Throw down your guns. The building is surrounded."

Marcel fired two more shots towards the bottom, persuaded that his answer was sufficiently clear. Silence again. The door to the general's apartment remained obstinately closed. Marcel told himself that if there really was anyone inside, as the bar owner had claimed, either they weren't very curious, or they were wondering how to get out. This thought amused him a little.

Several moments passed and then, suddenly, the police sirens wailed in all directions, interrupted by shrill whistles.

"Ah, the reinforcements," Marcel thought.

He decided to act.

He fired one bullet into the lock on the general's door and kicked. It opened.

"Don't shoot. We give up," begged a voice inside.

Marcel advanced, the revolver back in his belt, the rifle in his arms.

Seeing him, the men who were barricaded behind a couch and some chairs began firing.

"Shit, it's Héberti," grumbled a voice at the same instant as the first shots were drawn.

Marcel rolled to the floor, the rifle shielding his chest and arms, a reflex that he had never forgotten. No bullets found him. He gained shelter behind a bureau, then began to crawl back towards the door. The shooting had let up.

Almost at the landing, he heard *Le Boudin* being whistled in a hesitating manner, as if the whistler were having a hard time getting his breath.

"A moi la Légion," Marcel cried with all his heart.

A door opened halfway down the little hall, and a man with a face contorted with pain approached. Huge drops of sweat ravaged his almost unrecognizable features.

"Joe! My God. What the hell are you doing here?"

"I haven't betrayed you, Marcel, but my heart . . . my heart has betrayed me."

"Come on, Joe, come on."

Marcel held out his hand and moved towards his friend. Joe Torronto let go of the wall and also held out a hand. Marcel saw another hand, behind the couch in the living room. He didn't have time to yell. The shot was fired with an almost mocking burst and Joe collapsed, his hand groping forward. Marcel crawled back to the landing. Furtive, sliding steps in the stairwell announced that the police were making their way up the steps again, more discreetly this time. Marcel took out his automatic and fired, to show that he was indeed still there. Then he took time to imagine an exit.

An exit that wouldn't be shameful.

Of course he could shoot down the stairwell, saying that he had hostages. The cops would negotiate. He was sure of it; he had read it so many times in the newspapers. He would lead them to believe that the guys who had killed Joe were now his hostages. Or, he could arrange to slip out, leaving the two groups to face each other — no doubt the cross-fire would revenge Joe's death. Or yet again, he could go find hostages among the tenants in the maid's rooms. He would send the little student to warn the police, and he would barricade himself on the top floor of the building with a few terrified people whom he would try his best to reassure.

But he didn't want to involve people who had nothing to do with his business and towards whom any hositility would be a guilty offense.

He didn't even want to know who the guys were who had shot at him, probably killing Joe by mistake. He thought that they were probably cops too, or something like that. Anyhow, they were guys who didn't understand that he had a mission to fulfill, and to fulfill in spite of all obstacles.

Marcel realized that he could only flee.

Flee, not to protect himself, not to try to save his neck, but flee to reserve for himself the chance to come back to de Régenville's house some other day and find a solution for his revenge.

"Ribot? This is your last chance. This time the whole neighborhood is blocked off. Throw down your guns and come down or we're coming up."

The voice was very loud, a little nasal and slightly distorted by the echo. It seemed to Marcel that it came from just behind him and he instinctively jumped, at the same time realizing that it was being amplified by a megaphone or a loud speaker.

He still thought of calling out that he had hostages — even if it wasn't true — just to put off the assault. But he forbid himself this cowardice.

Abandoning his suitcase, hereafter useless, he opened the fake stone door and climbed the stairs to the sixth floor. A few startled silhouettes fled at his approach. Several doors slammed. The locks turned.

Marcel found his way to the fan window that opened onto the roof. He rested his rifle against the wall and leaned on the edge of the sink to reach across and grasp the iron handle that would allow him to swing open the glass panel. The window opened without much difficulty. Marcel grabbed the frame and positioned his foot on the sink to hoist himself up. The roof sloped gently down towards the masonry of a large chimney. Marcel bent his knees to reach back and pick up the barrel of his rifle with his extended fingertips. He held the gun in one hand and hoisted himself completely outside. He closed the window behind him. The noises of the intense and unusual activity reached him from the street below — sirens, whistles, strict commands, the herding crowd, and around the perimeter of all this, the horn-honking concert of the blocked automobile traffic.

Marcel descended towards the chimney. The roof was almost flat. Covered with zinc tiles in careful rows, it allowed a relatively safe passage. Marcel breathed the fresh air of the early evening and wondered if he would ever see the sun again. His heart beat heavily in his chest, but not irregularly, nor in trepidation; it was like a machine that had attained its full working rhythm.

He then oriented himself. He was on the side of the roof slanting towards the boulevard. Then it was the other side that he had to go to. He left the chimney and climbed back up to the top. Passing a few yards away from the fan window he noticed that it was now lighted . . . the cops already? Over the top, he allowed the slope of the roof to accelerate his course. He came up against another building, whose roof was a little higher, and he had to make his way along the extreme edge close to the gutter, in order to find a way down. He followed the edge just to the corner, where he found a sort of terrace in the middle of several concrete braces. Below, he saw the long lines of traffic stopped on rue Lecourbe. Most of the drivers had left their cars and were craning their necks, trying to find out what was going on up ahead. A group of police officers undertook the re-routing of traffic onto rue Leblanc. Several of the gray vans of the CRS couldn't get through. In spite of their flashing lights and sirens, they were stuck in the congealed flow.

Marcel experienced a kind of pride in discovering that he was the central figure in all this drama.

Then he continued rapidly and carefully on his way, descending by a few successive terraces connected by short stairs. He found a heavy iron door with a leaded-glass window that probably gave access to a stairwell leading to the ground floor of the building, or at least to an apartment on a lower level. He broke the glass panes in order to reach in and grab the bolt, and forced the door open. Then he went down in the darkness and ended up at another door, also locked. It was a wooden door — a single panel. He thought of breaking the lock; it would only take one shot. But Marcel certainly didn't want to signal his presence by firing his gun. He went back up the stairs to a very narrow window encased in the wall. A simple latch opened it, and Marcel realized that if it was possible to slip through the tight opening he would then be able to easily catch onto the supports of the Petite Ceinture railway tracks. From there he could regain solid ground. He stood his rifle against the wall.

* * *

Commissioner Mainguet directed the operation with the aid of his lieutenants Carouge and Carboni. Bertholier was there too, with his squad of marksmen. Boruti and Legriffe, invited to be present, followed in the wake of the commissioner, at the same time managing to keep out of the way and yet miss nothing of the spectacle. It was the first time that they had participated in such a deployment of forces, and as they were only probational inspectors, they congratulated themselves on being able to profit — in ring-side seats — from the experience. Commissioner Viliard would be unbearably jealous and furious, and they could expect at least a week's tedious assignment with administrative garbage. But, for the moment, they were very pleased with themselves.

The orders that Mainguet gave had been precise and decisive. A network of carriers and receivers now wound back and forth through the entire blocked sector. From time to time they came pounding back to the center, announced by an electric buzzing in the crowd or a breeze advancing suddenly before the panting runner.

Behind a double row of officers, the crowd grew rapidly, thrusting forward in spite of the exhortations for order and warning against the ensuing danger. But the taste for the circus was too strong. Sure that he wouldn't be "the victim," each one pressed and pancaked together, shoving with shoulders and knees to get the best view, or to preserve the one that chance and personal ability had won for him. The shouts were joyful, excited, friendly, like a big party. Those who knew, or thought they knew, informed the others in a loud voice and received their thanks with faces lightly posed for the gravity of the situation. Certain spectators remained silent and their faces affected an almost bored indifference, but their eyes clung to the unfolding events. Occasionally, cries of pain or resentment sounded in one place or another, where a hurried passer-by found himself pinched in the crowd, or when the police officers pushed back, without great caution, against the locked mass of thrill-seekers. The cries undulated like a wave, diminishing gradually, and finally dying off where the crowd thinned out, reduced to a few isolated individuals who stopped only briefly before continuing on their way, no doubt persuaded that nothing very interesting was happening, or that they were too far away from the show to hope to profit from it.

For a moment Boruti contemplated the face of this crowd — a face without a soul — and felt an almost hateful hostility rising in him. Didn't each of these men and women secretly hope that there would be a corpse — blood and death — of someone right at their feet?

"What chance do we have of taking him alive?" Boruti asked Commissioner Mainguet, who had just turned to him with a small smile, as if to ask him if he thought everything was going all right and if he was glad to be present.

"That, my friend, I simply don't know. The little that we do know of this fellow makes us believe that he won't let himself be taken too easily."

Boruti nodded silently. Several detectives came back to report to the commissioner. The radio in the black car that the two inspectors had decided to situate themselves alongside crackled, and a calm voice announced that the intervention squad had arrived on the fourth floor, and that there was one death and four prisoners, including an American.

* * *

Florence hadn't been allowed to take part in what the commissioner had termed "the conclusion of this case." An inspector had been charged with accompanying the young woman back to her home. She had been very careful not to mention that her own car was waiting for her in the parking lot. Inspector Boruti certainly hadn't forgotten this detail, but he said nothing, undoubtedly preferring to remain uninvolved.

Upon exiting the police building, Florence thanked her escort for his courtesy and immediately slipped away and jumped into her Autobianchi before he even realized what was going on.

She had heard the name Boulevard Victor being mentioned and that was enough for her. She got through the rush hour traffic without too much trouble and found herself on the scene quickly. At the edge of Porte de Versailles she turned towards rue Vaugirard, which was completely blocked. She abandoned her car and continued on foot. At the upper end of Square Desnouettes she ran into the crowd. She managed to pick her way through to the front row and realized that she had no chance of getting any further. However, it seemed that the mob was less dense at the other end of the avenue, nearer to the area where something was happening. She decided to make a detour and went off around by way of Avenue Porte-d'Issy.

* * *

Marcel had scratched up his arms and legs a little (the side of his thigh, especially, and his hip), but he succeeded in getting out of the window. He pulled his belt out behind him, with the rifle and revolver fastened to the end. His jacket, rolled in a ball and heavy with ammunition, lay in a heap a few yards off, on the gravel edge of the tracks.

The railway trench, cut in the middle of rows of buildings, offered only an illusion of liberty. The rails surrounded Paris in an infinite loop, like a snake swallowing its tail. Marcel knew that the trains rarely traveled on this part of the line. He didn't have to worry about being surprised by one, but neither could he hope to make use of one. He took the little path between the platform of the overhead bridge and the embankment, where the gravel and small stones wouldn't slip under his feet. The jumble of weeds and wild bushes lashed at his trousers. He advanced cautiously, his spine lowered. If he managed to cross the bridge without being seen, he could take momentary shelter between the gray walls of the buildings lining the tracks, then further on, he would find a place where he could climb safely back to lose himself in a quiet and darkened part of the city.

In the middle of the bridge he stopped. Under his feet, the CRS helmets and officer's *képis* made a surging carpet, so close that he had to hold his breath. There was some shuffling, a few orders and shouts, and Marcel saw a group of men coming around the corner, wearing handcuffs. He realized that the cops now knew that he wasn't among them. His superiority over those who were searching for him was all the more reduced.

Marcel examined the faces of the four manacled men. They were all strangers. Who were they, where had they come from, why had they killed Joe? He had no idea. And yet, one fact suddenly became clear to him: if they had preceded him to the home of General de Régenville, it was probably because they had known that he was going to come there. That meant that they were aware of his mission. If these men talked, there would no longer be any chance for him to carry on to the end.

Quickly, he knelt down on the ground and rested his rifle between two rails. The leader, a young guy, elegantly dressed, was about to climb into a van when, suddenly, he fell forward without anyone hearing a thing. There was instant confusion and some officers bent over him, no doubt thinking that he was ill. Marcel had already re-loaded and then another man crumpled a guy in a coal-gray raincoat who didn't seem to understand what was happening to him.

This time there was a panic. Some men flattened themselves on their bellies, others crouched along the walls, scanning the roof-tops, fingering the triggers of their guns, but most fell back, running to their cars.

Marcel's third bullet was lost on the sidewalk.

He had been seen.

The gunfire rained in his direction and he heard the bullets ricocheting, ringing on the steel girders. He crawled to the end of the bridge and ran. He came to a second bridge. The stairs leading to the ground were closed off by a fenced gate. He shot open the lock. He crossed Place Balard in a few wide steps.

Not all the way, however. Extremely rapid commands were immediately followed by gunshots, obliging him to fall to the ground. He rolled onto his side and fired instinctively in the direction of the voices and fire.

An order to cease fire was called.

Marcel saw the uniforms, helmets, boots, and guns waiting a few yards ahead of him, barring rue Leblanc and part of Avenue Félix-Faure where it crossed Boulevard Victor. There were still three possible exits, but Marcel knew that he wouldn't have time to get to them. He didn't have much longer now. He took up a marksman's position, lying there on the ground, and his gestures seemed to surprise the others. A few officers fell back, looking for shelter.

"For the last time, give up!" shouted a hysterical voice.

That was when Marcel noticed the woman in black.

She was young, blonde, and pretty, and she walked towards him without fear.

The folds of her long cape stirred gently in the evening breeze, the evening perfumed with the smell of gunpowder.

It was the Lady of the Grand Companies. The Lady of Spades. He recognized her right away.

He knew that he was going to die.

Then he wanted to attempt what others had attempted before him — he wanted to kill Death.

He took his revolver in one hand and the rifle in the other and stood up, leveling both arms towards the approaching figure.

He saw that Death was afraid and without firing, just to increase his advantage and to show that he was the stronger, he shouted the old combat order in a clear voice:

"Fire at will!"

He fell clutching to his breast the only friends he had, his guns.

No one heard the name that he pronounced.

It was the name of the son that war had given to him and then had taken away again before he'd even been able to prove how much he loved him.

16

Florence Bertol was personally invited by Commissioner Mainguet to participate in the follow-up investigation.

"But I thought pursuit of Justice ended with the murderer's death," she remarked as the commissioner, holding her firmly by the arm, invited her to get into the car.

"Who are you talking about?" Mainguet asked with a threatening ambiguity.

"My husband's murderer, of course . . . Ribot."

"Are you certain that Ribot was the murderer?"

"You yourself claimed as much. There's even all the necessary proof. Not to mention all the shooting, which will allow you to compare bullets."

"That's true. Just the same we regret that Ribot isn't here to tell us everything that he had to tell us."

"Yes. We'll probably never know the exact reason behind his revenge."

The commissioner prepared to light his pipe but then no doubt realized the danger of asphyxiation that he would be imposing on all the passengers. He shook out the match before it reached the bowl.

"Most likely not. The principal figure is dead, and all the minor characters as well. There are only a few secondary persons left . . . like you and General de Régenville and the two punks who escaped the bullets."

Florence pulled a little at her hem to cover her knees, whose ivory pallor, set off by the black of her skirt, seemed to fascinate the commissioner.

"That's true. What did they have to say?"

"Good lord, nothing much. The general is a complete dotard. We weren't able to get anything out of him, except for an allusion to some 'terrible sin' that he had committed long ago. That's probably why Ribot came to his home. As for the American's two buddies, they claim not to know much of anything. They were paid to get Ribot and not to ask questions."

"Exactly who was this American?" Boruti asked from the back seat.

"Now he's a corpse and just another puzzle. The general's nurse confirms that he was the head of the gang. As for Joe Torronto, he was taken to the general's place against his will last night. Again according to the nurse, it seems that the others were busy with a little 'work' during the night, trying to get some information out of him."

"That makes a lot of Americans and a lot of unanswered questions," Boruti commented. "Maybe the key to the puzzle is on the other side of the Atlantic?"

"Maybe . . . but for the time being, we're obliged to finish up here. And since Madame Bertol has been so kind as to come spontaneously to join us, perhaps first we can try to clarify some of the more obscure points in the Houdan case?"

Florence answered the commissioner's question with a slight nod of the head. Her lips trembled a little and her face turned suddenly pale.

"Is anything wrong, Madame?" the commissioner asked politely but without particular concern.

"No . . . it's just that when I think of this massacre . . . I'm still very upset."

"There probably wouldn't have been a massacre if you hadn't seen fit to interfere," Mainguet remarked dryly.

"I wanted to talk to him, just to talk to him," she murmured.

It was what she had said through her tears when Boruti had rushed forward after the last round of gunfire. The inspector had understood the meaning behind that senseless march. He too regretted not having been able to meet with Ribot and talk to him, to try to know, to attempt to understand what troubled emotions were hidden in the "mad killer" who had died with a hero's stance.

Mainguet shrugged. Obviously this answer didn't satisfy him, but he knew enough about the female mind to think that, after all, it might be true.

"All right. I would like, on the other hand, for you to explain to me why you hid the playing cards that had threatened your husband as well as the envelope that the anonymous letters alluded to?"

This was the confirmation of what Florence had suspected. Ribot's death wasn't going to put an end to the cops' curiosity, and they would finish by learning exactly what role she had played in this affair. She glanced at Commissioner Mainguet and understood from his steady gaze that, as she already knew, he wasn't going to be content with vague answers, nor allow himself to be evaded by false leads. With him, she didn't have any chance of being able to control the game and she wondered if it would be better to admit everything now, to acknowledge that she had played . . . and lost.

. . . And tell him that she had been burning for independence and with ambitions of her own.

Tell him that living with Xavier had been a relentless hell of frustration and waste.

Tell him that she wanted his death rather than a separation, because the Bertol fortune would fall to her.

Tell him that she had known that she was incapable of such an act, and that this terrible desire had stayed inside her unformulated for a long time, firmly repressed . . .

Until the day when old General Bertol, that infatuated old fossil whose confidence she had known how to win, had mumbled a few strange names in a semi-comatose sleep, curious hints that made her want to know more. When the general was feeling better, Florence — who cared for him with constant devotion — hadn't had any trouble gleaning the confession that, in reality, the old soldier wanted to make. She learned the name of Sergeant-Major Héberti and Legionnaire Cartier. The general hadn't wanted to betray the others. He hadn't said much, actually contenting himself with telling her that Héberti had promised Cartier that some day he would revenge him and that he himself, the old "Companion of the Queen of Spades," had dragged the weight of this threat through all his life. But Héberti had never come . . . maybe he was dead? . . .

Héberti wasn't dead. She had found him easily, through the *Képi Blanc,* approaching the paper in the general's name. Héberti now called himself Ribot. He lived in the 13th district of Paris. She had observed his habits for a while, and then one day, she decided to stop him on the street, a few steps from his home, because she didn't want to run the risk of being recognized later by a concierge or a friend. It was necessary that her existence remain unknown to everyone — everyone except Héberti.

They had gone to a discreet and busy café, so that their low-voiced conversation wouldn't be noticed. She had worn a brown wig and had disguised her face with thick, dark makeup and heavy eyebrows. She spoke of Cartier and Ribot had seemed shaken by a great shock. "Luc?" he had asked, and Florence, who had been ignorant of the first name, had lowered her eyes. "You must keep your promise," she had said with a pleading note in her voice that could only increase the old man's emotions. Little by little, sensing that Ribot had guarded the desire for revenge and his soldier's honor deep inside, she had guided him to propose to himself what she had come to demand of him. She had quickly realized that the former Legionnaire possessed a distorted notion of morality and justice, which contributed exactly to the success of her plan and, even furthered, her hopes. Ribot's slightly deranged mind served her design perfectly by eliminating the idea of "murder" in her conscience, even if she could have done so. When she had showed him the copy of *Terre-Air-Mer* relating the details of the already old promotion of the former Captain Bourges, Ribot's convictions and resolution had been such that she couldn't even think that he would fail. She had found the man that she needed.

Ribot had found the idea of revenge through another person excellent, and had agreed, although not completely understanding the point to the story of the playing cards. She had needed an alibi, and she had to be far away on the day of the crime. It was also necessary for Xavier to be at home, alone, and the circumstances surrounding his death had to be mysterious enough to confuse the police. That was what Ribot hadn't understood.

Of course, she could have come up with a simpler strategy, but finally, as it was necessary that the crime occur at a rather precise moment, she had known that mailing the playing cards would end in obliging Xavier to take the attitude that she could expect from him, leaving her perfectly anonymous regarding their significance.

She would return to see Ribot at the time when it was necessary to act, to give him his victim's address and the date of the execution. Ribot hadn't seemed to suspect anything at all. She had promised him money also, for his "expenses," but she had only offered it when she had been sure that the Legionnaire wouldn't see it as a kind of salary. With it he would be able to get away, after the crime . . .

The general had died a few months later, and Florence had attended to the funeral announcements, making sure that news of the death didn't pass outside of a certain restricted circle. The official announcement could come after the fact. She went back to Ribot, as arranged, on an evening when he was just leaving to follow his own business. Then the plan had been executed most perfectly, and she had suddenly found herself free, rich and happy . . . for a brief moment . . . until she noticed, lying on the carpet in the study, halfway slipped under the desk, a large manila envelope.

She had already called the police and she lost her head a little. The envelope contained the general's posthumous confession, destined for his son. It wasn't necessary that the police know of its existence. It was necessary that the killer also be the person to have stolen the playing cards, and the envelope too, if it came to that.

Before Boruti's arrival she had had time to hide all the incriminating evidence, and to imagine a few explanations.

For the rest, possessing an unassailable alibi and maintaining — so she thought — perfect mastery over the situation, she had played the role that most became her — that of a woman who was, at the same time, terrified by what had happened, but in control of her emotions. Everyone had known that she had hardly been on the best of terms with her husband and it would have been very awkward to have played the game otherwise.

She had only allowed herself the luxury of being distraught.

But something strange had happened. This new-found liberty, so terribly acquired, had given her the bitter taste of solitude and abandonment. She had reassessed the details of her problem minutely. She initially convinced herself that the scenario was infallible, but she ended by doubting. She hadn't counted on Ribot's independent action, and she had valued the cleverness of the police much too cheaply. Then, as much to break her solitude as to know what was going on in the official investigation, she had laid the trap into which young inspector Boruti had fallen.

She had played with him, like a cat with a mouse, holding him for a moment between the paws before letting him escape a little in the direction that she knew he would take, then suddenly drawing him in, throwing him out on another lead, before trapping him under her paw again.

In this way, she had learned that the police investigation was practically dead-ended. It was even more amusing to offer Boruti "possible" leads — two fingers from the truth — as much from arrogance as to scatter the suspicions a little further . . .

Ribot's letters came to play the role of the grain of sand in the machinery. Even if Ribot should be arrested, nothing said that her complicity could be established. Faithful to her manner of proceeding, she had wanted to preserve the advantage of her position, and so, she set out to do so. The general's confession had been replaced with bonds found in Xavier's safety deposit box (she had a proxy), and the playing cards had mysteriously reappeared.

When Boruti had come, she had decided that the explanation that was at the same time the most simple and the most stupid — an irrational move, a kind of whim — would add up to be the most plausible. It wasn't necessarily the sort of thing that would be suspected of being calculated.

Afterwards, events had occurred swiftly and she realized that she needed to be able to follow these events from as close as possible. She didn't, at any cost, want to be excluded from what was going to happen.

And now, with the only witness to her machinations dead, was she going to confess?

Was she going to reveal that she had approached Ribot with neither fear nor reservation, persuaded at the time that destiny had stepped in?

Was she going to give in to the bewildering terror that had seized her when she learned that Ribot wasn't going to content himself with the single moment of revenge that "Luc Cartier's sister" had suggested, but that he had also, unknown to her, committed a series of bizarre crimes whose unlikely path had caught the police officers charged with its investigation in a sticky web of conjecture and incomprehension?

Parallel to the game that she led, Ribot had played another, much more dangerous and dreadfully hurting. If the police ever learned of the part she had taken in the organization of this series of murders, there was no doubt that she would be charged with inciting a crime and complicity, not only for the murder of Xavier, but also for all the other murders that Ribot had committed outside of her direct influence . . .

Ribot was dead.

She remained alone.

Alone in the face of responsibilities and remorse that she had never meant to assume.

She didn't want to pay for another, nor abandon so easily the freedom that she had gained through so much hardship.

But this the cops would never know.

No one can know everything.

Commissioner Mainguet tolerated Florence's silence for a moment, then he posed his question again —

"I asked you, Madame, why did you hide the cards and the envelope?"

"I don't know," she answered, with a sad smile. "I've already answered that question. It was an unconsidered move on my part. To give Commissioner Viliard a hard time, I think. Stupid, wasn't it?"

The commissioner didn't answer. He looked at Florence Bertol with a small, frozen smile, his lips tightening on his unlit pipe, and then he absorbed himself in the dull contemplation of the city drowned in rain. The windshield wipers arched in sweeping swirls.

*
* *

Four young Legionnaires in formal dress — *képis*, spats, white gloves, red and green epaulettes, wide blue waistbands — mounted guard around the coffin draped in the tricolor flag. A cushion resting on top proudly displayed a number of decorations.

According to the wishes of the deceased, his services to the state were read at the end of the ceremony, and Boruti tried to imagine what kind of life these names and dates described: "1927 . . . Syria Campaign . . . Moroccan Campaign . . . 1935 . . . 4th Regiment, Foreign Infantry . . . Staff Corporal . . . Stripped of his rank . . . Narvik, 1940 . . . 13th Division, French Foreign Legion . . . Sergeant . . . Stripped of his rank . . . Bir-Hakeim, 1942 . . . Wounded in combat . . . Military Medal . . . Battle of the Aurunci Mountains . . . 1944 . . . Cross of War T.O.E. . . . Adjudant . . . Cross of War, 35-45 . . . Knight of the Legion of Honor . . . Commemorative Medal of the Italian Campaign . . . Phe-Tong-Hoa . . . Diên Biên Phu . . . Military Cross of Valor . . . Stripped of his rank . . . Commemorative Medals of Indo-China and Algeria . . . 1955 . . . Adjudant-Major . . . Wounded . . . 1956; by his rights honorably retired."

Thirty-five years in the Legion. A long record. An exceptional soldier. Dozens of friends killed in combat. And his final reward: more than twenty bullets received in the Place Balard on a sad September evening . . . the end of a bloody drama, self-mocking and pathetic, invented for himself, probably, as a reason to live . . . or to die.

"It's certainly the first time I've seen a murderer buried like this," muttered Commissioner Mainguet, with more wonder than acrimony.

A broken old man, stiff, in a heavy overcoat that made his low squat shape even more deformed, turned around. His hard face and unflinching gaze identified the former soldier.

"Héberti didn't betray. He served up to the end with 'Honor and Fidelity.' He was a true soldier."

"Did you know him?" asked Mainguet, whose inquiry into the reasons for the series of crimes had come up short.

"I knew him very well," confirmed the old man in a voice that wasn't weak. "I am Captain Ernesto Biaggi . . . twenty years in the Legion."

"Division Commissioner Mainguet, Judicial Police. And this is Inspector Boruti. Perhaps you know what revenge Héberti was pursuing?"

The small man tried to straighten up. He looked the commissioner deep in the eyes.

"Legionnaires' scores are settled by Legionnaires," he said proudly.

And he went off with short, shuffling steps behind the coffin carried slowly by the four white *képis*. Slowly enough that the old man with the uncertain march didn't find himself too rapidly outdistanced.